I0823296

THE SCAMMER

ALSO BY TIFFANY D. JACKSON

Allegedly

Monday's Not Coming

Let Me Hear a Rhyme

Grown

White Smoke

The Weight of Blood

Blackout (coauthor)

Whiteout (coauthor)

Quill Tree Books
An Imprint of HarperCollins*Publishers*

HarperCollins Children's Books,
a division of HarperCollins Publishers,
195 Broadway, New York, NY 10007

HarperCollins Publishers,
Macken House, 39/40 Mayor Street Upper,
Dublin 1, D01 C9W8, Ireland

Quill Tree Books is an imprint of HarperCollins Publishers.

The Scammer

harpercollins.com

Library of Congress Control Number: 2025941755
ISBN 978-0-06-327127-2
Typography by David Curtis
26 27 28 29 30 LBC 8 7 6 5 4
First Edition

For my Bison Babes:

Nicole J., Nicole W., Tiffany S., Tiffany T., Tonia, Simone, and Adana.

Thank you for the countless times you've saved my life.

ONE

THROUGH ALL THE college preparation—the SAT courses, applications, essays, GPA fights, and interviews—no one ever mentioned how you had to fit your entire life into two suitcases and a duffel bag. Maybe people assume you don't have much of a life to pack. As if we spent the last four years of high school twiddling our thumbs.

I heave my suitcases off the Amtrak train, sweat dripping down my neck, and immediately twist my hair up into a claw clip. Don't know the next time I'll be able to have it straightened, so this silk press needs to last as long as possible. Shouldn't there be a bellhop or something?

Scanning the platform, I grip the handles of my bags and roll them toward the direction of the foot traffic, not wanting to stand around like some clueless tourist. A guide on our summer vacation in Italy once said, "That's how you are taken advantage of. Appearing like easy prey instead of a worthy adversary."

I know I don't look like I carry an ounce of street smarts.

More suburban-Connecticut, private school chic. Skinny jeans, a simple white T-shirt, and black ballerina flats. I own one pair of sneakers for gym, which I barely used since it would require me risking sweating out my hair. Like I'm about to do in this train station as I head for the exit, breaking a nail in the process.

Outside, the humidity grabs me by the throat. But I'm too busy taking in the picturesque view of the marble domed US Capitol Building, only a few short blocks away, rivaling Greek temples and architecture. It looks just like it does on countless news stations.

Washington, DC. I've made it, Kev.

Around me, the world goes on, indifferent to my presence. I hoped that I would see other kids in a similar predicament—fresh meat, arriving alone to a new city, with no family to help them settle. But it's just me on the sidewalk, with her life inside a few matching pieces of luggage. The fear I've been ignoring starts to boil up again.

Maybe I am making a mistake, just like everyone has said. Maybe it's not too late to jump on the next train, back to what I know, what's familiar, what's safe. But there is something inside me so hard it could crack teeth if you tried to bite it. So empty that the air smelled old, carrying the echoes of heartbreak and grief. If I don't go . . . it may never soften.

Above my head, a giant American flag smacks the wind like a whip, and I straighten. The new backbone I acquired won't let me turn around. Especially since I may never get this chance again.

* * *

The cab drives by the official school sign bookended by short pillars. Frazier University. It looks so much smaller in person. Online, it's a sprawling campus, with bright chrome-green lawns and redbrick buildings soaked in history. It's touted for being a college up on a hill, surrounded by a bustling city.

Frazier University is one of the most established, well-known HBCUs, or Historically Black Colleges and Universities, in the country, located smack in the middle of the nation's bustling capital. The complete opposite of my all-white high school deep in the wooded suburbs. I once mentioned Frazier to a white classmate, and she had never heard of it, which wasn't surprising.

The car pulls up to Rockland Hall, a coed dorm at the bottom of the hill. For a moment, all I can do is stare at the front door, busy with students flowing in and out. A rainbow of Black and Brown faces, laughing and smiling, donning school colors, sneakers, and T-shirts. I look down again at my wardrobe, well overdressed for freshman orientation, and fidget with my hair.

The driver grunts as he grabs my bags out of the trunk. I slip him a tip, not as much as I would usually. I have to watch the cash I have on hand now. I pass by a security booth and weave through the lobby, straight to the desk with the Welcome Freshmen banner swooped overhead. A girl in a Frazier crewneck clicks her pen, smiling.

"Hey girl, hey! Name?"

"Jordyn Monroe," I say, scoping out the scene of scattered lounge chairs, dinging elevators, and giant posters of football and basketball games with roaring crowds.

She flips through her clipboard. "Okay. Got you right here. This is your welcome packet and your key. You'll be in a quad on the sixth floor. Suite 610, room A. The loading dock is on the side of the building for you to bring up the rest of your stuff."

"This is all I have," I mutter at the table.

She glances at my bags, her mouth making an "oh."

"Mmmkay. Well, all of your roommates have already settled in, so they'll give you the rundown before you meet your RA at tomorrow's house meeting. Oh! Almost forgot. A mug! Welcome to the Rock!"

I palm the black mug like a new bestowed heirloom, thumb tracing over the school logo.

"Thanks," I mumble and head to the elevators.

Today is the last possible day to move into the dorm. Most kids moved in four days ago. It was still a question of whether I was going to go through with this crazy plan of mine. But here I am, practically vibrating with adrenaline. The elevator dings and I hold my breath up the six flights.

The moment I open the suite door, I'm accosted by a scent so strong it burns my eyes. Smoke billows out of the end of incense sticks tucked into a wooden holder sitting on the coffee table. Thumping music beats out of a shaky speaker behind one of the closed bedrooms. I set down my bags, taking a moment to appraise my new home. The small living room has two yellowish love seats forming an L shape, facing the tight kitchenette.

I've never seen a fridge and oven that narrow before. And no dishwasher?

Across the room are four doors, two facing the others, with a small bathroom between them.

Just as I'm about to enter room A, the door to room B opens and out pops a tall brown-skinned beauty queen, her hair in a puff crown.

"Ahhhh! You're here!" She spins around, tapping on the other doors before enveloping me in a tight hug. "Hey y'all! She's here!"

I freeze under her touch, stunned by the immediate affection of this familiar stranger. I have to tell myself to breathe so I can hug her back as naturally as possible.

In seconds, the other doors swing open. Two girls let out giggly screams. One dark-skinned, short and curvy, the other thin with honey copper skin.

Principle number five: Smile.

I widen my grin and hit them with my best "Heyyyyy!"

I spent the summer reading *How to Win Friends and Influence People* by Dale Carnegie, hoping it would turn me into a chameleon, soften my metal bones. Because that's how you make friends . . . you have to be likable.

I stopped being likable so long ago that I didn't think I could do it again. But here I am, peppering them with compliments.

"Your room looks great! Oh, I love your room too. You're so pretty!"

Principle number two: Give honest, sincere appreciation.

Not one lie told. Just me putting on a show.

"Okay, wait wait wait. We need names, y'all!" The beauty queen says, "Hi, I'm Vanessa."

"Loren," the skinny one says while wrapping her braid up in a bun.

"Kammy," the curvy one sings, hair hidden under a purple bonnet. "And OMG, you're so pretty too!"

"What's that smell?" I ask. "I don't recognize it."

Vanessa beams. "Frankincense and myrrh. My brother told me it's the best for working on good vibes."

"Nice," I say, trying to keep my voice lighthearted.

I've always had a hard time fitting in. But I have to try. The last thing I want is college to be another version of high school.

Vanessa plays with my hair. "We thought you were never coming!"

"Yeah, we've been waiting forever," Kammy adds. "What took you so long?"

I let out a nervous giggle. "You know. . . . life be lifeing."

"Facts," Loren agrees, and I notice her thick New York accent.

"Okay. I have the BEST idea," Kammy sings. "How about we pregame tonight before heading to that welcome party."

"Ooo, I love that!" Loren agrees.

"Aye, hold up," Vanessa laughs. "Let's let our girl get settled first. While she doing that, what am I going to wear!"

They file into Vanessa's room, rummaging through her closet that almost seems to be busting at the seams.

I step aside with a smile and dig the key into the door of my new room. The space is narrow, with dark gray carpet and one long window that faces the front, so you can look down into the courtyard. The standard-issue wooden desk and twin bed look like they've been through a war or two and Vanessa's incense does little to fix the dank scent. But it's home and it's mine.

I push my suitcases by the closet, open my phone, and text the parent chat.

Hi! Made it.

I slump on the unmade bed, noting how hard the mattress is, and wait. And wait. But there's nothing. I know they're not busy. It's Saturday. All they're doing is sitting in the den, watching golf or some documentary on PBS, phones within reach on the marble side table next to their lukewarm coffees. Black with three sugars. Probably already made their dinner reservation at the country club. No one knows my parents better than I do. Wish they could say the same about me.

Mom and I talked about decorating my dorm room for over a year. We wanted to raise the bed, string Christmas lights on the walls, hang pink curtains to match some throw pillows, maybe even add a furry rug. Now, the sight of the bed reminds me that I forgot to pack sheets. Not that I had much room for decor in my suitcase.

I open my backpack, taking out my laptop, chargers, and the few books I could fit. I clutch my journal, flipping through the last few pages. On the train ride, I managed to work on another short story. It helped the time pass, the longing and uncertainty fading. When I'm caught up in a story, I can ignore the world around me.

"I'm here, Kev," I whisper aloud. "I'm actually here."

My phone buzzes in my pocket and I scramble to snatch it up. It's a message from Dad. A thumbs-up response to my text. I swallow the bitter disappointment with my head held high, as if they were here, watching me. I refuse to let them see me cry.

"Uh, is that what you're wearing?"

My new roommates, gathered in the living room, crane their necks to look at me.

I glance down at my outfit, a simple white tank top over jeans, and a blazer. "What's wrong with it? You said it was a house party, right?"

"Yeah but . . . ," Kammy starts.

"It's giving . . . stick up your ass," Loren says with a laugh.

"Don't you have some, like, cute earrings or something that shows a little skin?" Kammy suggests. Now without her bonnet, I see she has a brown twenty-four-inch wig with blond highlights.

"Um, no." In fact, nothing in my closet would match their vibe of tight dresses, skirts, and crop tops, their faces painted, lips juicy like models, hair styled to perfection.

In an instant, my face flushes and I'm ready to crawl under the carpet. Why didn't I think of outfits when I packed? Probably because I never go out at home.

Vanessa waves a hand. "Y'all, it's fine! You just gotta . . . lose the blazer. And you can borrow a pair of my hoops!"

"Dang! We don't have shot glasses. But we DO have mugs!"

As Vanessa runs in her room, Kammy pours vodka shots in each of our mugs. I gulp, slipping off my blazer, plopping down next to Loren. She digs into her bag and taps my shoulder.

"Ooooo, girls would kill for these lips, boo," she says, gripping my chin and staining my lips red.

Kammy passes around our drinks. "Yas! That color is perfect on you. Alright! Cheers, y'all! To the suite!"

I grip the mug with a nervous smile. My first drink. Of course, I can't admit that. This is my opportunity for a fresh start. A whole new me. And a new me would have friends, people who like her, a life. A new me would drink, responsibly of course.

Act normal, act chill, I coach myself before taking it to the head, letting the liquor burn down my throat, holding back a cough as my eyes water.

"Okay, I have a confession to make," Loren says, smirking. "I looked y'all up. You know, I had to check on who I was gonna be rooming with. Can't be stuck with no nut jobs. I've heard too many horror stories." She turns to me. "But there's, like, no pics on your Insta. You don't even have a Snapchat. What's up with that?"

The girls turn with curious stares, and I shrug.

"Guess I'm kinda private," I say, not wanting to admit that there is nothing in my life worth posting.

"Okay, back up. Can we go through the basics. You know, to catch Jordyn up to speed," Kammy giggles, with a happy clap. "State your name, your sign, where you from, your major and why. Then a little about your family."

"Okay. I'll start. Hi, I'm Loren. Cancer, from Harlem, some call me Lo. Public relations major. I want to do PR for artists and movie stars. I have six brothers and sisters that all still live at home with my moms but I'm the first one to go to college."

Vanessa's mouth drops. "Wait, did you say six?"

"Yep. And one damn bathroom," she says, pouring herself another shot.

Kammy cackles. "Okay, guess I'm next! Hi, Kamara, but everyone calls me Kammy. I'm from St. Louis, Missouri. Pisces. I'm a psychology major. I'm going to be a child therapist. I got three older sisters, five aunties, and dozens of cousins. My boyfriend still lives back home. He's studying to be a pastor so he can take over his father's church. I've been going there all my life."

"You plan on staying with him?" Loren chides, bumping her shoulder.

"Of course! Once I graduate, we're getting married. I'm going to have like eight bridesmaids. Maybe nine, if my cousin Shay-Shay act right."

Loren raises a mischievous eyebrow at Vanessa while sipping her drink, as if to say, "We'll see about that."

"My turn. Hi, I'm Vanessa, some call me Ness. From Oakland, California. Accounting major, planning to own my own firm. No man, but they say college is the best place to meet your husband. Parents are dead, long story, been living with my grandma. Outside of that, it's just me and my brother. Well, will be . . . once he gets out of prison."

I notice the ache of longing in her voice, so similar to my own that my breath catches.

"Prison? What he do?" Kammy winces, covering her mouth with her hands. "Shit, can I ask that?"

Vanessa laughs with a wave of her hand. "It's fine. He was framed for some credit card fraud bullshit. I haven't seen him in two years. But he's getting out real soon then he promises to visit."

A sting of jealousy rips through me. At least he can still visit. So caught up in my thoughts I almost miss the question thrown at me.

"Helloooo? What about you," Kammy says.

"Oh, yeah, right. Hi! I'm Jordyn. Most call me . . . well, Jordyn. I'm a Virgo from Westport, Connecticut. Poli-sci major on the prelaw track."

"And family?" Loren asks.

I shrug. "Uh, small. Just me and my parents. With three bathrooms."

The girls laugh as I take a relieving sigh. I want them to like me, not pity me. I want them to be my friends. I don't want them to know about Kevin. I want to leave my past buried under the fresh dirt I swept over it.

"So where's this party anyways," I say, desperate to take the focus off me. "Should we call an Uber?"

"Nope." Vanessa jingles a set of keys. "I have a car!"

TWO

VANESSA PARKED DOWN the block from a dark red row house on the corner in the Adams Morgan section of DC. The overflow of partygoers hang outside, cups in hands. Music thumps out of the open windows.

Not many freshmen brought their cars to campus. Student Housing all but banned them, claiming there wasn't much space in their lots. So just like high school, having your own car wins instant popularity. And having a roommate with her own car is a major plus.

"Whose party is this?" I ask, as we climb out of Vanessa's brand-new green Jeep Wrangler.

"Some guy I met in the Rec yesterday invited me." Vanessa grins. "He's a junior."

"So it's gonna be a bunch of upperclassmen," Kammy squeals, practically skipping through the gate, noticing red and white Greek letters above the door.

It's a frat house.

Inside smells heavy of spilled liquor, perfume, and sweat. The lights are dim, but it's not dark enough that I can't see the swell of students flooding the place. It isn't like those old teen movies, with kids dancing and drinking. More like kids gathered in clumps around the living room, on the stairs, and in the kitchen toward the back. The DJ is set up in the corner near a boarded-up fireplace. Most of the boys are wearing red-and-cream jackets or T-shirts.

We huddle by a wall near the staircase, fixing our hair and makeup in our camera phones, pretending like we're not. I've never been to a party, much less a college party before. Out of my element, I can only dream up a fantasy.

"Okay, girls, be chill," Loren instructs us. "It's all about the way you carry yourselves. Like you belong. Fake it until you make it."

"What are we trying to make?" Kammy whispers, and I let out a giggle, the alcohol finally buzzing through my system.

"We just don't want to come off like some corny-ass freshmen," Loren warns, turning to me. "And thank GOD you're all pretty in person too. Can't have no fugly girls in my crew."

"Thanks? I guess," I say with a chuckle.

"Do you have a man back home?" Vanessa asks, bumping me with her shoulder.

"No. I like to travel light."

The girls laugh and I love the ringing sound to these practiced answers.

"What about friends?"

"Not really. I like to keep my circle small." A perfect noncommittal answer.

"That's exactly what my brother says." Vanessa laughs. "Along with, 'keep your friends close and your enemies closer.'"

I point at her with a laugh. "Exactly!"

"What enemies you talking abo—OMG! I love LOVE this song!" Kammy shouts, hand in the air, swinging her hips. Within seconds, a few guys start to notice us.

"Yo! My brother was in the studio when they recorded this," Vanessa says.

"What? Really?"

"Yeah! Nas and my brother are tight. His manager introduced him. He used to work in the hip-hop industry for a long time. Knows a lot of rappers! Used to tour with them and everything."

"That's fire!" Loren exclaims.

Vanessa nods proudly, going on about her brother's accomplishments. How he helped rappers with their albums, produced songs, met with executives who still call him for advice to this day. I gaze down, realizing my fist has rolled into a ball. I want to be able to talk about my brother that way, with the type of glowing pride that even the sun would be jealous of. He was going to be a doctor. He was going to find a cure for the breast cancer that almost took our mom. He was going to be famous one day. He was, he was, he was . . .

I look up, stunned to see a group of boys forming a semicircle around us. The tallest one has dark brown skin with tight black curly hair and a crooked smile. Unsure of what to do, I clutch my soda with two hands and smile.

"Kareem is from Baltimore, so not far," Vanessa goes on to explain. I must have missed his introduction.

"Was your dad in your frat? I heard most of y'all are legacy," Loren asks.

Kareem shakes his head. "Nah, he got locked up a while ago, along with my uncle. Doing dumb shit, you know. I'm the first in my family to do the school thing."

"That's cool."

His friend group is inspecting us with mischievous grins.

"So y'all live at the Rock?" one of them says. "So do we. You should stop by our spot and chill sometime."

"Um, I got a man. Can't be just chilling in some boy's room." Kammy hits them with a flirtatious smile. She has a man, but she's loving the attention.

"Ha! You're definitely a freshman. Bet your man be gone by Thanksgiving. Maybe even Columbus Day."

"Um, no we don't celebrate that Colonizing Murderer," Vanessa snaps.

"No, but we celebrate a three-day weekend!"

Vanessa lets a small smile leak through her outrage and the boys melt, their eyes roaming every inch of her. Standing next to Vanessa, I feel childlike in comparison. She has the body of a grown woman, with hips and curves; of course she would draw attention. Not to mention a smile that lights up her entire face. I wonder how long she's been this beautiful and how much she's gotten away with all her life.

"Hey," Loren says, eyes on the rest of the party. "Who's the white boy?"

Across the room, I spot him. Tall with broad shoulders, his long blond hair down to his chin, wearing a boyish grin. He's familiar in many ways, the type of boy I went to high school with. But I wasn't expecting to see any of them here. I thought I left that part of my life back in Connecticut.

"Oh, that's White Boy Nick! He's a Kappa."

Kammy does a double take. "What?! He goes here?"

"And he's in your fraternity?" Vanessa asks, a disgusted look crossing her face that she wipes clean before Kareem notices.

"Yeah. He's a sophomore. Hey Nick!" Kareem waves him over. "He's cool peoples, I'm telling you."

Nick hears his name, his bright blue eyes scanning the four of us. As he makes his way over, I notice the other girls at the party noticing him too. Not like when you spot a pink elephant in the room, but more like hungry lions eyeing their next meal.

"Um, he's actually kinda cute," Loren whispers in my ear. Vanessa gives him a once-over but doesn't seem moved.

Kareem puts his arm around Nick's neck. "Yo Frat, I want you to meet some new friends of mine."

"New?" He chuckles, taking a sip of his drink. "Ohhh I see, so y'all are fresh meat!"

There's a slight twang in his voice. Definitely from the south.

"Tell us what you think." Kareem looks at Vanessa. "He's good at reading folks."

Nick taps his chin with a pensive squint.

"This one . . ." He points at Loren. "Reminds me of a Big Sis. Probably beat up a bunch of kids when she was little."

Loren takes a small bow and the guys laugh.

"This one . . ." He points at Vanessa, winking at Kareem. "I don't know, man, looks like Trouble."

Vanessa rolls her eyes, but a smile breaks through.

"This one . . ." He points at Kammy. "Reminds me of sunshine. All sunshine and rainbows all the time. Loves to love."

"Wow. You're good," Kammy giggles, twirling her hair.

"And this one . . . ," he says, pointing at me with a devilish grin. "She reminds me of Bambi."

"Bambi? Like Disney?" Kammy asks.

"Yeah, 'cause she has big gorgeous eyes and thick lashes, just like Bambi."

The ladies look at me, impressed, and I drop my eyes to the ground, cheeks on fire. No one has ever said something like that to me before.

"Plus, she looks like a deer in headlights, like most freshmen."

The girls have a hard time holding in their giggles. A scowl takes over my face. I was used to being made fun of back home by white guys. But I refuse to take it here, at the one place I should be safe from them.

"So, I guess you have a nickname too," I spit, more than annoyed.

"You're close. The name is Nick. Nice to meet you," he says, offering his hand.

I roll my eyes. "Whatever."

He laughs. "I was just joking with you."

"Well, I don't think your jokes are very funny. In fact, your whole presence is an insult."

He blanches. "Whoa. What does that mean?"

"You're clearly just some boy who's taken an admissions spot from a Black kid who rightfully belongs here. You probably swindled yourself a minority scholarship too. Typical white privilege behavior. Thinking that you have the right to go anywhere you want, even if that makes people uncomfortable. You even had the audacity to join a Black fraternity. Clearly your fetishization of Black culture has led you here but no matter how much rap music you listen to, or Black schools you go to, or fraternities you join, you'll never be one of us. So, for once in your life, maybe you should read the room."

At first he just stood there, frozen stiff. Then his eyes narrow.

He steps closer, as if to scare me. But I raise my chin and meet his glare. We stand facing off, two boxers in the ring for what felt like hours. Finally, he scoffs.

"You don't know a thing about me." The words come out low and covered in ice.

And with that, he breezes by, disappearing into the crowd.

Kareem shakes his head. "Damn, that was cold-blooded."

"Yeah, take it easy!" another one of the guys adds. "Nick's a cool dude! He's always invited to the cookout!"

Pulse racing, I keep my eyes on my cup. That was so stupid. Showing anger like that, and this early, turns people off and that's not part of the plan. They probably think I'm an uppity tight-ass now. Or worse. Back home, my old classmates would roll their eyes.

"There she goes again, making everything about race."

Why couldn't I just keep my mouth shut?

But when I turn to the girls, they're beaming.

"My girl read that man for filth," Loren laughs.

Kammy cheers my cup. "I know that's right!"

A rush of relief and love fills my chest.

Vanessa lurches forward and grabs my wrists with a mischievous grin. "You are gonna LOVE my brother!"

"After convincing him I was Beyoncé's cousin and crying my eyes out about missing my flight, he let me go. My brother almost had a heart attack. And that is how I got out of my first speeding ticket."

The next night, we four girls laugh over our giant pepperoni pizza slices and cans of Sprite, laid out in our cozy living room, rocking pajamas and face masks. Vanessa's going over her wild LA driving tales. We talk about everything, from movies to first celebrity crushes, the convos flowing like we've been friends for years rather than a few days. I had very few friends . . . before Kevin. But, if I was honest, I felt more like a token piece, someone they could point to and say, "I'm not racist! See! My friend is Black." Being the lone Black girl in the room always brought its own set of issues when I'm not busy dodging microaggressions or blatant racist questions. Here, it all feels so natural, so . . . safe. Is this what I've been missing in my life?

Kammy finishes pin curling her wig and hugs her knees. "Guys . . . tomorrow's it. First day of classes!"

"Anything I should know?" I ask. "I haven't even taken a tour around campus yet."

Between the last-minute decision to attend and battling my parents, I missed most of freshman orientation. Our RA gave me a crash course of the map in her room but wasn't much help past that.

Vanessa stuffs her pizza crust in her mouth. "Alright, here are the main things I've picked up: First, the cafeteria food is garbage. Absolute trash!"

"I heard the best time to go is dinner," Loren adds. "That's when the athletes meet up. But if the café is crazy bad, then we're better off just snacking here."

"Number two," Vanessa continues. "Everybody chills in the Rec, that's in the basement of the Malcolm Center. They serve mostly burgers, fries—"

"Mozzarella sticks," Kammy adds. "YUM!"

"But! They don't take dining dollars. Only cash."

I deflate a bit. Don't have much cash to burn on burgers. I already blew through about half of the graduation money my grandparents gifted, so I need to be smart about the rest. I'll have to skip the Rec as much as possible.

"The Malcolm Center is where all the clubs and stuff meet too. Three, which you kinda found out last night, the Kappas run this school so try not to piss them off. They throw the best parties."

"Got it," I mumble, still reeling over my exchange with the lone white boy on campus. So much for not attracting attention.

As if reading my mind, Loren pats my shoulder. "Girl, you straight. By next week, no one's gonna remember you. You ate him up though!"

The girls giggle and I bury my head into my hands.

Loren slaps my arm. "I'm messing with you! Anyways, we got classes in the same building so you can just follow me tomorrow."

"Thanks," I say. Loren has a way of putting people at ease quick. She must have so much practice with all her brothers and sisters.

Vanessa sits up on her knees. "Yo, do you realize that when we graduate from here, we're gonna be Frazier alums? That carries some serious weight."

Loren stretches out. "Right! I've always wanted to come to Frazier U. I have an auntie who went here who told me all about homecoming. They're legendary. This was my first choice and I got in, early decision!"

"Girl, I couldn't believe I got in. My grades are . . . special,"

Vanessa says, wide-eyed, and we giggle. "But my brother says it's straight up THE best HBCU to go to. When he was touring with Hit Makers, they said our campus had some of the best parties and finest women. This place is full of Black excellence!"

Kammy squishes a cheek to her knee, gushing. "My parents came and fell in love here. I'm a legacy baby."

"Aww that's so cute," Loren says. "Maybe I'll meet my hus-bae here. What about you, Jordyn?"

I shrug. "I always wanted to come here. Plus, I went to private school with nothing but white people so I was definitely looking for a change. And who knows, maybe I'll meet my husband here too." Two truths and a believable lie. Not the worst.

The girls nod in agreement.

"My aunt is still best friends with her college roommates. They go on all kinds of girls' trips together."

"Hey! That's gonna be us," Kammy says, hugging up Loren. "We're gonna be sisters for life now!"

"Facts," Loren agrees.

I take in their glowing faces one at a time, full of hope and love.

Yes, sisters. What I always wanted.

I stand up, heading for the kitchen. "Anyone want any tea?"

"Tea? Girl, what?" Loren laughs.

"Yeah," I laugh, giving a sheepish shrug. "I can't go to bed without having some tea."

"Sounds like my brother." Vanessa laughs. "He loves his tea too."

THREE

WITH ONE LAST look, I close the photo album on my computer and slip it into my bag. So many memories, so much history, so much a part of me hidden and tucked away. At least for now.

Packed and ready, I check the time. One hour before my first day as a college student. Feels like I've been preparing for this since middle school. All my parents ever talked about was how every decision that I made, from how I wore my hair to my GPA, was going to lead to college. This is the first day of the life they've been warning me about.

While Vanessa and Kammy went for high-fashion looks for their first-day 'fits, I settled on my typical uniform—a black tee, straight dark denim jeans, and flats. I comb my hair perfectly in place, listening to the girls giggling in the kitchen over bowls of cereal. I'm too nervous to eat.

I'm really doing this, Kev . . .

Just the thought of him makes me slump on my bed. I check the time again and dare myself to dial the number.

"Yes."

The moment I hear her voice, my heart leans toward it.

"Hi Mom," I say, my tone desperate.

There's a brief pause on the line before she sighs. "Hello Jordyn."

Her voice is icy. Not the usual Jordy or JoJo. She is using my full name.

"How are you?" I ask, remaining cheerful.

"I'm well. Thanks."

I wait for her to ask some questions, Like, how's it going, how's my room, how are my roommates . . . but nothing.

"Um, so I was just calling because today is my first day of classes. Intro to Ethics."

"Okay."

"And . . . I guess that's it."

"Okay."

The "okays" were in the same inflection. Dad must be standing by, listening. The silence stretches.

"Well, we got a letter from Yale yesterday," Mom states. "Confirming your deferral."

I swallow. "Oh. I . . ."

"Guess you'll see if this year will all be worth it."

It's as if she etched the underlying meaning of her words on the walls of my dorm.

"Okay. Talk to you later then. Bye." I hang up quick so I won't hear her hang up on me first. I'm too tender for that.

According to the psychiatrist Elisabeth Kübler-Ross, there are five stages of grief: denial and isolation, anger, bargaining, depression, and acceptance. I read about it in her book *On Death and Dying.* Right now, I can't tell if my parents are in the anger phase or the depression phase with my decision to go to Frazier U.

I held a proverbial gun to their heads in order for them to agree to pay for college. If they didn't, all of Westport would have known. It would make them look bad. And after Kevin . . . that's the last thing they would want: more attention. Outside of tuition, room, board, and a small stipend, they made it clear that I wouldn't get a single dime from them otherwise.

I take a deep breath and scroll down my meager address book, daring myself to call him. It's selfish, but I just want to hear a familiar voice. Everything is so new, exciting yet nerve-racking.

"Yeah what?" he snaps, answering on almost the last possible ring.

"Hi! How's it going?"

He scoffs. "Do you really wanna know?"

"Jack, I just thought we could—"

"Jordyn, did you expect me to be happy to hear from you? You pull this last-minute stunt to go to that ghetto school when we've been planning for YEARS to go to Yale. I worked my ass off to get into the school. You barely broke a sweat. And now we're . . . well, I don't even know what we are anymore."

"Friends?" I offer.

"Friends?" he spits. "Right. Well, FRIEND. I have to go."

Click.

Clearly Jack is still in the anger phase.

I guess I shouldn't be surprised that my boyfriend of the last four years doesn't want to hear from me. Not after just telling him two weeks ago that no, I wasn't going to college with him. I shouldn't have even been surprised that he immediately dumped me. I wasn't even surprised when he showed up the night before my train, begging, pleading with me to change my mind.

There's not a single person back home that is happy that I chose Frazier. Shock and disgust was the typical response, the question always being why? Why would I give up Yale for some "'Black school"?

And I don't have an answer for them. Or at least an answer that I can tell them right now.

I've always loved the balance beam. It requires flexibility, grace, poise, strength, and, of course, balance. Mom said when I was younger, I would find anything to tight rope across—curbs, benches, logs, walls, random lines of chalk. By the time I was seven, she enrolled me in gymnastics, hoping it would help me wean off the habit, with hard work and a few hard falls. Instead, just made me hungry for more.

That's how I feel, walking through Frazier's campus. Hoping that if I just go for it . . . it would put an end to my curiosity. This plan of mine was going to call for a delicate dance on a beam. The issue becomes when I eventually fall in front of a crowd, how hard it might hurt.

Frazier's main campus is a quadrangle, known as the Quad. It's a rhombus-shaped yard, flanked by vine-choked academic halls, with a flat grassy expanse and network of paved walkways painted a dull gold. Students follow the yellow brick road to classes.

I rush toward the stairs in Baker Hall, taking two steps at a time. First day, and I'm already going to be late to class. The trek to campus from our dorm up steep hills was a bit more intense than I thought.

My schedule says it's in room 2012 but these room numbers are not in order. Soon as I round the corner, I bump right into him.

"Ooff!" Nick grunts, stepping back. "Bambi?"

I straighten my hair. He's the last person I want to see right now. "That's not my name. It's Jordyn."

He grins with a bored sigh. "Same thing. You lost?"

"No," I shoot back defiantly.

He rolls his eyes and snatches my phone, scanning my schedule. "Oh. You have Hammond. I had his class last year."

"You're prelaw?"

"Ummm yeah." He scans my schedule. "Huh. Looks like we have Ethics together. How'd you get in that without the prerequisite?"

I snatch my phone back, slipping it into my pocket. "I took

pre-college courses over the summer."

"Figures you'd be an overachiever. Come on, walk this way or we'll both be late."

Begrudgingly, I follow. It's my fault. Instead of partying and hanging with the girls, I should have been doing a practice run-through of my day. I should have looked up my professors, read their syllabuses, ordered their materials.

That's what old Jordyn would do. Because old Jordyn couldn't just be herself. She had to work ten times as hard to get half the recognition. New Jordyn can just . . . exist. At least without the same fire under her feet. A new drive is here.

Nick walks into class first, sitting in the back row, garnering stares from the other classmates. Wanting to create a canyon-size distance between us, I sit in the front but notice a few girls peek over their shoulders at him.

On second glance, Nick is cute, in a preppy white boy kind of way. Baby-faced, but his blue eyes twinkle with mischief, which only makes me wonder . . . why is he here?

The conversation around going to Frazier went a little something like this . . .

Dad: What kind of education are you going to get there? It's not going to help you get a job! A Black school doesn't even represent the real world. There's no place in this country where the predominant is Black. Certainly not successful places.

Mom: Colleges like Yale can offer you better opportunities,

guaranteed job security, and career prospects. True success can only be found at elite institutions. Not at a Black school.

Dad: How can you embarrass us like this? After everything we've been through!

Despite the resounding evidence that going to an HBCU has the opposite effect of their assumptions, it doesn't matter. They've already been conditioned to think that white spaces equal white success.

But sitting here among my peers . . . it all feels so worth their belittling.

"That's what I'm saying!" Kareem shouts, his arms around Vanessa's shoulders. "You putting Lil Wayne in the same box as Lil Baby is wild crazy, bruh!"

"Baby, be easy on him," Vanessa coos. "He don't know no better."

It's been just a week, yet Vanessa and Kareem already look like the perfect couple. The two ooze chocolatey sex appeal. When they walk across campus, heads turn. They don't even hold hands, but their energy speaks volumes. When they're not in classes, Kareem just about lives on our love seat, staring at Vanessa.

Beside me, Loren is trying not to have a meltdown over a sophomore boy she met last week.

"But he said he'd call, then he just texted. Now I see him walking around with some other girl. I can't believe he ghosted me like that."

"Girl, he ain't worth it." That's Kerry, Loren's friend from her Intro to Comms class. Kerry is from Atlanta, with long golden locs and cute apple cheeks.

"Tell her!" That's Legacy, Kareem's old roommate. I think he has a bit of a crush on Loren, who pretends not to notice.

"Anyone need more ice?" Kammy asks from the stove, as she turns over some chicken legs with one hand, popping open the fridge with the other. She always flutters about like the perfect host. "You got ten more minutes until I finish this chicken. Corn bread almost done too."

"Girl, I ain't trying to gain that freshman fifteen in a month," Loren chides with a grin. "But add some extra honey to my butter please!"

Loren is equal parts silly as she is no-nonsense. Kammy is a warm hug, a bowl full of southern sunshine. She feels like home, which, for a school full of homesick kids, makes her a beacon to our kitchen.

Almost every other day, Vanessa is inviting new friends to our suite. We've become the cool hangout spot, the place others in the dorm come to kick it.

There are always people around, but I don't mind. I love that I'm friends with the popular girls. People want to talk to me and not in a perfunctory manner. For once in my life, I'm just Jordyn. Not "Jordyn, the Black girl in my AP Chem class."

Some would also confuse me with Google, the way I'm used to fact-checking just about anything we talk about. That and tech support.

"Hey Jordyn, why can't I send this file?" Kammy asks, tapping her laptop. "I swear. Oh! Now I've deleted it. Great."

I laugh, pulling the computer onto my lap. "I keep telling you, you have to compress these big files before you try to send them. And it's not deleted, it's in your cloud. Kammy! How many files do you have in here? And have you ever emptied your trash?"

"Girl, you speaking French," Kammy laughs.

I wave her off. "Just let me handle it."

"Jordyn, could you clean up my computer too?" Vanessa asks. "It's slow as hell. And I definitely can't afford another."

I grin. "Of course!"

I can't believe it took leaving home to find friends like this. Ones who I'd do anything for and the same for me. As I look around the room, all I want to do is start taking pictures, so I never forget this feeling and post my new life for everyone back home to see and think, maybe I was wrong about her. My classes are great, my friends are amazing, I have a life worth being jealous of. Maybe I won't need to transfer to Yale. Maybe I can really make it work here.

"My brother could tell you some stories about YG," I hear Vanessa say and tune back in, straightening. "They used to party together. They're still real tight. He'll tell you all about him when you meet him."

Vanessa is the closest thing we got to a music historian, thanks mostly to her brother.

"So wait, did your brother really roll with Snoop Dogg

back in the day?" Legacy asks.

Vanessa whips out her phone. "Check this!"

She shows us a few photos. Everyone oohs and aahs. Her brother looks young, maybe fifteen. But he's really there.

"Damn! Your brother been everywhere!"

"Come on, y'all," Kammy calls, wiping her hands. "Let's say grace and thank the Lord for this food. Amen, amen!"

Vanessa goes on to talk more about her brother's music industry dealings. Everything I know about hip-hop I learned from rich white boys who used it as fodder in their privileged lives. They'd come to school, rattling off one-hit wonder artists as proof that I had the personality of dry bread.

"You don't know XYZ? HA! See, that why I'm blacker than you."

But here at Frazier, no one knows that version of Jordyn. Just assumes we've all had the same Black experience when really, I'm here to learn and feel everything I didn't at home.

"Hey hey! Hold up, y'all. Listen!" Legacy stands, plays a news clip on Twitter from his phone.

"'Tonight, we have shocking news out of Southeast DC. Footage of an unarmed man shot by an off-duty police officer last spring has been released. The officer claimed he was—'"

"Damn, not again," Kareem mumbles. "I swear, shit like this happens every day."

"You think there're gonna be riots and stuff?" Kammy asks.

"Why you ask like that?" Vanessa snaps.

"It's just . . . you know how folks get and I've lived through enough of these," Kammy says. "They burned down my auntie's hair shop after a kid got killed in our neighborhood."

"Pfff! Who you telling," Vanessa says. "Not one of us are in here without a story."

"Breonna Taylor in my city," Legacy agrees. "They did her so dirty. I remember the curfew."

"Ahmaud Arbery in mine," Kerry says, shaking her head. "They burned down a CVS around the corner from my house."

"I was in kindergarten when Trayvon Martin happened," Loren adds. "New York was on fire. I'll never forget it."

Everyone looks at me and I don't have a specific story to share.

"Uhhh, George Floyd," I whisper.

The room nods. Not one person in the room doesn't remember those days during COVID.

"Damn. It's like nothing ever changes," Kareem grumbles, taking a sip of his drink, his eyes hard. "Can't ever get a break. Even at school."

* * *

JOIN THE FRAZIER U STUDENT ASSOCIATION
First Town Hall of the School Year
Meet Your Student Executive Leaders

The large yellow flyer is pinned on a bulletin board in the lobby outside the Rec Center. It's been just shy a month of classes and between keeping up with assignments and bouncing from party to party with the girls, I haven't had time for much else.

But I've been a part of student government in one way or another since middle school. Freshman year I lobbied to have more snacks added in our school's vending machines. By junior year, I was being invited to school board meetings and was already planning a presidential run.

Of course, I abandoned most of my extracurricular activities once Kevin happened. Maybe this is a chance to start over. Something to ground me in reality. It'll also look perfect on my law school résumé. That's what my parents would say. Every step I'm supposed to take should be toward their ultimate goal.

Lost in my own thoughts, I don't hear Loren sneak up beside me.

"Hellllllloooo?! What you doing? Didn't you hear me calling you?"

"Oh . . . uh, my bad. I was in my own world," I say, shouldering my backpack.

"Sure was. Ready to go?" she asks but her breath seems a little labored.

"Hey, are you okay?"

"Uh, yeah," she croaks with a staggered step.

I hold out my arms. "Whoa, Loren! You don't look so good."

"No I'm . . ." She trails off, her eyes widening, as if she realizes what is happening to her, before they roll back. Then, she tips over, collapsing right into my arms, and we fall backward to the ground.

"LOREN!"

FOUR

"LOREN, ARE YOU sure you're okay?"

Loren, Kammy, and I amble from the Malcolm Center like drifting leaves in the evening breeze. Loren insisted she didn't want to go to the infirmary but agreed to eat dinner in the café instead.

"Yeah," she says in a groggy voice, flashing a sleepy smile. "That was mad embarrassing tho. Can't believe I forgot to eat today."

Despite her words, she still looks gray in the face.

"Why didn't you tell us you were diabetic?" I ask.

She shrugs. "I didn't want to make a big deal out of it and y'all treat me all different."

"We would never," Kammy insists, rubbing her shoulder. "You're one of us."

Loren nods, her eyes glassy. "Thanks, boo. And I promise, I'll keep my shit in check. No more fainting."

Kammy sucks her teeth. "Hmp. Better not."

The weather has finally started to cool, fall close to joining us for our first semester at Frazier. We walk down the hill, toward the Rock, arms linked. Mostly to keep Loren on her feet. I don't think I can stomach seeing her faint again.

"Anyway, the café wasn't the worst tonight." Loren brightens, trying her best to change the subject. "At least there were veggies."

Kammy huffs. "I only ate there for you."

I laugh. "Kam, the food isn't that bad."

Kammy sucks her teeth. "That chicken could've lit a forest fire it was so dry. I'm mad I prayed over it. And I know you ain't talking, you barely ate!"

Loren and I crack up. Kammy is a bona fide picky eater, which makes sense given she's the cook in her family. Loren mostly eats for sustenance. I have a feeling she isn't used to food being this readily available to her all the time. And me, well I guess food and I have always been acquaintances rather than lovers.

Screaming sirens pierce the air as four police cars fly by, weaving through the busy street. We cross the road, watching their lights dim in the distance.

"They must be heading to the protest," Kammy mumbles. "I've seen a few on the news."

We walk through the lobby of Rock Hall, everyone waving and making plans for later. No one seems too overly worried about the protest. We ride the elevator up and I slip my key into the suite door, stopping short at the man sitting on our sofa.

"Uh. Hello?"

Loren and Kammy gather beside me, defensively.

"Who are you?" Loren snaps with a wobbly voice.

He slowly stands and we all take a step back.

Vanessa runs out of her room, beaming. "Hey girls! This is my brother, Devonte. I know! We don't look alike. Same mom, different dads, you know how it goes."

Devonte takes us in one by one. When his eyes land on me, I flinch, as if hit by a static shock. He's much taller than I thought he'd be. Thin, but muscular, with veins raised a touch beneath brown butter skin. His long locs cascade down the side of his face. He has dimples, which bring a youthfulness to his demeanor. But his dark shiny eyes hold a unique power.

Above all . . . he smells amazing.

Kammy and Loren stand dumbstruck. None of us were prepared for this type of Greek god–like man.

"Hey," Kammy utters, then shakes her head, as if waking up from a nap. "Welcome! Would you like a drink? We got it all."

"No thanks, sis. I don't drink," he says, with a light wave of his hand.

"Oh. Okay. My bad."

"Nothing to be sorry about at all, love."

Kammy just about clutches her pearls, taken aback by his smooth baritone voice. The way his tongue moves when he says "love" is mesmerizing.

"Uh, hi," Loren lets out with a small choke. "What's up?"

Vanessa straightens, her face turning serious. "Lo, you okay?"

"Yeah I'm . . ."

Loren sways and before I can yelp, Devonte swoops in, scooping her up into his arms, effortlessly.

Kammy stumbles back with a "Whoa."

Vanessa runs across the room petting Loren's hair and forehead. "What happened!"

Kammy gives a recap as Devonte struts over to the sofa, placing her down like a baby in her crib.

"Yo, Ness, pass me my bag," he says.

Vanessa rushes into her room, procuring his satchel.

"Vanessa said y'all might be hungry." He motions to a bag of groceries by the kitchen. "Figure I make a little something."

"You know how to cook?" Kammy seems both impressed and skeptical at the offer.

He grins. "I learned a thing or two." He glances at Loren. "But for you, Queen . . . you need something a little different."

As Vanessa and Devonte set up in the kitchen, Kammy plays bartender, mixing drinks for the rest of us. I watch Devonte boil water then add some dried herbs from his bag, never taking my eyes off the cup. He sips, approving, then carries it to Loren.

"Drink this." He places the mug into her hands and I resist the urge to slap it away. She JUST fainted, who knows what the hell is in that tea and what it can do to her. But I have to play it cool. Plus, Loren said she wants to be seen as normal. I can appreciate that. Don't want to come off like some helicopter mom. I try turning my attention elsewhere.

Principle number eight: Talk in terms of the other person's interest.

"Um, so, Vanessa said you used to work in the hip-hop industry," I say in my best friendly voice.

He lets out a low laugh returning to the stove. "Not work. I wouldn't call it work. I was a part of creating the culture. I'm an architect."

His deep throaty voice is intoxicating. The kind you could listen to on audiobook all day. Kammy hovers nearby, as if worried about someone being in her kitchen. I hit her with a silly face, trying to lighten her mood.

"What are you listening to now?" Loren asks from the sofa.

"Little of this, little of that. Mostly stuff that ain't out yet. People send me tracks for feedback."

"Even when you were in prison?" Kammy asks, and we all flash her a look. But Devonte only chuckles.

"My ears were free, sis. They locked up my body but they could never take over my mind."

He shuts her down softly, a light feather tap.

"Yo, let me ask y'all a question," he says. "Do you really know how the music industry works?"

He begins breaking down the major players of labels, the producers, the tour managers, the marketing teams. . . . He refers to them on a first-name basis, all while cooking us sautéed veggies with red potatoes. Loren begins taking notes on her phone, hanging on his every word. He speaks with such passion, authority, and vision. If our professors talked with this amount of knowledge, we'd never leave their classrooms.

"The thing you gotta remember is . . . music breathes life into people. It has a heartbeat. You gotta take it seriously when you create it. But before I go into all that . . . let me take a look at my patient here."

Devonte crosses the room and kneels beside Loren. She lets out a bashful laugh.

"Oh! I'm good," Loren insists, trying to shoo him away. "Don't worry about me."

Devonte cocks his head to the side, his gaze on her firm and intense. "I bet it's frustrating, not being in full control of your body the way you want."

Loren's mouth drops. I don't think she's ever admitted that to anyone.

He smiles, brushes a few braids out of her face. "How are you feeling now, love?"

Loren takes a moment, eyelids fluttering as if she's doing a full-body scan.

"Actually, much better." She peers into her cup. "What is this stuff?"

Devonte chuckles. "A little of this, a little of that. I studied under a bushman doctor in Cuba."

Kammy frowns. "Cuba? Thought we weren't allowed to go there."

"I have my ways and my connections. Some of the best doctors in the world are in Cuba. One of the many reasons this country tries to keep us from going there. Our healthcare here is shit. And expensive."

"Facts," Loren mumbles, taking another sip from her mug.

I nod, as an alert buzzes on my phone. News headline: **Protests erupt in DC following release of deadly police body cam footage.**

"'It's a very tense situation out here between DC police officers and protesters. As you can see, we have officers in riot gear. . . .'"

The next morning, the smell of fresh biscuits fills the air. We stayed up past three a.m. with Devonte, talking about music and life, until we slowly drifted into our rooms and fell asleep. I figured maybe Kammy decided to make breakfast. But when I step out of my room, I find Devonte pulling a tray out of our tiny stove.

"Grand rising, Queen," he says in a soft voice. "Made some breakfast. You slept good?"

I blink back in surprise. "Uh, yeah. You?"

"Any night outside the chains they had me in is a gift."

Suddenly self-conscious, I rush into the bathroom to brush my teeth, wash my face, and compose my thoughts. When I step out, he's there, waiting with a plate.

"For you." He hands me the plate, thumb grazing my knuckles, and I flinch.

"Thanks," I murmur just as Loren and Kammy come out of their rooms.

"What! Breakfast!" Loren exclaims.

"First meal of the day is the most important one," he says, his smile glowing. "You know breakfast stands for breaking your fast. What you put in your body helps knowledge absorb in the mind. Beyoncé and Jay-Z are all about that shit."

Loren almost drops her plate. "Wait, you know Beyoncé and Jay-Z?"

"Who do you think helped with that On the Run tour?"

"Wow," she gasps, astounded.

"What's the green stuff?" Kammy asks, poking it with a fork.

"That's callaloo with saltfish. You need nutrients in your body. Summer Walker put me on to that."

He continues on, name-dropping celebrities we've all heard of. So caught up in his stories we lose track of time and go running for the elevator to class.

"Okay, this is gonna be a crazy question," Vanessa says on the way down to the lobby.

"I'm all for crazy," Loren says, applying her lip gloss.

"Y'all mind if Devonte stays with us for a few days? I haven't seen him in so long and I really miss him!"

Kammy beams. "What, of course he can stay!"

"Duh! I mean, he's your brother!" Loren adds.

The girls look at me and I smile wider. "Yeah. The more the merrier and all that, right?"

"Right!" they say in unison and burst into laughter.

Who in their right mind would say no to her?

My parents had a very specific agenda for me:

- Parker Academy for first through twelfth. A's the only acceptable grade.
- Gymnastics, ballet, Jack and Jill, Honors Society, debate team, Junior Law Club.
- My hair was to be straight at all times. Clothes neat, clean, proper.
- No boys. Unless they were from a good (read: white) family.
- Major: political science. Yale or Stanford, with a straight track to Yale Law School.
- Work at Dad's law firm until I'm cold in the ground.

And even though I followed this agenda for the most part, any small deviation would send them reeling. They couldn't understand why I would waste my time reading novels. Anything that wasn't for educational purposes was considered trivial.

And this was all before Kevin. After . . . it only got worse. Because now all their hopes and dreams were stuffed into the shoulder pads of my uniform blazer, weighing me down. The pressure so severe, it made it impossible to eat.

At least, that's what I tell myself.

I'm ten minutes late to Ethics, which sucks because attendance is part of my grade and I want to nail an A. Especially in front of Nick. There's been a few times we sparred during class discussions and I never backed down. I played small in high school with white boys like him. I refuse to do that here.

Just as I reach the stairs, a tidal wave of students come flowing down, rushing out the building. I spot Nick in the crowd, heading for the doors.

"Hey what's going on?" I ask, following, trying to keep the panic out of my voice.

"Classes are canceled," he says without stopping. "School closing early due to the protest. Giving people a chance to get home before curfew."

"Really?" I didn't check the news before leaving. Too preoccupied with Devonte. "Are you going?"

He shakes his head. "No."

I scoff. "Figures."

He stops to face me. "No, I'm going to the police station. I'm a jail support volunteer. They're going to be arresting hundreds of people and folks don't know their rights. We remind them what to say and ask once inside. Try to catch people's names and birth dates before they are bused away so we can track them in the system, then greet them when they're free, with hot coffee or tea, anything they need."

"Wow." That's something I would love to do. Something I never thought or heard of.

"You should go home, Bambi. It's only going to get worse before the National Guard is called in."

He doesn't wait for my response and walks off.

In the lobby of Rock Hall, a group of students are dressed in all black, painting posters and signs . . . *No Justice, No Peace!*

Overnight, the protests exploded in Southeast, spilling farther into the city. The school buzzed with the news, resulting in the same question being tossed left and right. . . .

Are you going?

The truth is, I don't know. My parents hate protests, think they are the biggest waste of time and energy. Both lawyers, they can't wrap their head around breaking the law to prove a point in the name of justice. Living in the suburbs, we are always far from the fray. Now, I'm in the thick of it, locked inside the protected bubble of school, where students are planning to cut their way out, and I'm not sure if I should follow.

What would you do, Kevin, if you were here?

I stop to read another sign right before spotting Vanessa at the front door, rushing over with a grin.

"Girl! Thank GOD they canceled class! My ass did not study at all for that accounting quiz." She stares into her phone, scrolling through messages, and I find myself wondering of all careers . . . why accounting?

She nods at a message. "Okay, cool. There's a happy hour at this bar on V Street. I met a security guard who can slip us in."

Some bars and lounges aren't big on letting in underage students. Especially freshmen.

"You really want to go out tonight?" I ask, waving at the posters still drying by the windows.

"We'll be fine! It's all going down in Southeast and by the White House anyway. Nothing over here to be worried about. We'll be home before curfew."

I take a deep breath. "Is your brother coming?"

"Nah," she says with a wink. "It's ladies' night!"

There is a thick unease in the air, as if the whole city is collectively holding their breath.

But at the bar, I watch Kammy flirt her way through two rum and Cokes. Feels like we're partying on the edges of a war zone, with choppers flying overhead and black smoke billowing in the distance. Vanessa didn't want to drive so we took a car service to the bar fifteen minutes from campus.

Loren grabs Kammy's hand, dancing her closer to us and away from some guy who's been in her ear all night.

"Aye, girl, don't you have a man you're all in love with," Loren says with a laugh. "Not me out here trying to save your happy home!"

Kammy gives us a coy smile. "I do but . . ."

"But?" we all say at once.

Kammy gives us a sheepish grin, sliding a piece of hair behind her ear. "It's nice feeling so, I don't know . . . wanted. Nobody used to check for me like this back home. I'm not built like Vanessa and got the boys wrapped around her finger."

Vanessa giggles. "HA! I wasn't always this cute. Check this out." She flips through her phone and pulls up a picture. In the photo is a young Vanessa grinning with braces and thick glasses, sitting in a cluttered living room. On the opposite side of the flowery sofa is Devonte, his expression stoic.

"That's me, freshman year of high school. A hot mess! And that's Devonte. He was just starting his locs. My dad HATED them."

The picture seems ancient in comparison to what I see and know standing before me that I have to laugh.

"What was your brother like as a kid?" I ask.

"Mmm . . . I guess a deep thinker. Always had wild ideas and plans."

Just like me, I think, and take a sip of my drink.

The bright bar lights pop on, blinding everyone. The music shuts off with an abrupt snap before someone jumps on the mic.

"Everyone . . . you need to leave, right now. Bar is closed."

A chorus of grumbles comes from the crowd, as people make their way to the door.

"Aye, what's up?" Vanessa asks one of the bartenders.

"They shutting down the bar," a woman in black says. "Protesters are making their way up here. They don't want no smoke. Y'all better get home. Now!"

This sobers Kammy up. "Wait, the protesters are coming this way? What do we do?"

Vanessa remains composed but her lips wiggle.

"Well, we're already out here. Maybe we should just . . . join them," Vanessa suggests with an innocent shrug. Was this her plan all along?

Loren and I exchange a look, clearly thinking the same thing. We need to get home. This isn't the right time to be justice warriors. I check my phone, no service. There must be too many people around. No way to call a car.

"Everyone is talking about going." Vanessa shrugs. "Maybe we should get in on the action!"

I feel my facade begin to slide off and shrug it back up my shoulder, remaining mute.

Kammy bites her lip. "I've never been to a protest before. My momma wouldn't let me. She said we should just pray for everyone's safety."

Vanessa has a hard time holding in her disgust. "Nah. We don't need no thoughts and prayers. We need to be about action!"

Loren's brow furrows. "I feel you, but I can't afford to get arrested."

"Me either," I add, calculating what's left in my bank account. My parents would have to come bail me out. That would just about ruin everything. I can't risk it.

Then again, I keep thinking what would Kevin do versus what he would want to do.

"No one's getting arrested, y'all," Vanessa says, nonchalantly. "What are we going to do? Just stand by while they murder us in cold blood and not say nothing? We'll be fine! Trust me."

I study Vanessa, a thousand thoughts running through my head, the loudest one: I wish I could syphon just a fraction of her audacious confidence. Then I would have no issues making friends. She probably could talk her way out of a prison sentence. I'll have to keep that in mind.

Outside, I hear chanting coming closer.

"NO JUSTICE, NO PEACE! NO JUSTICE, NO PEACE!"

Everyone files out of the bar. Outside, V Street is packed. Every spot shutting down, lights off, doors closing, people spilling out into the middle of the road. Up ahead, police lights swirl, a barricade put up, blocking off traffic. The opposite end, protesters marching toward us, in one straight line that takes up the entire street. Hundreds of people as far as you can see.

We're sandwiched in. Trapped.

A few feet away, a newswoman stands in front of her cameraman. . . .

"It's a very tense situation out here between DC police officers and protesters! As you can see, we have officers in riot gear. . . ."

"Shit," Loren mumbles behind me.

"No, no, no," Kammy whimpers, head shaking. "I don't like this. I wanna go home!"

But which way do we go, toward the police or toward the protesters? Without cell service, I don't even have GPS to tell me how to get back to campus.

The crowd of partygoers twist and turn around, lumping

together in the middle. Vanessa looks both ways, eyes panicking, as if realizing her mistake.

"Uh, this way. I think." Vanessa grabs my hand and heads toward the protesters. I grab Loren's hand, who grabs Kammy's, linking us like a chain.

But before we can take two steps, a bottle launches up, forming an arc in the sky, landing right at our feet, glass exploding in every direction. The girls shriek.

"Y'all partying in our city while they kill us!" someone in the crowd yells.

"Fuck you and your school, you bougie-ass Negroes!"

Behind us, the police form a tight line, shields held up, batons in hand at the ready.

"Go!" Vanessa screams and starts running. We dive straight into the crowd, weaving through signs, posters slapping our faces, blocking our view, the chants deafening. But it's like swimming through oatmeal. The crowd becoming thicker with every step.

Behind me, I hear Kammy cry out, "Wait!"

I spin around and see Kammy and Loren stuck a few feet behind. I wring my hand loose from Vanessa to backpedal.

"I can't move!" Loren screams, her eyes bulging. By the time we reach a hysterical Kammy, I can barely breathe. We're laced in a corset of people, the strings pulling tighter.

And I can't see Vanessa. She's gone!

My arms are pinned to my sides. I can't move, can't yank

myself free. My hair unravels as I stretch up and realize what's happening. The police are marching forward, the crowd is squeezing us tighter to the point that no one can move. I stare into Kammy's horrified eyes, as she tries to push people off her. If someone yells "run," if a gun goes off . . . we'll be trampled.

At that exact moment, there's a small wave, the crowd falling like dominoes. Loren loses her footing, toppling down.

"Loren!" But she's gone, drowning in the sea of people, vanishing from sight. My bones turn to icicles, heart trying to explode through my ribs.

Through all the screaming and shouting, I hear the echoing of cans bouncing on the concrete. Smoke plumes and surrounds us like an oncoming fog. A billion onions are sliced at once. My eyes begin to burn and sizzle. In the height of my panic, my thoughts drift to him.

This is it, Kevin. I've failed . . . before even trying.

I frantically spin, searching for a way out, thumping into a hard chest.

Devonte.

He takes a giant stride, plucking protesters off one-handed, and pulls Loren to her feet, scooping her to his side.

"Don't let go," he shouts into my ear. His thick calluses scratch the inside of my palm as he tightens his grip. Then, like a bulldozer, he charges through the crowd, moving fast, a hot knife through butter, heading straight for a parked van.

"Wait!" he orders, positioning us behind the back of the van.

"Cover your nose and mouth. Just wait."

And as if on cue, a stampede erupts, everyone running, screaming following. Kammy sobs into her praying hands. But Devonte seems to be calm, careful . . . calculating.

When the crowd thins, Devonte pushes us toward the sidewalk. "Go!"

On the corner, the crowd eases enough for us to push through and run away from the madness. Down the block, Vanessa waves by the open door of her truck.

"Get in! Get in!"

I grab Kammy's hand and scramble into the back seat, Loren dives in after us.

Devonte jumps into the driver's seat, throws the car in gear, and speeds off.

"I'm so so sorry, y'all," Vanessa says for the millionth time, eyes swollen with tears. "I didn't think it was gonna be like that."

Back at the dorm, Devonte helps us tend to our stinging eyes. Other than a lost shoe, a torn shirt, and buckets of tears, we managed to make it out unscathed.

"So why did you hide behind the van?" Kareem asks as we recount our night of terror.

Devonte sips his water, taking all the attention in stride. "They were in the middle of a crowd crush. A stampede was the next thing coming so I hid us behind something and let the majority of the crowd pass. You don't want to get caught up, trip, and run over. Trust. Been to enough concerts to know how to survive."

Kammy shakes her head in awe. "You saved our lives."

Devonte gives a modest nod. All in a day's work for him. Still, I find myself so grateful. A strange feeling. How did he even know how to find us?

"It's my fault we were out there in the first place," Vanessa admits, shaking her head. Kareem kisses her cheek. "We could've been locked up. Then . . . shit."

She looks at Devonte, something passing between them.

"It's nobody's fault," Devonte corrects her, eyes flickering to Kareem's hand then back.

"How'd you know where we were?" I ask, trying not to sound suspicious.

"Vanessa told me where y'all were kicking it tonight. I had a sense something was up. I've seen this movie too many times. The police set a trap, trying to lock up as many brothers and sisters as they can get their hands on. More numbers, more overtime, more pay. You probably would've stayed locked up over the weekend."

I think of Nick at the police station. What would he have said if he saw me being carted off. Would he have tried to help? Would he be impressed?

"Nothing is gained by looting and burning down businesses owned and run by our own people," Loren says, and I tune back into the conversation. "These riots are just gonna keep setting us back."

"It's an uprising, sis. Not a riot," Devonte says gently. "Words have power. We have to use them wisely, and not use the enemy's language for what is going on right now. See, calling it a riot makes it seem like fighting against oppression is wrong. And that ain't it."

Loren processes this for a moment, giving him an appreciative nod. "Facts."

Kareem continues to comfort Vanessa while Kammy stares at the floor, still in shock.

"This is just gonna keep on happening," she mumbles.

"Yeah, and they just gonna keep getting away with it," Kareem hisses.

Devonte scans the room. "Y'all are young and have seen this type of injustice more than you should. Before, there were no cameras to catch our people being gunned down, attacked, and framed. Y'all are a generation who've seen lynching and police brutality in real time, in color and surround sound. You've had to deal with the burden of witnessing those same people get away with it. Murderers in navy uniforms. Then, folks expect you to go to school, function like it's just another day. Teaching you to be fair and follow the rules, in an unfair world that stays cheating. It's no wonder y'all fed up and ready to take to the streets, ready to burn it all down. It ain't right and you deserve better."

The room simmers, a dark cloud over our thoughts and memories. The images shoved in our faces every day. It's all we've seen and known. It's like he understands the feelings we have had no real words for. The violations that have been done to our childhood, the proverbial peace promised yet never experienced. Seems like we're always sitting on the edge of an unsaid war; if it's not one thing, it's another. It's not right and we do deserve better.

"But believe me," he continues. "There will be a day where we, Black people, will inflict the same violence that was done upon our people to them. No one should be surprised when that day comes very soon. A few burnt buildings will be the least of their problems."

Kareem sits on the sofa next to Vanessa and, for a change, is not mesmerized by her beauty, but fascinated with Devonte.

"Okay, tell me again how you helped produce Kanye's album," Kareem says. "'Cause that's my favorite album of all time!"

Devonte sits on a love seat arm, trying to hold back a coy smile, as if he's nervous about being the center of attention.

"Albums," he corrects. "I know people think Kanye ain't right in the head but they said that about every genius who walked on this earth. We'd be in the studio for hours, vibing to a beat, and I make a suggestion then . . . POOF! Art."

Kareem leans forward like a little boy eating up a good picture book. Can't say that I blame him. I, too, wanted to hear more about his time with Kanye. Kareem spread word about Devonte helping us the night of the uprising and some of his friends were eager to meet him. With a city-wide curfew still in effect, we hunker in our suite, riding out another wave of protests as the National Guard struggles to maintain control.

"What was it like, being locked up?" Legacy asks. "And couldn't Kanye help get you out? Pay for lawyers and stuff."

He shrugs. "He knew the real reason, he knew what I was up against. Sometimes the mission needs its strongest soldier."

I glance at Vanessa who nods in agreement. The way she admires her brother . . . seems unearthly. Their relationship doesn't fit the traditional mold of big brother/little sister. They don't make fun of each other, roll their eyes when one or the other is being annoying. They're like a team, one unit.

That could've been us. . . .

"What you mean by 'the mission'?" Legacy asks from his seat on the floor.

Devonte stares at his palms. "It's hard being a Black man in this country. Damn near impossible. Haven't you ever wondered why? I bet your pops had 'the talk' with you once or twice. You know, the talk about what to do if you're stopped by an officer?"

Kareem and Legacy nod.

"You ever wonder if white boys ever had to have 'the talk'? You ever wonder why you're treated so different? Why your fathers, grandfathers, uncles, cousins were all treated so different? Aren't you tired that no one is able to answer the question why?"

The room falls silent.

"The moment you start questioning a system that's aimed for your demise is the moment you become an enemy of that system. Then the mission becomes clear. You can't be sold or indoctrinated. That's when you learn none of this shit is real and you got to wake the people up!"

Legacy nods. "Like in *The Matrix*."

The room giggles. Everyone except Devonte.

"Funny you should say that. Did you know the original creator of *The Matrix* was a Black woman?"

"What?"

"Yep. White people stole her idea. Think about all the other inventions and ideas white people stole and took credit for. But when they stole her shit, they didn't know they were sending a secret message . . . the truth, to Black kings and queens everywhere."

"Damn, that's deep," Kareem mumbles as Vanessa rubs his knee.

Kammy, scanning the room, lets out a sigh. "Anyone need anything to drink? More ice?"

The evening carries on, Devonte sharing more of his adventures in music, handing out life advice like sweet candy. The way he's able to command attention, while his points fly over heads, is fascinating.

Around two a.m., as the boys get ready to leave, Devonte has one more thing to say.

"Hey brother, before you go, can I ask you something?"

"Yeah! What's up," Kareem says eagerly, his face lighting up.

Devonte wiggles a finger at Kareem's arm. "What do those

letters on your jacket mean to you?"

Kareem looks down and laughs. "Oh! They're from my fraternity. Kappa Kappa Psi."

"Hmm. Why do you think you need to be in a fraternity?"

Kareem laughs, eyes toggling from us then back to Devonte. "Well, why not? It's a brotherhood. And there are fraternities all over the world."

"Fraternities were originally founded by white men exclusively to trade secrets."

That's not true, I think but don't say out loud.

"You ever question," he continues, "why after all these years, Black folk still trying to live up to an image of them?"

Kareem blanches. The thought never crossed his mind.

"Wooo Lawd, answer that question and we'll be here all night," Kammy says, trying to interject humor into the moment. Not that it feels tense. It feels as if we have still so much to learn.

Exhaustion begins taking over. I slyly move away from the group saying their goodbyes, dumping my plate in the sink. Devonte volunteers to clean up. He's always cleaning, straightening, even offering to iron our clothes.

As I head to my room, I notice Kareem, Legacy, and Devonte in the corner, whispering. Devonte seems to be explaining something and Kareem's face pales.

Two hundred and fifty people were arrested over the course of a few nights. The protesters simmered as pastors and community members bound together to restore order. Classes were back in session. And as the world returned to normal, I realized my parents didn't call once. Not to check on me or make sure I was safe. They'd never dream of their daughter being involved in the melee. That's not who they raised. We were to be apolitical. They didn't want us to be confused with Black people who did nothing but complain rather than pull themselves up by their bootstraps. If people were struggling, it was their own fault.

After dinner in the café, Loren and I decide to head to the library. With Devonte's visit came many nights of no studying and papers waiting until the last minute. I even skipped a few morning classes when my bed felt too comfortable to abandon. Back home, my mother would've been on my neck, pestering me to the point that I would rather sleep outside in a freezing car than inside my own home.

We pick a table in the old stacks, books, papers, and tablets spread out like a feast, our heads down and hyper focused. About an hour in, Loren yeets a pen at her laptop.

"If I fail this class, I'm going to lose my merit scholarship and will end up scrubbing toilets at the Holiday Inn."

I laugh. "Dramatic much?"

She smiles. "I'm not like you. You're smart, probably will graduate with honors and a job already lined up. The entertainment industry is cutthroat. It's all about who you know. And Frazier is the best place to make those kinds of connections.

But I gotta stay in school to make that happen."

Principle number two: Give honest, sincere appreciation.

"But you're really pretty! And brilliant. You can do anything!"

"Thanks, girl." She sighs and drums her nails. "Sooo . . . Devonte's pretty cool, huh?"

I raise an eyebrow at her and she laughs.

"Ew! Don't get it twisted. I'm not into him like that!"

I would hope not. Then again, he is extremely good-looking. Charming in a way that's not overbearing or gross. Starting to understand how anyone could fall for his spell.

Principle number four: Become genuinely interested in other people.

"Well, what do you like about him?" I ask.

"I don't know. He just knows so much. Yesterday, we were talking about how scientists used to do all these crazy experimental surgeries on Black people with no pain medication. They were stealing people's organs and stuff!"

I blink. "You were? When was this?"

"I wasn't feeling well yesterday so I skipped class and went back to my room. Devonte was there. He made me some tea and we talked for like four hours straight."

"Oh," I say, trying to ignore the feeling that I have been sucker punched in the spleen. She's had time alone with him that I didn't know about. Things are happening behind my back, and she didn't tell me. What else have I been missing?

Loren goes on, unaware of my unraveling. "You ever hear

about Henrietta Lacks? They stole tissue samples from her arm and made all these vaccines, earning millions yet never gave her family a dime."

"What? Seriously?"

"Yeah! And the Tuskegee experiment, how they injected all them Black people with syphilis just to watch them die!"

I swallow. "Well, they didn't inject them with syphilis. They already had it and withheld treatment."

"Who knows if that's even true tho!"

But I do know. I read science papers about it. Still, I hold my tongue.

Loren shakes her head. "It's amazing how much they don't teach us in school. But Devonte, he's been spitting some facts. It's like everything he says . . . makes perfect sense, you know? He's been giving us the real tea, the background, telling us things we should've known!"

"That's true," I agree.

"But you know what I really like about him." She leans closer, elbows on the table. "He doesn't talk down or at us like we're some little kids. He talks to us like we're his equals. And for a guy who's been around the world and did all these amazing things . . . it's mad cool, knowing we're not just some whack-ass freshmen to him."

I smile at her. "Facts."

"Well. What do you like about him?" she asks, eyes roaming my face. The question feels off. Like it's not hers to ask.

I keep my voice light. "Uh, just like you said, he talks to us like we're real adults."

She brightens. "Right . . . like, what did your parents tell you before you left for school?"

I shrug since my parents didn't say one word to me when I left. They didn't even offer to drop me off at the train station.

She chuckles. "All mine said was, 'Don't get pregnant.' At least that's all I remember them beating in my head. Nothing about how the world works. There is too many of us for them to pay any kind of real attention to me. They would get mad aggravated when I used to get sick that I would just hide it from them. Meanwhile, Devonte is schooling us on life without making us feel stupid or we're a . . . a . . ."

"A burden?"

"Yeah, that. He keeps it real. And I guess, I appreciate that. So when I do make it big, no one can try to play in my face. I'll know what's up from jump. I don't got to rely on anybody."

"Well, except your girls," I counter. "You can always rely on us. Sisters, remember?"

She nods with a grin. "Facts."

She turns back to her notes with a satisfied smile. I watch her study and suddenly have the inexplicable sensation to protect her at all costs.

The next day, Loren invites Kerry over for dinner.

"I've seen you walking around campus," Kerry says, shaking

Devonte's hand, giving him a hard once-over. "Just strolling and hanging on the Quad. What's up with that?"

Loren shoots her a look.

"Girl, don't be rude," she snaps, mouthing a "Sorry."

But Devonte takes it in stride, stepping back into the kitchen to fix her a plate of his rice and beans.

"When you've been locked up for as long as I have, fresh air is all you crave. So since I've been out, I like taking long walks, even at night. Your campus is real nice but what makes it beautiful is seeing all these Black faces. It's like being back in Africa. It's heaven for me."

"Hmmm," Kerry says, tapping her chin, and slips out her phone. "What's your Insta?"

"I don't like using phones. The type of radiation going through our bodies leads to all sorts of cancers. Especially cervical cancer. There's been several studies."

Kerry purses her lips. "That sounds made up."

He shrugs. "You gotta do your own research, Queen."

"Okay, Jordyn. Google that!"

I grab my phone, but Devonte's voice stops me.

"Nah. That ain't something you gonna find on Google. And for someone at such a prestigious university, I'm surprised you would use Google as your main source of information. Think about who owns and controls Google. Who owns and controls most of the high-traffic search engines. Why would the enemy give you access to such knowledge when their whole goal is to keep you ignorant. Remember, they didn't even want us to read."

Kerry watches him, skepticism floating in her eyes. Vanessa seems to notice and jumps in.

"Devonte, go easy on us, damn," she says with a light laugh. "How about you give us some real-life advice."

"What kind?"

"How about dating!" Kammy says, with a mischievous grin.

Devonte chuckles. "Well, I've been around the block a few times and one of the first things women tell me is if they could go back, they'd tell their younger selves to get closer to their feminine energy source. That's the key to it all."

"A few times," Kerry echoes. "So how old are you?"

He chuckles. "I'm old enough to know never to ask a woman her age. When I was young, I made the mistake of asking a shorty at the train station her age. Shorty almost took a bite out of my neck."

The girls giggle. Kerry's icy walls seem to melt just enough for her to smile.

"You ever been in love?"

"Damn, in love?" He ladles soup into bowls, passing them out. "Well, love lives in that place between souls where the light just blinds you. So who knows if you're in love or in ecstasy?"

His eyes fall on me, and I look away, fearing my cheeks will redden.

"Well, we all know what ecstasy is," Kerry cackles, giving Loren a high five.

"Facts!"

"Not me," Kammy says, all proud. "I'm still a virgin."

Loren drops her spoon on the floor. "You're a what?"

Kammy straightens her shoulder, holding her head high. "We're waiting for marriage. Well, me. He's already lost his before me."

Vanessa slaps a hand to her forehead. "And you're just telling us this now? Girl, how long have you been with that preacher's son? Six years?! And never . . . not even once?"

Kammy looks to me for back-up but I'm a little shocked myself. The way she flirts with anything that gives her an ounce of attention, I assumed she's had more experience.

Devonte's face doesn't falter. "That's commendable, sis. It's good that you're trying to stay virtuous for your king."

Kammy beams, triumphantly.

Devonte goes on to talk more about men and women, the roles they should and shouldn't play.

Kammy pulls up a chair, eating his words, her soup all but forgotten.

With so much going on in the dorm, I almost forgot about the first student government meeting at the Malcolm Center. After dinner, I scramble to the conference room on the first floor, joining a small crowd of students filing in.

In the front of the room, I spot Nick talking to a few of the other officers. Of course he would be involved in politics.

"Hi everyone, I'm Nneka Young, president of FUSA. Welcome to the first all-hands Frazier U Student Association meeting. Gonna let everyone introduce themselves before we get into the agenda."

Student officers announce their various titles. Vice president, secretary, etc. Next, they allow the individual school councils, like School of Education, School of Fine Arts, School of Engineering, to introduce themselves with updates.

Nick steps up to the mic. "Hey, I'm Nick Chandler. President of Arts and Sciences. We'll be having a small town hall next week to discuss the recent police shooting to see how we can better support the community. But we need more volunteers to help with fall programs and gearing up for homecoming. . . ."

"All student government offices are located on the first floor of this building," Nneka says toward the end of the meeting. "If you're interested in joining the councils for your respective schools, please gather at the tables placed around the room and sign up. Thank you!"

The council for Arts and Sciences meets near the front. We sit in a small circle and do quick intros.

"Hi, I'm Mercy."

"Brianna."

"I'm Jordyn."

"Hey! I'm Neveah, your vice president. Welcome! Like Nick said, we're looking for people to help in the office, volunteering a few hours a week, doing admin work, answering phones, emails, and help with programs. I head the homecoming committee and I definitely can use the extra hands with the parade float. That's about it. Just fill out the application with all your contact information and availability and we'll put you on the schedule!"

As we sit scribbling, Brianna tips her nose across the room. "That's White Boy Nick," she whispers to Mercy.

"Yeah, I figured that," she says, shaking her head with a laugh.

"You sure he's all the way white?" Brianna asks. "I heard some seasoning in that voice."

Mercy grins. "That is the finest white boy I've ever seen."

"He's aight," Brianna says, combing back her hair. "Too bad he's not into the swirl."

"Wait, seriously?" I ask. "He goes to a Black school and he doesn't date Black girls?"

"Oh no, I heard he loves himself some chocolate now," Mercy corrects, raising her eyebrows. "Maybe a little too much. He just doesn't do 'the girlfriend thing.' Our luck the one white boy on campus would be a fuck boy."

"But he's cool," Brianna says. "Heard he's big on social justice and advocacy work. Interned with the NAACP last summer and—shhh."

I look up as Nick passes. He gives me a knowing grin.

"Bambi." He nods.

"Nick," I shoot back without an ounce of warmth.

He shakes his head and moves on.

Brianna turns to me. "Girl, I thought your name was Jordyn?"

* * *

A few of the students from my Intro to Prelaw class planned a study session at the library. It's a chance for us to exchange notes on case briefs before our big midterm. If I was at Yale, I bet my parents would be salivating at the idea of me studying cases. It's how they met at law school, at Columbia. They've retold the story about a thousand times: Two lone Black students, two only children, first in their immigrant families to graduate from college, learning from their elders that the key to success and survival is assimilation. Between their drive and their upbringing, they had so much in common, it only made sense to marry and carry on the tradition of pinning all their hopes and dreams on their children's proximity to whiteness.

Of course, my interest in case briefs is abysmal but my notes are spectacular, so I have something to contribute. Neveah is there, and it's cool to hang out with peeps outside of class. But even as I sit there, trying to focus, I keep obsessively thinking about Devonte. How everything out of his mouth has some morsels of truth to it.

We wrap up our study session around ten p.m., deciding to make it a weekly date. The chilly air and glowing streetlights greet us as we spill out onto the darkened quiet campus. And just as I wave bye, I hear someone call my name.

"Hi Jordyn."

Devonte steps out of the shadows, hands in his pockets, a pleasant smile across his face. My body goes completely still.

"H-h-hey," I stutter, trying to calm my nerves.

He has on his typical uniform of baggy jeans, white T-shirt, and green army jacket, his locs pulled back off his face.

"Is everything okay?" I ask. What is he doing here?

"Vanessa mentioned you were working late on something tonight. She asked if I could walk you home. Late night, woman alone on campus, you know."

"Oh." When have we ever worried about each other like that? But maybe Vanessa's just being nice or overprotective. Especially after the protest, she probably still feels pretty guilty.

He extends his arm, as if to say, "After you."

"Oh. Um, okay," I mumble, and we head down the hill. He gently touches the crook of my elbow, moving me to his opposite side.

"Men should always walk on the outside, closest to the curb. Just in case anything happens, we can protect you."

I nod, appreciating the thoughtfulness.

Devonte saunters like he's a poem; you can count two Mississippis between each footstep. I grip the straps of my book bag, skimming all the principles I can remember, trying to find a way to strike up a conversation to hide my nervousness.

"Nice night," he says, glancing up at the sky. "I noticed you didn't eat the breakfast this morning. Was it my cooking or you just weren't hungry?"

"I, uh, don't eat much to begin with. But thanks anyway."

"Hmm," he says, as if making a note of it. "You know, I'm actually glad we can find some time to be alone together. You know, to get to know each other."

I grip my tingling fingers tight. "Well . . . what do you want to know?"

He rubs his chin as if thinking.

"When you were a kid, what did you want to be when you grew up?"

"Besides a princess, I wanted to be a writer. I've settled on being a lawyer."

"Hmm. Settled?" He tries the word out, feeling it on his tongue. "Law school does not seem for the weak. Why not writing?"

"Law school ensures a career and money."

"And you think your writing wouldn't?"

I shrug. "It's just a hobby."

"Hmm." It was just a sound but it carried heavy judgment.

I cross my arms. "You know how hard it is to be a writer. It's like a rap career. A one-in-a-million chance!"

I hear myself echo the same reason my parents gave me when I told them I wanted to be a writer. Now away, out of their orbit, and up from under their thumbs, it's strange to think how my dreams didn't align with their vision for me. How I had no say in my future.

Kevin had no say in his dreams either.

I realize I'm daydreaming and turn to Devonte, watching me silently with a sly smile, his deep dimples holding all of his thoughts and nefarious plans.

"I think you'd be an amazing writer," he says. "Maybe you can write my life story."

I laugh. "Sounds like you've been through a lot! It would be a duology."

"Okay. Maybe not my whole life. But the last few years. While I was in prison. It's a horror story, really."

I dare myself to ask the questions I've been thinking since laying eyes on him.

"Why did you steal those credit cards?"

Devonte lets some silence pass, then smiles at me. "You've met me. You've heard about my life. About the people I know. Does it look like I need to steal credit cards? I could buy a condo tomorrow if I wanted to. In cash. I was framed, sis. Like most Black men."

I nod. "I see."

"What people don't know is that private corporations run prisons for profit. It's part of the prison industrial complex. The more beds they fill, more money in their pockets. You know why they really wanted me? 'Cause they wanted to shut me up. I was spitting too much knowledge in the streets. I was putting people on to the game."

"Oh," I mumble.

"Do you want to know what prison's like?"

I nod.

"They serve cold slop for breakfast, lunch, and dinner. The water tastes like rusted metal. The conditions are just . . .

inhumane. Dogs are treated better than humans. You know what they also do with prisoners? They harvest organs. For wealthy people. Think about it, have you ever seen a really sick rich person? No."

I give him a skeptical look. "That can't be real. That has to be illegal."

"Sis, I knew a brother in there, doing life, who had both of his kidneys taken. Most evil things men do are illegal but they're never punished for it."

I stare at our feet, shadows dancing on the concrete, resisting the urge to tight rope on the curb.

"I'm really sorry you had to go through that."

He doesn't say anything and we continue our walk in loaded silence. But as we approach the doors to the Rock, he stops in his tracks.

"Jordyn? Can I ask you a question?"

Bracing myself, I turn to face him. "Yes?"

I never noticed how intense his stare can feel on the skin. Searing yet not an uncomfortable burn.

"Who. Are. You?"

My stomach drops. "What do you mean?"

He crosses his arms, relaxing his stance. "I feel like I can't see you, can't connect with you. Like you're holding back on your true self. So, I'm wondering . . . who are you, really?"

Pulse racing, I lower my eyes. "Um. No one special. Just a girl."

"Words have power, sis. You're not just a girl. You're a woman, a Black queen."

My head gives a little nod, conceding to his point.

"What's stopping you from loosening up," he asks, "losing control, being free?"

I chuckle. "What? I am free. I'm here!" And that's true. I made the decision to go to Frazier all on my own. There's no one here breathing down my neck every second.

He taps his temple. "You're here, but your mind is trapped back wherever you came from. Mental freedom is the only way to true liberation. You still are under the control of your parents, the invisible leech of expectations holding you back. You were expected to be perfect, weren't you? Straight A-ing your way straight to college. I bet your parents already told you what you were going to be before you learned how to walk. I'd love to meet the real Jordyn, if she's brave enough to come out and join us."

He smiles and enters the lobby of our dorm, dapping up the security guard on the way to the elevators. As if he's a student who really lives there, which doesn't bother me.

What bothers me is how he seems to see right through my act.

FIVE

THE SCENTS OF rosemary, garlic, lemon, and thyme fill our suite. Welcome guests after a few weeks of living off ramen noodles and Cap'n Crunch.

Devonte is stirring some type of concoction in a pot on the stove. I watch his motions, a slow lyrical dance, tossing in ingredients, taste testing in the small dent of his palm. He's made our tiny kitchen feel like a five-star restaurant. I wonder what his apartment is like. He's mentioned it a few times, but I haven't seen him stray away from our dorm for more than a few hours.

"You know you don't have to cook for us," Kammy says, placing bowls out on the counter. "You're our guest. We should be cooking for you!"

He smiles, dimples deepening. "I'm never too cool to not step up and add value to wherever I'm at. You ladies don't have a man in the house. A lot of feminine energy. You need a stabilizer. Someone to provide and protect. Women, especially young women, weren't made to develop in this world alone."

Kammy agrees, nodding eagerly.

Tonight, there was a student mixer at the Malcolm Center, but all we wanted to do was hang out in our spot with Devonte. You can't help but be drawn to his serene strength, his soothing presence, like a palm tree by the beach soaking in the sun, facing the breeze or hurricane winds just the same.

"Thing you gotta remember is, you're not just females, you are queens. Original mothers of this civilization. Society has spent a lot of time and money trying to erase that from your ancestral DNA. You genetically are the first living being."

"Well, that's actually Adam," Kammy corrects him with a nervous laugh. "It's in the Bible. Women came from his rib. Genesis."

Devonte looks amused. "The Bible, huh? So you fell for those magic tricks too?"

Kammy's smile falls. "Magic tricks? No."

"Bible is nothing but a book of magic tricks, a distraction from the real war that's going on. A war between men and gods."

Kammy chuckles. "Okay, now you talkin' crazy. The Bible stands for Basic. Instructions. Before. Leaving. Earth."

Kammy's whole family goes to church every Sunday. She's the epitome of a church girl.

"Alright, let me ask y'all something," Devonte says. "Who taught you the Bible? Who taught you to fear God? Who taught you to forgive?"

"Well . . . white people," Vanessa says, hesitantly, avoiding Kammy's gaze.

I glance at Loren, who remains silent, staring at Devonte.

"See, Christianity is how slave masters controlled our enslaved ancestors," he says. "Kept us from our roots. Christianity is merely a tool used by the whites to keep you blind to your true heritage. It's a form of mental slavery. Christianity serves its own interests, not God's interests. You're smarter than that, Kamara. You just gotta open up them pretty eyes."

I smile, leaving Kammy to defend her religion, and walk into my room, looking for my sweatshirt. But as I dig through my dresser drawers, I notice how stuff seems to be out of order. I glance at the closet, the door ajar.

My bag zippers are open, pockets turned inside out. Someone has been digging around in here.

In the living room, I hear the girls giggle.

It's a soggy Monday morning. The kind where umbrellas do nothing to protect your hair from the surrounding elements. I tie my mane up in a tight bun. Once the week is over, I'll have to ask Kammy to help me straighten it again. She has amazing flat iron skills. She probably could open up her own salon. As we file out of the suite, waving bye to Devonte in our kitchen, I notice Kammy is unusually quiet. By the time we pile into the elevator, I see a single tear stream down her face.

"Kammy? What's wrong?"

"I called Micah last night," she sniffs.

The moment she mentions her boyfriend's name we gather around her like a cocoon.

"What happened? What he do?" Loren asks, fluffing Kammy's hair.

"Did you break up with him?" Vanessa asks, and seems too happy at the prospect.

"No. I tried to talk to him about, you know, church being the white man's religion, and he got all upset. Do you think I'm being stupid?"

"No!" I say, fixing one of her curls. "Not at all. You're just being curious. You have the right to ask questions."

Kammy blinks up, patting her eyes dry.

"It's just . . . I've been following the word all my life and now . . . I don't know. I just feel lost. All this new stuff, new people, new food. Maybe I'm homesick. They say that happens."

Vanessa takes a deep breath and rubs Kammy's arms.

"Listen, don't read too deep into Devonte, okay? He just . . . telling you what he's researched. You can still go on, marry Micah, and live happily ever after just like you planned. Nothing wrong with that."

Loren hesitates to agree, glancing from Vanessa back to Kammy.

"And if you're still confused," Vanessa goes on, "just talk to Devonte about it. I'm sure he'll clear stuff up. He can be passionate but he's cool. Right?"

"Yeah," Loren adds.

Vanessa straightens, her smile gleaming in the low elevator light.

"Speaking of Devonte . . . do y'all mind if Devonte stays with us for like a bit longer?"

I hold in a breath. It's already been two weeks. It's not that he's worn out his welcome. It's just that he is . . . intense. The suite feels warmer with him in it and not in a good way. He radiates on a nuclear level.

Loren avoids eye contact.

Principle number one: Don't criticize, condemn, or complain.

"He did save our lives," Vanessa quips. "We kinda owe him."

Kammy bites her lip. "Oh. Uh . . ."

As if reading our mind, Vanessa jumps in to explain.

"Y'all it's so hard for Black men to get back on their feet after being locked up. Especially in this cruel, unforgiving, racist society. He just needs a little time around me, his family. The only family he got. I don't want to lose him."

Kammy's eyes fall to the floor in shame. Loren sighs, her shoulders softening in surrender. Neither one of them wants to say what they're thinking about the impossible positions she's put us in.

The elevator opens with a ding that finalizes our fate. So, I paste on a smile and speak for all of us.

"Of course he can stay. He's your brother!"

And I, of all people, know what it's like to lose a brother.

* * *

I volunteer in the FUSA office twice a week. Anytime people need anything, I'm able to run around the building and get it. Order cookies for the town hall? Got it! Ice cream for the social? No sweat! AV equipment for the African Art presentation? Not a problem. I'm almost on a first-name basis with the Malcolm Center staff.

But tonight, I'm out in the parking lot by the football field with Neveah and Nick, trying to figure out how to put the custom-designed backdrop up on the homecoming parade float bed.

Nick stares at the wobbly sign, hand under his chin, as I hot glue tassels around the bed's edges.

"It looks dumb," Neveah groans.

Nick grunts.

"Maybe we can just paint over it?"

Nick grunts twice.

"It cost two thousand so we gotta use it."

Nick grunts again.

"I'll go get some paintbrushes."

He turns to her. "That'd be great. Thanks!"

Neveah chuckles and walks back into the Malcolm Center. Nick hops on the float, testing out the sign.

I wait until Neveah is out of range before making a comment. "You know, you're really nailing the whole down-ass broody white boy act."

"Who said it was an act, Bambi," he says, pulling the sign across the bed.

I've worked a couple shifts with him in the office. He's a man of few words. Ask him any questions about himself, he'll either ignore you or laugh it off with a flirtatious smile, melting hearts all over campus. But when you ask him about business, he's all in. I was really impressed with the town halls he put on, advocating for more student involvement and brokering a meeting with local police officers after the protest.

"Bet you've been listening to hip-hop all your life."

He winks. "And country too. Are you just gonna sit there like a bump on a log or you gonna help?"

I laugh. "Bump on a log? HA! What Black woman raised you?"

He hesitates before taking a steadying breath and ignores the question.

I climb up onto the float. "Why are you so pissed about a sign?"

He pushes the frame down. He is stronger than his slender frame gives him credit for.

"The money could've gone to better use. Fund programs. Not a sign that's going to be thrown out by the end of the weekend."

We grab each end of the banner, stretching it over the framing, but it's like playing a game of tug-of-war. He pulls a little too hard and I'm yanked forward, falling right into his hands.

He grunts. "Did you do that on purpose?"

"Seriously?" Can he be any more full of himself?

We right ourselves and try again.

"Well, you can still do that if you make some cuts on other stuff," I say, moving the banner diagonally, and it fits perfect. "Who makes budget decisions?"

Nick notices my changes and nods appreciatively. "We do."

From our position in the parking lot, I can watch the band practice under the giant bright lights in the middle of the field. During homecoming, they'll lead the parade down the main street toward the Frazier stadium, followed by a procession.

Nick peers over my shoulder, so close that I can see how long his lashes are and the specks of gold in his blue eyes. I can't lie that there is something . . . to him. But I didn't come to a Black school to fall for the only white guy around. That's something old Jordyn would do. New Jordyn needs to keep focused.

"Wait, is this float for you, Mr. President?" I laugh. "Are you gonna wave like this?"

He smirks. "I prefer a cool head nod."

"President of a school is a pretty big deal. What are you going to go for next?"

"Don't know yet."

There he goes again. Being cagey. He knows. He's just not saying. What do girls see in this aloofness?

Nick hops off the float, grabs my waist, and lifts me down with ease. He dusts his hands, standing back. "Okay, it's a little better."

I turn back to my glue gun, hoping to keep him from seeing me blush.

Around eleven, I enter the suite, surprised to find the living room empty. Maybe everyone's asleep or studying. It's been a wild few days. I haven't asked about anyone else's classes but I wonder what our grades are looking like now.

I open my door and throw a hand over my mouth to keep from screaming.

"Oh! Hi! How did you—"

"You left your door open," Devonte says. He's sitting at my desk, hands folded on his lap as if he was waiting for me.

I shoulder my bag, gripping the strap. "Oh, yeah? That's . . . weird."

He measures my response, eyes trailing my every move as I flutter about, snatching up clothes, remaking my bed. Grateful I didn't leave my laptop alone.

"So, Vanessa tells me you joined student government."

My back stiffens. I don't remember telling her that. "Yes. It's looks good on my résumé."

He raises an eyebrow. "For the job you don't really want?"

I don't have an answer for that. My balance is off with him in the middle of my room, a space too small for his larger-than-life presence. His scent suffocates my senses. He's too close. I open the window, hoping to let a breeze in.

He reaches over and touches my wrist, his fingers warm and slightly moist.

"You know, Jordyn, I really care about you," he says, softly. "You're different than the other girls. And I want to make sure you're making the right decisions about your life. I want to help you, just like I'm helping Loren and brother Kareem. But the only way we can work together is if I know the truth about who you really are."

I gulp, wondering how far I can stretch my act. "The truth?"

He nods. "I want to read your work."

The room squeezes tight. I've never let someone read my writing before. But saying no to him doesn't feel like an option. The moment is a monumental turning point I can't mess up if I'm to earn his trust. In a daze, I hand him my journal.

Devonte sits on my bed and delicately flips the pages of my journal like one would handle a biblical scroll.

I sit on my desk, trying not to hover in anticipation. But I can't help it. My restless legs hit against the bed frame as I twiddle my thumbs.

Finally, he flips the journal closed, handing it over, and gives me a quaint smile.

"It's good."

I blink. "Good?" It feels like a subtle criticism. A backhanded compliment.

"Yeah. It's good," he says, nonchalantly, as if he just finished reading a fast-food menu. That's it! After everything . . . that's all he has to say??

I clench the journal, my nails digging into the leather cover.

Don't tell me it's *good*, I want to scream. Tell me it's missing teeth. Or tell me it's a masterpiece. You owe me that! You owe me at least one of your beautiful lies!

He shrugs. "I just . . . think you can do so much more with your voice. Write something real."

"Real?"

He stands, towering over me.

"You and I, we're gonna write a book. And we'll publish it."

Cold, crisp air hits my lungs. "You want me . . . to write your life story?"

"I said the story is good. But your writing . . . your writing is breathtaking. You shouldn't be wasting your time on law when you're the next Toni Morrison. I think it was meant to be that I came here. That we met. Do you believe in coincidences? 'Cause I think this was fate. That I met you at this crossroads, not just in your life but in mine. I don't think I could take the steps needed without you."

He smiles and slowly floats out of the room, leaving me in awe, thoughts muddled and clashing with pure rage, and yet I can't help but wonder . . .

Is it possible that he really sees . . . the real me?

SIX

KAMMY, LOREN, AND I giggle over the lone mirror in the bathroom with the terrible lighting, doing our makeup and hair, while Vanessa tries on various outfits in her room.

"Ugh! I have nothing to wear!" Vanessa pouts over the music. "I knew I should've went to the mall this week."

"My nails look a mess," I say, swiping extra coats of mascara over my lashes.

"I'll do them tomorrow before the game!" Vanessa yells from the other room. "Don't worry about it."

I glance at Kammy, grinning, and she lets out a laugh.

"Yes girl, I'll do your hair on Sunday!"

"After you all finish helping me take out these braids," Loren warns. "With three people, it'll take maybe two hours tops. We can watch *Love Island*!"

For some reason, tonight feels special, like we're back to our regularly scheduled program. Probably because Devonte has been gone all afternoon and it's homecoming. Legendary parties are happening all around the city and the whole dorm is buzzing. The mini concert on the Quad was like a fashion show. Tomorrow is the big game and Loren was able to score us some tickets. But tonight, we're heading to the Kappa party at their frat house.

Nick will be there. As much as I say I don't want to think about him, I definitely don't want to make a fool out of myself. Again.

I can't stop smiling as we doll ourselves up, like a girls' night straight out of the movies, what I've watched on hundreds of social media posts with brutal envy. Only a few short months ago I didn't have any of this. The love, the friendship . . . it's everything I've ever wanted.

Music plays out of Vanessa's room, mugs are set up for shots. Everyone is in the best mood . . . until we hear the front door open.

Devonte strolls in, standing in the middle of the room. He takes us in one by one, his face expressionless.

"Where are you going?" he says, his voice no louder than usual but still filling us with dread.

Loren and I exchange a glance in the mirror.

Vanessa turns down the music, giving him an easy breezy smile. "Uhhh . . . the Kappas are having a party tonight. But you probably don't want to come and see all the ratchetness, right? What d'you think?"

"I think you should stay home," he says plainly. "All of you."

Kammy slowly puts her eyebrow pencil down on the sink. She takes a deep breath and steps out of the bathroom.

"But it's a Kappa party," she says, as if it should mean something to him.

His face doesn't change. It reeks of disappointment.

"Devonte, we're freshmen," Vanessa starts, slowly entering a lion's den. "This is supposed to be the time of our lives."

He sighs. "Well. I guess I was wrong about y'all. I thought y'all were different. Maybe I'm wasting my time trying to teach you the truth."

Kammy twists her fingers. Loren looks to me and I don't know what to say.

"Devonte," Loren pleads. "We love everything you've taught us. We just hoping to have a little fun, that's all."

"How can you think of 'fun' when there's thousands of innocent Black men in prison and families being torn apart. Do you really want to contribute to the capitalist machine and fill the white man's pockets? None of the money that will be made this weekend will go to the people in need."

He shrugs, not meeting our eyes, seeming wounded.

"But I'll respect your wishes. Whatever you do is up to you. But if you really loved me, you wouldn't go out tonight."

The words hang in the air like a threat.

He glances at Loren. "And are you sure you want to go out, dressed like that?"

The light fades from Loren's eyes. I want to step across the room and hug her, but I'm afraid it would come across as pity.

"If fun is all you care about, then go. Drink the white man's liquor. But remember it came from a store that was specifically put in the hood, infiltrating our community to keep us from knowing the truth about ourselves. To keep us from succeeding." He shakes his head. "After all I've done for you, taught you. This whole weekend is another trap by the system. And this time, I won't be able to save you."

Vanessa looks at us, her lips pressed in a hard line. We stand frozen, waiting for someone to make the first move. Finally, Vanessa nods toward the sofa.

Loren sighs. She shuffles her feet and sits on the very end, Vanessa plopping down next to her. Kammy blinks, unable to contain her shock, but she too moves in its direction. She looks back at me and I don't know what to do.

Devonte stands up straight, the light of the bathroom behind me highlighting the youthfulness in his skin.

"How will you rewrite history, Jordyn," he says in a low voice, "if you're outside with the masses who don't want to learn it?"

I glance at the girls on the sofa, sitting there sullen and shamed . . . and confused. Are we really going to just skip homecoming?

Principle number ten: The only way to get the best of an argument is to avoid it.

I give him a wide smile. "You're right. Of course you're right. I'm sorry."

Loren takes a deep breath. "Okay, so what should we do instead?"

Devonte gives us an approving nod. "I think it's time we open up your minds."

Loren's candles flicker on the coffee table, casting shadows on the walls. As drumming music hums out of Vanessa's speaker, Devonte doles out a special mix of tea.

"This is powerful, powerful stuff. Once you have it, you should lay down immediately on the floor, let the effects take you. Surrender to them."

Loren and Vanessa slurp up their tea immediately. Kammy winces through her sips. I stare at the brown-reddish water with a sickening feeling.

"What is it?" I ask.

Devonte shakes his head with a smirk. "Always a curious one. It's a powerful medicine that will clear the clogged-up thoughts in your mind."

As I gather his meaning, my neck tenses. "We'll be high?"

"High is too basic of a word. It's transformative. Don't worry. I studied with a great shaman in Mexico. I'll be here to guide you through your fears. Trust me, I've been able to help Loren, haven't I?"

I look at Loren, who's already lying on the floor, her smile full of content.

This is not a part of the plan, my mind screams. This is

dangerous, this is how you'll get burned. But if I don't walk through the fire, how will I gain the girls' trust? His trust? How will I be one with them?

"Can I add some sugar to this?" Kammy whines. "It tastes nasty!"

With his back turned to reassure her, I quickly pour half of the cup into the corner of the sofa and shoot back the rest. It tastes like a mix of coffee and wood, bitter and mud-like. I have to take several deep breaths to keep from gagging.

Devonte smiles proudly, taking my empty cup. "Lay down and close your eyes."

I do. And within minutes I'm awake.

But I'm not on the floor of my suite. I'm in my bed. The pure white walls of my room glow in a haze. I cuddle the fluffy lavender down comforter, the color matching my curtains, throw pillows, the bench at my vanity next to my walk-in closet. A whistle rings through the air.

That's my teapot. . . .

My toes grip the plush rug as I rush into the hall, down the grand stairwell, wind flowing through my satin pink pajamas.

I walk into the kitchen and . . . there he is. Wearing that orange sweater with the teddy bear I bought him for Christmas. He looks at me, teacup in his hand, and smiles.

He left me. He left me. He left me.

"No," I gasp, squeezing my eyes, and deep, dark river water takes me under, until I come up for air, arms flapping, reaching for anything to hold on to. I open my eyes and I'm back in the suite, ears clogged with screams.

I turn toward the noise. Kammy is keeling over on all fours, a mumbling, bumbling mess. Devonte is beside her, whispering into her ear. But I can't catch a single word. The suite is sitting on a ship in the middle of the ocean, rocking back and forth.

No, don't, I want to scream but the words are trapped.

Across the room, Loren jerks, as if something knifed through her, her face glazed with tears and sweat. She rolls to her side and vomits up flowers; the room reeks of its stench.

Then, there's Vanessa, sleeping soundly. Or is she dead? I'm not sure.

I try to peel myself off the floor until I hear my name miles away.

"What does perfect mean to you, Jordyn?"

I arch my neck up, and there's Devonte, hunched over me, eyes twinkling.

"What?" I croak out.

"Seems like you're chasing this illusion of perfection when in reality that doesn't exist," he coos, every word vibrating. "What would happen if I said you could let go?"

Blaring alarm bells go off inside me but my legs won't cooperate. He's trying to unearth emotions I long since put in the ground and had a funeral for. I look at the door, my trembling lips shout the word "help" but no sound comes out.

Please help us! The man is dangerous.

Devonte stoops closer to me. "Your parents abused you, Jordyn."

I shake my head, the motion causing the room to rock harder. I'm falling off my balance beam, the floor hundreds of stories down.

"No, no, they didn't," I croak, voice covered in slime and glue. He knows nothing about my parents. I made sure of that.

Didn't I?

"Yes! They did," he insists, his voice like massive church bells. "Mentally, maybe even physically. All they've done is try to force you to be who they want you to be. To them, you're nothing but a doll, a plaything, a puppet, and they're your masters. It's very clear they abused you. The damage, the trauma has blocked your memories, and you are hiding them behind your perfection. They probably told you what to eat, what to drink, what to wear . . ."

"Don't listen to them, JoJo, you're not fat!"

My eyes strain to pop out and roll across the floor. Or at least they feel like they do.

That wasn't him? It couldn't be him. He's dead.

He left me. He left me. He left me.

The floor is burning, we're lying on top of radiators, my skin is covered in lava.

"Please, no," I beg.

"What are you hiding, Jordyn?" he whispers, petting my head. "You can tell me."

I can't feel my face. My stomach is full of lava. Someone is screaming. That someone is me. The sob I've been holding back, maybe for years, comes busting through the dam.

"He left me! He left me! He left me! How could he leave me!"

"Who left you, Jordyn? Your father? Did your father leave you after he assaulted you? It's okay, Jordyn, let it out!"

I shake my head, the room spinning. I can't say his name, won't say his name, I can't bear it. The rage inside me is still in control. And no drugs can penetrate it. No therapist, no specialist. I tried them all. So I just nod, giving Devonte whatever he wants. Hoping that person who caused the pain can take it away. But I want to claw the skin off his face, I want to rip out his tongue. I want to . . .

"I hate you! I hate you!" I scream, snapping like a rabid dog at his fingers, ready to kill him!

"Yes, that's it! Let it out," Devonte says, rubbing my back. "You hate your parents. You hate what they've done to you. Yes!"

Then it hits, the vomit racing up my throat like exploding lava. Purging my guts, I can taste his name on my tongue, but never let it hit the air.

"You see that white cloudy line that plane is making in the sky?"

Outside the Rock, we gathered in the empty courtyard in our sweaty, sticky clothes, too weak to change or wipe the mascara off our cheeks. Most of the dorm is up at the stadium, cheering on our football team for the homecoming game, which makes me realize I missed the parade and all the hard work on the float.

No one is around to see our disheveled state. But I also feel . . . lighter. The heaviness I carried, the anxiety, the guilt . . . all replaced with a sudden burst of cool, refreshing air.

Devonte points and we all look up at a plane flying overhead, a plume of white trailing behind it.

"That's them chemtrails. The government been releasing toxins in the atmosphere, spraying our communities, causing death, mind control, even sterilization. See how we haven't been seeing it."

Kammy lets out a horrified gasp.

Vanessa stares up in bewilderment. "How can you just . . . stand out here and take it? How can you let us stand out here!"

"'Cause I've been infusing your food with nutrients that act as a shield against it," Devonte says.

Loren's face is sweaty, palms clammy. I think she's sick but won't admit it. I'm too sluggish to help her.

"I want to go back in," she says in a shaky voice. "I don't want to be out here."

Devonte moves us toward the door. "I keep telling you, we are in the middle of biological warfare. That's what I was protecting you from this weekend. Trying to keep you safe. See how they wait until this weekend, homecoming weekend, where thousands of brothers and sisters would be, to drop that shit, spray us like bugs."

Vanessa grabs Kammy's arm, rushing back inside, but moving in slow motion.

In the distance, I hear the crowd at the stadium cheer. Devonte hears it too, head motioning toward the sound. The effects of the tea still lingering, his smile seems to be splitting his face open like a melon.

This isn't right, something inside me says. This isn't you.

But I ignore it. I have to. Because Vanessa promised to do my nails. And Kammy my hair. And Loren eats with me in the café so I'm not alone. And Devonte needed us all to be a family.

How addicting it is to be a part of something that's more than you.

SEVEN

THE TURKEY AND cheese sandwich sitting on my tray in the Malcolm Center looks disgusting. Last week, it was my favorite lunch. Now, the sight of the white roll makes me queasy. I shouldn't be surprised. My mom always said carbs are the devil. She put me on a keto diet in the sixth grade. It took years to be able to nibble on a bagel without guilt.

You're not fat, JoJo!

I toss the sandwich and walk outside to get some fresh air.

"Jordyn!" Kerry waves me down. "Hey girl! What's up? Didn't see you at homecoming."

"Oh! I . . . came down with a bad cold. Couldn't even get out of bed." Which wasn't exactly a lie. It still feels as if all the blood has been drained from my body and pumped back in slowly.

"Damnnn. You missed everything. It was our first homecoming. They had all these artists on the Quad. And the band went IN during the halftime show!"

I shrug with a laugh. "Well! Maybe next year!"

"Aight. See you later. Tell Loren to hit me up! She left me on read."

"Oh, I think her phone was broke. But I'll tell her."

"And is Vanessa's brother still in town? He's kinda creepy."

I let out a weak laugh. "Yeah. But he's not too bad."

Kerry shrugs, walking toward the Fine Arts building.

I drop my fake smile, too exhausted to keep it up. While everyone else was out partying, Devonte had us doing practice drills in our suite. Sit-ups, push-ups, planks. Kammy started crying. Loren threw up. I slipped her a granola bar, worried about her blood sugar. But I do feel stronger. For a change, the walk up the hill to campus is a breeze.

Last night, when we finished our exercises, Devonte and I retired to my room, so I could transcribe his philosophies on life. It's amazing the way he leaned into my knowledge of memoirs and biographies. I could really see myself writing an entire novel, imagining my name on the cover, next to Devonte's, of course. I outlined several chapters before he came up with the brilliant idea of creating pamphlets to pass out, subsequently testing my writing prowess on other people. Practice makes perfect and I'm down for the challenge!

We didn't finish brainstorming until close to four a.m. I could barely keep my eyes open in my ten o'clock class.

I stand at the top of the hill, looking at the Rock in the distance, and take a deep sigh. There's no way I can make it through this day without a nap.

* * *

Devonte asked us to stop locking the suite door, so he can have twenty-four-seven access to come and go as he pleases. I didn't mind, since I only lock my room door. With a yawn, I slug down the hall, twist the handle and bust in, ready to kick off my shoes and crash for a few hours.

"Oh!" Kammy yelps, jumping out of Devonte's arms on the sofa.

Devonte's . . . arms?

The scene replays over and over. My feet can't move from the spot by the door. Devonte looks at me, his arm draped over the back of the sofa, unbothered and unfazed while Kammy yanks down her shirt.

"Uh . . . hey girl," Kammy says, a quiver in her voice. "What are you doing here?"

"I live here."

"I mean, so early," she says with a sheepish smile, playing with her hair. "Don't you have class right now?"

Devonte stares at me, holding in a laugh, as if amused by Kammy's humiliation. In fact, it feels like he wanted me to see.

"Yeah," I mumble and shuffle quickly into my room.

My pen bleeds through the page of my journal. I can't take my eyes off the spot, the ink spreading away from the tip into swirling tentacles. As many times as I try to tell myself I was seeing things, I remember a new detail from the scene—his missing shirt, her hanging bra strap, his smug smile. . . .

Loren hit me up about going to the café a while ago, but I can't possibly stomach food. Not after what I saw. I'm still trying to erase the image of Kammy and Devonte out of my mind but there's a pulse in my ear. All Kammy talks about is her boyfriend. Their connection felt cemented. She couldn't possibly . . .

"Hey girl. What cha doing?"

I jump at the sound of her voice and snap my notebook closed.

"Oh! Hey. Uh, just writing a story."

Kammy walks in wearing her p.j.s, hair scooped up in a bonnet for the night.

"Story? I thought you wanted to be a lawyer."

"I do! I do. It's . . . just a hobby. That's all."

She plops on my bed. "What's this story about?"

"Well . . . it's about a girl and she's like . . . a con artist, trying to play a prank on her classmates until one day she meets her match."

"Ha! That's cool." She glances around. "Your room is so . . . empty. You don't have no pictures or nothing from back home?"

I shrug. "Maybe I'll print some of us. My new family."

In fact, that's a great idea. I don't have a slew of pictures from high school with a bevy of friends. I only appeared once in my senior yearbook for my graduation portrait. Now, I have tons of photos, ranging from silly to cute to hilarious, and find myself so eternally grateful for the way these girls have changed my life.

Kammy grins and clasps her hands together. "Soooo . . . about what you saw . . . with Devonte."

"Saw? Oh, I saw nothing."

Kammy rolls her eyes. "Girl, quit playing. I know you. And what you saw was totally natural. In fact, destined."

Funny how a statement can sound so right yet surrounded by something so ridiculous.

"But . . . what about . . ."

"Micah? I broke up with him," she says proudly. "We're just going in two different paths. He wants to be a pastor and I'm . . . not sure what I believe in right now. You wanna know the truth? I think he's been brainwashing me, gaslighting me. Him and his family. That's why I'm so sexually suppressed, you know? I should be exploring more."

A cold chill creeps up my arms.

"Are you . . . sure about that? Like, that's what you really think?"

"Well, yeah. But my memories are all mixed up. I bet I'm not remembering everything exactly."

I nod, feeling sick. "But . . . isn't Devonte a little . . . old for you?"

"Not you trying to be my momma!" She laughs. "Age is just a number. It's what you feel inside that makes you twin flames. This was fate. I was meant to meet him. To learn about myself."

Words fall dead in my mouth.

"But we're not together like that, like that. He's just helping me . . . process some things. And until I'm ready, I don't think I should be open to exploring with other boys. Especially ones that I don't trust, don't you think?"

I swallow. "Yeah. That makes a lot of sense."

Kammy smiles and jumps up, giving me the tightest hug. "Thanks, girl!"

I cough out a laugh. "For?"

"For not judging me. Duh!"

EIGHT

"NO, I DON'T think you get it. They were . . . kissing kissing! His hands were all over her!"

Vanessa laughs as we jump out of her car. "You were probably seeing things. You know Kammy, she's all touchy-feely. She gives crazy long hugs to everybody!"

Loren throws me a nervous glance, closing her back door.

It took some major convincing from Kerry, but after chilling in the Rec, we decided to stop by a party off campus, just us three. Kammy has been MIA all day. I fear she's stuck in her room with Devonte. I don't want to imagine what they're doing.

But with just the three of us, it gives me the perfect opportunity to raise a giant red flag. The girls HAVE to see how . . . wrong this is.

Vanessa reapplies her lip gloss. "Girl, it's no big deal, don't be a hater."

Loren shrugs. "She's grown. She knows what she's doing."

I expected that response from Vanessa. But not from Loren. I swallow the rest of my thoughts as we head inside to a ground-level apartment in Hyattsville, Maryland. They're calling it an "old-school rent party." They're either trying to raise rent or using any excuse to have people over.

Loren shrugs out of her coat as we enter. "It's hot as hell in here."

A girl appears by the door, with a red cup. "Hey ladies! Gimme your coats, I'll put them in the back."

We're herded in the living room, a DJ's set up in the kitchen by a makeshift self-serve bar. I spot a few people I know from FUSA—Nneka, Brianna, Neveah, and, of course, Nick. He wouldn't miss a party.

Loren scans the crowd, fidgeting with her top. "We shouldn't stay long."

"What's wrong?" Vanessa asks, looking around for a threat.

She shrugs. "Nothing. Just . . . not in the mood to party like that anymore. And . . . we don't want Devonte wondering where we're at. He'll be worried."

"Oh. I told him we were here," Vanessa says matter-of-factly.

Our necks snap in her direction.

"Seriously?"

She laughs. "What! I didn't want to lie to him. That'd be hella wack."

Vanessa turns, already mingling with a few girls I haven't seen in our suite since Devonte's arrival.

Loren tenses, eyeing the door.

"Don't worry about it," I urge, bumping her shoulder.

"But I do worry about it," Loren whispers, looking sheepish.

"It's just Devonte. He's not gonna ground us until the middle of next week."

Loren's eyes narrow. "I know you think everyone's being ridiculous. But his opinion of us matters to me. I'm surprised it doesn't matter to you just as much."

In an instant, I sober up. Maybe I am coming off as a hater. I don't want Loren to think I don't believe in Devonte's guidance, that I'm disloyal, that I think differently than them.

"You're right. I'm sorry."

Loren holds her breath until her shoulders sag. "Nah, I'm sorry for snapping at you like that. You're right. Let's just . . . get a drink."

"One drink," I offer, cheerily. "Then we could go?"

She smiles, happy with that plan, and nods across the room at Vanessa, cuddled up with Kareem in the corner.

"That's if you can drag her out of here."

We laugh and make our way to the kitchen.

"Wait, I see Legacy. You go on. I want to holla at him for a second."

I weave into the narrow kitchen, watching people searching for clean empty cups. On the counter is a giant cooler, with a spout, squeezing out red punch.

That . . . does not seem safe.

I grab a fresh bottle of cranberry juice off the floor and pour myself half a cup. I don't really need to drink tonight. I don't really need to drink at all, but holding a cup makes it easier to fit in.

In the middle of the crowded room, Nick is sandwiched between two girls, laughing and dancing. Most of the crowd is people from FUSA, and a few of his frat brothers. I stand back sipping my juice, trying to absorb the joy in the air. This is what I thought college would feel like, taste like. But since Devonte moved in, things have changed, a striking difference in a matter of a few weeks.

Loren and Legacy are still chatting, their faces serious. Legacy glimpses over at me, then back at Loren. She almost seems annoyed.

What are they talking about?

Glass breaks behind me, pieces scattering around our feet. A few of us offer to help clean up, trying to be respectful of the place. Not many students have off campus housing. I grab a trash bag, holding it open. Once done, I turn back to the party and freeze.

Devonte is standing by the door.

In a split second, the world goes quiet. What's he doing here? How long has he been watching? And where's Kammy?

The crowd doesn't notice him, just another body in a sea of bodies. But he's the only person I can see.

We lock eyes across the room and my pulse begins to race. He swims in my direction, and as he nears, my spine goes rigid. His scent, once so intoxicating, sends alarms throughout my entire body.

"Hey," I sputter. "W-w-what are you doing here?"

"It's a party," he says, towering over me, seeming upbeat but his eyes are dangerous. Somehow, I know we'll pay for this later on. Somehow, he'll make us regret we ever stepped foot in this place.

As if reading my mind, he smiles. "Relax, sis. You're allowed to make your own choices. You chose this, so I thought I'd join you. You've been so busy with school lately. Don't got much time for me."

His smile is pleasant, but his tone reeks of sarcasm.

He leans an elbow against the counter, his legs crossed, eyes glued to mine. As if I am the only person in the world he wants to talk to. Maybe I am.

"Your shoe is untied," he says, grabbing my cup.

"Oh, thanks," I mutter. I'm not used to wearing sneakers to parties. Well, Loren's sneakers that I borrowed. I double knot with shaky hands and pop back up. Devonte hands me the cup and I take a quick glimpse around the room, both searching for an escape and wondering if the girls notice he's here yet. But Loren is busy with Legacy, more like arguing. And Vanessa is boo-ed up in the corner. Nick is still dancing in the middle of the living room with a bunch of girls from FUSA.

My eyes return to Devonte, who is staring at my lips.

"You know," he starts, fingers touching the ends of my hair as he leans in closer. "Sometimes I look at you and I feel like I know you. Like I've met you in another lifetime."

At that moment, I stop breathing and focus on steadying my hand so my cup won't spill.

"Really?"

He nods. "It's your spirit, your energy. I know it. That's how I knew so much about you. But there's so much I think you're still holding back. Don't you think we should explore that? Alone. Just you and me."

Memories of tea and his voice in my ear make me quiver. Not sure if I could go through that again.

"I, uh, told you everything," I say with a nervous laugh.

Devonte holds an expectant expression. "I knew you would say that. That's why I—"

Voices rise above the music enough to distract us. I stand on tiptoes, peering over the crowd gathering as the party comes to a halt.

In the middle of the room is Vanessa. Her cup empty and another girl wearing its contents on her face. She snatches the girl's braid with brutal force. Her face contorted in rage. They lump together, falling to the floor, a ball of braids, hair, and limbs flying.

Everyone rushes to see the fight, the DJ on the mic trying to calm the party down. Legacy holds back Loren, seeming transfixed.

Devonte suddenly springs into action, crossing the room. He ropes an arm around Vanessa, lifting her as if she's light as a feather. This is the most attention I've ever seen him give his sister. The fastest I've seen him move. He's stronger than I imagined him to be.

As more people gather to watch, Nick strolls over to me, grinning.

"What are you doing back here?" I ask.

He shrugs. "I'm a lover, not a fighter."

I scoff. "Yeah, I bet."

"Well, what's a party without a little . . . punch?"

A laugh escapes my lips. "Oh brother."

Nick looks over as the fight dies down, the crowd still circling. "That girl's mouth wrote a check her ass can't cash."

I gape at him, stunned.

"What?"

"My grandma used to say that. And she was the oldest woman from the south that I knew. Where are you from?"

Nick runs his fingers through his hair. "Hey, who's that guy you were talking to?" he asks, ignoring the question.

I didn't think anyone noticed Devonte or maybe I was so busy being lost in him. "Why do you want to know? Jealous?"

Nick laughs. "No. I've seen him around. He's a bit old for you, right?"

"Shut up," I mumble, rolling my eyes.

Nick tips his nose down, grabs the cup in my hand, and takes a sip, licking his lips.

"Mmm. Thanks for the drink. I was thirsty."

And with that, he walks off. I shake my head.

That boy is trouble.

Loren pushes her way to me, the music picking back up.

"What was that about?" I ask.

She shrugs, pouring herself a cup of cranberry juice. "That girl used to date Kareem, I guess. She was trying to . . . tell him to leave Vanessa."

"Why? She doesn't even know her."

Loren sighs. "Yeah. But she's met Devonte."

I notice the slight reservation in Loren's tone. Maybe Devonte has a reputation around campus that I'm unaware of. They couldn't know him the way we do, of course. In the corner, Devonte and Vanessa are arguing, Kareem standing by awkwardly, eyes toggling between them while Kerry makes her way to our spot in the kitchen.

"Damnnnn. I wasn't expecting Vanessa to throw hands like that. She's a beast. Who knew!"

Vanessa's eyes are cold, unrecognizable, violent, still staring at her prey.

After a few people lighten the mood with some TikTok dances and '90s R&B sing-alongs, the party is nearly back to normal, more people piling in. If this was a club, the place would be at capacity. Loren, Kerry, and I hold down our spot, gossiping about ratchetness happening in the other dorms. Pranks, love triangles, daily midnight fire alarms. I can't help but crack up at all the shenanigans.

Devonte continues to whisper in Vanessa's ear, soothing and taming her, like a coach with an unhinged boxer. He rubs her arm one last time and turns, eyes landing on me.

His mission is clear. He hasn't forgotten he wants me alone. Maybe the same way he's been alone with Kammy. My stomach plummets at the thought.

"Going to the bathroom," I spit out to no one in particular, and slip toward the back, before he has a chance to make a move.

Heart racing, I rush down the hall, bumping right into Mercy.

"Hey!" I say, glancing behind me, wondering if Devonte will follow. Something tells me he doesn't trust me the way I'm supposed to trust him. I know what Loren and Vanessa said, but him and Kammy together is unsettling and . . . weird. Whatever counseling he's giving, I'm not ready for. Don't think I'll ever be ready for.

"Girl, what was I thinking coming out tonight," Mercy says, fanning herself. "I have a whole paper due on Monday that I haven't even started. And it's crazy hot in here. I'm about to dip."

"Same," I say, letting out a relieved laugh. "Plus, I don't want to sweat out my hair."

"Me too, girl! I still haven't found a hairstylist I trust down here."

"OMG! Me either."

We cackle and it feels good to talk to someone about something normal. Vanessa's, Loren's, and Kammy's chats have been hijacked by Devonte's sessions. He has us reading so many different books, I barely have time to fit actual schoolwork in. Maybe Mercy can be another outlet, another friend I can rely on. But the thought instantly makes me feel like I'm cheating on my girls.

Brianna runs up to us. "Hey, y'all. Do you know where they put all the coats? The cops are probably gonna show up any minute. There's too many of us up in here."

"Think they in the bedroom over here," Mercy says. "I just about opened every damn door looking for the bathroom."

Brianna swats at the wall, clicking on the light to a large master bedroom, with a sliding glass door leading to a patio facing the parking lot, and a four-poster bed, a mountain of jackets piled on top.

Brianna groans. "I knew I shouldn't have given that girl my coat."

Mercy climbs onto the bed, combing through the jackets, until something moves beneath them, like a worm under dirt, and she scrambles off.

"What the fuck?"

"What is it ? A mouse?" Brianna cries, hopping in place.

A sneaker pokes out. Mixed in with the coats . . . is a body, lying face down in the middle of the bed. But not just any body . . . I would recognize his blond hair anywhere.

"Nick?" I say, shaking his leg. "Come on, wake up. We need our coats."

Mercy and Brianna bust out laughing. "Damn, White Boy Nick is White Boy Wasted!"

Nick doesn't move. Doesn't even flinch.

"Nick, this isn't funny, come on!" I shake him harder, turning him onto his back. Nick's mouth hangs open, eyes still shut tight. I shake his shoulder, his skin sweaty.

"OMG! He's out cold. Maybe we should find his roommate, brothers, or something?"

Brianna nods in agreement. But a sly smile spreads across Mercy's face.

"Orrr . . . maybe we should check things out."

I stand up, suddenly on guard. "What do you mean?"

She shrugs, feigning innocence but eyeing his belt buckle. "I always wonder what white boys . . . you know, looked like."

Brianna catches her meaning and cackles. "Girl, what? You bugging."

"Oh, come on, you're not a little bit curious to just . . . see it?" She wiggles her fingers in his direction.

Heat rises to my neck.

"He's unconscious," I point out. Though I can't imagine he'd want girls touching him inappropriately either way.

"Girl, relax. We're not raping him or nothing," Mercy says.

The word makes me flinch. He can't give consent. He can't even fight them off. This isn't right.

And if he was a girl . . .

Mercy reaches and I instinctually, block her way.

"Don't touch him," I spit, my voice low but firm.

Mercy recoils, the heat behind my words startling. But then, she regains her composure, and crosses her arms, neck rolling.

"Or what? What are you going to do?"

Brianna's eyes toggle between us, the tension palpable.

"Girl, we're just taking a sneak peek," Brianna says, with a laugh. "It's no big deal!"

My hands bunch into fists, my heart a racehorse. I may have to fight these girls off him. I've never fought anyone in my life and I probably won't make it out unscathed. But there's no way I'm letting them touch him.

Mercy must come to the same conclusion. She flips her hair, eyes rolling.

"Whatever," she hisses, snatching a nearby jacket, and storms out of the room. Brianna throws me a confused glare.

"You trippin'," she mumbles, combing through the pile. "It ain't even that serious."

She finds a blue tweed coat and slams the door behind her. It takes me five full seconds to release the breath I've been holding, my muscles aching from the anticipation.

Quickly, I climb onto the bed, hovering over him.

"Nick. Wake up. Come on!"

I pat his face a few times, but he only stirs. How much did he have to drink?

I can't do this alone. I need reinforcements. But as soon as I touch the bedroom doorknob, I remember who's out there. Just about everyone from student government. And Devonte.

Drool slides out the side of his mouth, noises gurgling up. By now, Mercy and Brianna have probably told people he's back here. He's the president of Arts and Sciences. He has a code he has to follow, even off campus. And I know he's interested in another officer position. Word of mouth is everything. I can't let them see him like this.

I run back to the bed, shaking him.

"Nick, what dorm are you in? We gotta get you out of here," I say, pulling him to his feet, checking his pockets for a dorm fob. He must live off campus. He slumps into my arms, weighing a thousand pounds. I struggle to keep him up before looking over at the patio doors.

Me: Hey, not feeling well. Took a cab home.

Loren: What? Why didn't you wait for me?

Me: Cause I had to 💩

Vanessa: Ew girl. Ok. We'll take our time coming home then.

The cabdriver has a nasty attitude, but I don't blame him. The last thing anyone wants is some drunken college students in the back of their car.

But Nick doesn't throw up. He leans against the door, his mouth ajar, and I check several times to see if he is still breathing. I'm surprised the liquor slushing around his belly doesn't run up his throat during the ride.

I pull Nick out of the cab, his legs more stable than when I pushed him off the patio. I'm able to maneuver him inside into the elevators with few witnesses.

In the suite, Kammy's door is closed but music hums through the walls. I quickly rush Nick into my room, dumping him on the bed.

"Nick," I whisper, with more pats to the face. But he's out cold again.

This is ridiculous.

Exhaustion overwhelms me. I snatch the comforter and pillow off my bed, lie on the floor, and close my eyes.

The sound of jiggling metal wakes me. The room is still pitch-dark. Nick's arm is draped over the side of the bed, unmoving. I check if he's breathing. He's still unresponsive.

Jiggling again.

Light from the common area leaks through the sweep. Someone is standing in front of my door, their shadow stretching into my room. The handle twists with a frustrated yank as if it was expected to be unlocked.

Maybe it's Loren. Or Kammy. Maybe they need help. But one look at Nick, and I realize I would have a lot of explaining to do.

I wiggle back into my makeshift bed, playing dead.

The doorknob pings back and forth, echoing in the silence. I want to cover my ears, tune out the frantic sound. Back and forth, back and forth. Just when I think they may break it open, it stops.

The person walks away, slowly.

NINE

"BAMBI?"

Sun streams through the open blinds of my window. I still have no curtains to hang. Nothing to make my room homey like in all those dorm shows Mom and I watched on HGTV. An ache blooms at the thought of her. Grief looks different on everyone . . . but losing my mom while she's still alive hits different.

Nick hovers over me, his bright blue eyes panicked, hair askew.

"It's Jordyn," I groan and turn over.

"What . . . where am I?" he asks in a groggy voice.

I sit up, my neck stiff and throbbing. "You're in my room."

He looks down at his clothes, rubbing his face.

"What happened?" His eyes widen. "Oh shit. Are you okay? Did we . . . did we . . . um . . ."

"No, nothing like that happened," I insist, noting he seems more worried about me than about himself. "You were drunk and incoherent. I didn't know where you lived so I brought you back here. There were tons of people from FUSA around. I didn't want them to see you like that."

I stand up to stretch and check the door. Still locked.

Maybe it was a dream.

Nick stares at the floor with a slight shake of his head. "I don't remember anything from last night."

I throw up my hands. "Well. That's what happens when you drink too much."

"No. I wasn't drinking."

I suck my teeth. "I saw you dancing and had a big red cup in your hand."

"It was soda," he mutters, rubbing his forehead.

He grabs his phone. "Shit, sixty new messages. Everyone's probably looking for me."

He tosses the sheet aside and tries to stand but falls back down.

"Whoa," he mumbles.

I grip his arms to steady him. "Are you still drunk?"

"I am telling you," he says, voice hard. "I wasn't drunk. This is . . . I gotta go."

He rummages around, managing to slip on his sneakers. What I know of him, this doesn't seem like him. He's always so put together, humble, and chill. This Nick is a disheveled, sweaty mess.

"Well, at least have some water," I insist.

He doesn't respond. He quickly unlocks my door and throws it open before I remember what's out there.

"Wait!" I shout, trying to stop him but it's too late.

Kammy and Vanessa are on the sofa, having tea. Their mouths drop at the sight of Nick.

"Uh, hey," he grumbles then bolts out the suite door. I step into the hall, staring at the spot he just left. But when I turn, Devonte is in the kitchen . . . shirtless. For a moment, we stand there staring at each other, his expression unreadable.

He crosses his arms. "You slept with him."

His voice calm yet lethal. It renders me momentarily speechless. Nerves making my teeth chatter, like a bunch of marbles in my mouth.

"N-n-n-no," I manage to croak out.

"No?" He chuckles. "You really plan to stand there and lie?"

I've been called a lot of things, but never a liar. A corner of my sticky facade peels off the knuckles of my clenching fist.

"I'm not lying."

"You slept . . . with him. Admit it."

I take a deep breath, deciding to be practical, and face the girls. They'll understand. "He's just a friend from FUSA. He was really drunk and I was just trying to help him out."

Devonte creeps forward, slowly, bare feet slapping the floor.

"You wanted to sleep with him. You wanted him inside you. You couldn't help yourself."

"What? No!"

"You've been having lustful thoughts about him, haven't you," he says, his tone buttery soft. "And now they're forcing you to lie."

"Just tell the truth, Jordyn."

Loren is standing behind me, arms crossed over her pajamas. I can't place the look in her eye. Is she mad at me?

"Yeah, we won't judge," Kammy offers. "We're your friends, girl."

"More than friends. We're family," Vanessa adds, sweetly.

Devonte takes another step closer. "Maybe you're misremembering the night. Too much drinking has your brain all mucked up."

I shake my head, once again looking at the girls. "No, I would remember sleeping with someone."

Devonte slams his hand on the counter, and we all jump at once. His eyes are hard black stones.

"So, he didn't touch you. How can you be sure? You can't be sure, 'cause you were drinking. Do you even know how much you drank?"

"I . . . I . . . I only had juice." I turn to Loren. "You saw me."

She shakes her head. "Only for a little while. Then you went missing."

I gape at her in disbelief.

"Girl, you have been drinking a lot lately," Kammy adds, like she wasn't drinking right beside me.

"What can you really remember?" Vanessa asks, pleading with her eyes, as if to say, "Give him what he wants."

It wasn't like that at all. Why won't he believe me? And why does it feel like these accusations are multipurpose . . . like he's trying to make me look bad, pitting the girls against me? Twisting my words the way one would twist a pen between their fingers.

The questioning went on like this, from every angle, for what seemed like hours. Devonte's interrogation growing more intense. Like a rabid dog, he has his teeth sunk into an image in his mind and he won't let go.

"So you were alone in the room with him. In the bed together and you don't think he woke up in the middle of the night, touched you? How can you be positive? How do you really know what happened?"

My lungs feel too hot to be in my body as I try to breathe. I need space, air . . .

"I . . . I don't feel like he touched me."

"But devious men have devious intentions. You played right into his hand. How do you know he was drunk? How do you know if this was his game all along? He was conscious enough for you to walk him in here."

My arms are still sore from holding Nick up as I carried him out of the party. His body was so limp. Could he really have been pretending?

Devonte sees the doubt in my face. "The enemy is good at confusion. Your weakness and drinking has made you blind."

I steal a glance at the sofa. I can't tell if the girls are staying quiet out of fear or out of confusion.

"I wasn't drunk," I insist, exhausted. "He was drunk! Like, couldn't-even-stand drunk. And these girls were trying to—"

"So you weren't drunk and yet you left your family to tend to some white boy's needs? Someone that means nothing to you." Devonte starts pacing around me. "You ditched your friends, your family . . . for him. Could you say he would do the same?"

I open my mouth, but nothing comes out.

"I just . . . thought we could trust you," he sighs with a shrug. "But this isn't what a good friend would do."

My neck snaps.

"No! I am a good friend!" I turn to the girls. "I swear I am."

They remain silent. They don't believe me. They don't trust me.

Panic pushes common sense aside.

"Please," I beg. "You gotta believe me. I wasn't thinking right. But you ARE my friends. More than my friends. Sisters, remember."

Remember who we were before we met Devonte, I want to scream. But the look on their faces tells me it's too late.

"Friends don't abandon each other," he sighs.

Tears spring up as I recognize the hurt in Loren's eyes. I did lie, I left her when she didn't even want to really be there. I put them all in the middle of this. He's right, I'm not a good friend. A good friend would tell them the truth about me. A good friend wouldn't keep secrets. A good friend wouldn't abandon her friends.

Principle number twelve: If you are wrong, admit it quickly and emphatically.

"I'm so sorry," I say to the girls and turn to Devonte.

He gives me a half smile, shoulders at ease. "Relax, sis. I'm not angry at you. I'm angry that some white boy took advantage of you. Let him come between you and your family. Isn't that something white people been doing for a century, separating us? After all the money I've spent, the time, dedication to teaching you to know the enemy . . . I don't think you can be trusted on your own."

I lower my eyes. "I'm sorry. I didn't mean to . . . I mean, I didn't know what I was doing."

Devonte shakes his head. "This is why I keep you close, this is why our sessions are so important. If you were serious about committing to change, to being a part of this family, you would commit to being home, every night, at eight p.m. It's time we un-program your miseducation about the white devil."

The curfew feels like a corporal punishment and it's all my fault. Not wanting to bring any more strife to the girls, I make sure to be back in the suite fifteen minutes early, if not sooner.

Devonte passes out the pamphlets that he and I created to a small group of us: Kareem, Vanessa, Kammy, and Legacy.

"Liberation is an urgent matter. In order to fight the psychological warfare being waged against you. You don't understand what's going down out there, what the government and all those people in power have planned. This is a game of chess, and the white man holds all the pieces. That means, I'm gonna put myself at risk again, teaching you what I know. I can't stay silent."

We nod in understanding. He's doing this for us. At least, that's what I'm telling myself. And that makes sense because he cares about us.

"Tonight, I want to teach you about the Willie Lynch papers. That way, you can teach others. The goal is to spread knowledge to every brother and sister that will listen."

Kammy nods eagerly, digging into the pamphlet.

Devonte stops to give me a look. "There's a misspelling on page three. I thought you were better than that."

I sit up rod straight. "Sorry!"

"Let's not let it happen again. The mission is too important for carelessness. That's how the white man wins."

Vanessa gives me a sympathetic smile, mouthing, "It's okay."

I flip to page three, noting the simple mistake. Devonte's scolding has a familiar air to it, similar to my parents. An A– on a test would result in a lecture on attention to detail. The same seething annoyance I have had for them begins to bleed through. I dig my nails into my palms.

"Willie Lynch was a slave master in Virginia, who gave a speech telling other slave masters how to control their slaves. The secret was setting the slaves up, pitting them against each other. Dividing us . . ."

The suite door flies open and Loren rushes in.

"Hey," she says, winded. "I know. I'm sorry. I was waiting for notes from—"

"Excuses are tools of incompetence," Devonte says. "We've been going over this in our sessions, haven't we?"

Loren's eyes widen and I can't hide the shock on my face.

Sessions? What sessions? Is he having private sessions with her too?

I glance at Kammy, who looks like she's having the same thought.

Loren swallows, choosing her words carefully. "Yes, but . . . it wasn't my fault. I got held up after class."

Devonte stares at Loren then slowly rises to his feet. The room collectively holds its breath.

"Do you know that Muslims wash their face, hands, arms, and feet before performing their prayers? It's a beautiful purification practice. To show respect to God, to pray in a pure state. See, cleansing the body and soul leads to enlightenment. That's why I clean and fix everything around here. Because I'm trying to save your souls. Rappers pay thousands of dollars for the guidance I've been giving you for free. Teaching you to be pure!"

Everyone nods, tension in the air rising.

"So why is this queen sitting here, talking to me . . . with makeup on her face?"

Loren gasps, touching her bright pink lips. A beautiful color on her. Until now.

"Kareem, why don't you help her get rid of it."

Kareem blinks, pointing at himself. "Me?"

"Yes you, help her. Get a rag from the bathroom, my black soap, and water."

Kareem looks nervously at Vanessa, but she nods in approval. He scurries into the bathroom, procuring the items.

Loren sighs, holding her hand out to Kareem, but Devonte pushes it away.

"Not you. Him. You wash it off her."

Kareem's eyes bulge, casting another panic-stricken look at Vanessa, her mouth gaping in shock. He takes a deep breath and begins to softly wipe Loren's face, as if hesitantly petting a feral dog.

"Scrub harder," Devonte orders, grinning.

Kareem, unsure, moves a little faster. Loren whimpers.

"Harder!" he barks, and Kareem's muscle flexes as he overpowers her. Loren cries out in pain.

Time seems to slow to an aching pace, Loren whimpering with each stroke. Kammy reaches over and holds my shaking knee still.

"Stop," Devonte says. Kareem stumbles back, panting.

Loren's face is bright red, rubbed raw, eyes flooded with tears.

Devonte brightens. "Ah! There you are, Loren. Now we can see you."

Loren nods, tears streaming down her face as she takes her seat. My stomach clenches with guilt.

He's right. I'm not a good friend.

TEN

ON MONDAY, MERCY is at the front desk in the FUSA office.

"Hey y'all," I say as I enter, testing the waters, flashing a giant grin.

Principle number five: Smile.

"Hey," Mercy says dryly without looking up from her phone. Brianna doesn't speak at all.

They can't still be upset about the party? Their sober thoughts must have caught up to them by now, telling them it was a bad idea to take advantage of a drunk guy. If the shoe was on the other foot, Nick would've been arrested and canceled within forty-eight hours. But their coldness speaks volumes.

Nick walks out of the office. I hadn't seen him since he ran out of the suite. His eyes land on me, face blanching.

"Uh, Jordyn. Hey."

"Hey?" I gulp, fidget awkwardly with my bag. How am I supposed to act around him? Do we even acknowledge what happened?

He points a thumb at the conference room. "Would you help me with expenses from homecoming tonight? I'm looking for a specific amount of savings and Neveah said you're good with numbers."

"Tonight?" He wants to be alone with me again? "Um. Yeah sure."

Mercy snatches her bag under the table.

"Later," she grumbles. She walks out of the office, shooting daggers with her eyes, Brianna following.

Nick frowns. "Something I missed?"

"Nope! Ready to start?"

Nick spreads out worksheets and invoices on the conference room table while I input them into the ledger. But whoever put the ledger together before made a mess of it. I spend most of the evening recalculating and reinputting with one eye on the computer and one eye on the wall clock.

"What's up?"

Across the table, Nick stares, his eyebrow raised. I almost forgot he was there.

"Huh?"

"You keep looking at the clock. Got a hot date?"

I gulp. "No, just keeping track of the time. Don't want to be out too late."

"You got a curfew or something?"

Trying to keep it cool, I force a laugh. "Seriously? What's with all the questions?"

"You don't live with your parents anymore, Jordyn. You're an adult. At college. You can stay out until the break of dawn if you wanted to."

I shrug. "Well, I have . . . other obligations."

Devonte made it clear that he expected us back in the suite by eight every night. Women shouldn't be out after dark without a man supervising them. How do we expect to be wives if we can't be ladies? How can we say we are committed to our community if we're not serious about our studies and unlearning our ways?

Dedication. Discipline. That's how you succeed in the world.

So why am I still going to FUSA?

Guess I'm still holding on to a small part of me that feels this will help in the future. The one place I have to breathe easy between classes and meals. Devonte is passionate but suffocating. Plus, his views on women seem a little archaic. Shouldn't he be empowering us, not taking power away?

Nick runs a hand through his hair. "Listen, I want to talk . . . about the other night."

My throat tightens. I've been dreading this. I don't want to talk about it. I don't even want anyone else to know.

"What about it?" I say quickly. "Nothing happened. Let's just call it a day."

He blows out some nervous air. "I know nothing happened between us but . . . I think I was drugged."

I purse my lips. "That's a little far-fetched, don't you think?"

"Not on a college campus, no. But that's not all. I don't remember much, but the last thing I do remember is grabbing a cup from you."

"So you think I drugged you?" I snap.

He blanches, holding up a hand. "No! I think that whatever

I was drugged with was actually meant for you."

I stop for a moment to think, retracing my steps. I poured myself some juice and never left it unattended.

But . . . Devonte did hold it for me for a brief few seconds.

No . . . he wouldn't.

Suddenly, I feel faint. Across the table, Nick watches me then nods, resolve settling. "So . . . should I call campus police or go straight to the DC Police?"

The word *police* snaps me back to my senses. I sit up straight. "Do you have any idea what it'll look like if the one lone white kid on a Black campus starts accusing people of drugging him?"

The fact is a slow sinking ship and Nick deflates.

"Shit," he mumbles, tossing his pen on the table.

If he contacts the police, they will start asking questions, tracing last steps, and that will lead to Devonte, throwing him on their radar. It could be bad . . . for everyone.

"Just drop it," I insist. "You don't want that type of heat."

He snarls in disgust. "Drop it? But what if it happens again? What if someone's assaulted or taken advantage of?"

I shake my head. "I . . . I don't know. But you need hard evidence before you start opening your mouth."

"Maybe we should ask around," he suggests. "See if anyone else had the same experience. Word of mouth, nothing official, will keep people on their toes."

I chuckle. "Once again . . . just you asking these questions is asking for trouble."

"I rather get in trouble than let anyone get hurt! I would

think you'd want other girls on campus to stay safe too."

I swallow hard but remain silent, Devonte's voice echoing.

You're not a good friend.

"Fine! Just . . . be careful," Nick fumes, snatching up his pen. "And if I didn't say it before, thanks. I owe you one."

I bite my lip, the shame sticky on my skin. It couldn't be Devonte, he has no reason to drug me, I would do anything he asks.

So why can't I shake the feeling that that night he had so much more in store for me?

I fly through the lobby of the Rock, pushing the elevator button. I'm thirty minutes past curfew. I don't want to make him mad again. Or not mad, maybe disappointed. And the looks of judgment from the other girls . . . I can't go through that again.

Exhausted, I push open the door to the suite and the handle hits someone in the back, the door only opening a crack.

What the . . .

Legacy peers out, spots me, and nods, allowing me in, as if he was club security.

There are students, most I've never seen before, packed in the living room scattered about, leaning against the stove, one even sitting on the toilet. Maybe thirty people in total.

All there to listen to Devonte.

"I'm afraid to tell you the nasty truth," Devonte says as he walks in a circle, hands behind his back. "That officer that killed that Black man in cold blood, he'll be acquitted. They're always acquitted. When the police police themselves, it's always the same outcome."

Murmurs erupt.

"See how they scooped up all those protesters? Sprayed them down like dogs!"

"Some bullshit!" someone shouts.

"It is, brother. But just because we live in the system doesn't mean we have to be another sheep in the system. There is another way." He taps his temple. "Knowledge of self."

He goes on, preaching from an invisible pulpit. Everyone is transfixed, eyes locked in rapture.

"What you got to remember is your roots! Your power. That's how you separate yourself. Why would you tell a white man your plans when it's in their DNA to sabotage you, conquer you, destroy you. Hell, why would you allow the white man into your sacred space, around your women? That's like letting a wolf sleep in a hen house."

The air in the room is electric as everyone whispers to one another. In the corner, Vanessa nods eagerly. I can't tell if this is new to her or she's resoaking it all up like a sponge.

Legacy whispers into my ear, "Isn't this dope? Everyone's waking up!"

I lean back against the sink full of dishes, listening as Devonte casts his magical spell, conjuring new admirers, controlling a room without ever raising his voice.

ELEVEN

EVERY TIME I'M about to walk back to the suite, I hold my breath for five seconds. The dread sinks and spreads to every part of my body, covering every organ in tar. One day, I'll be too heavy to move. That's when I'll know it's gone too far, I tell myself. But for now, I take another sip of fresh air, grip my keys, blades between my fingers, and softly step in.

Kammy is sitting on the sofa, peeling potatoes into a bowl. I don't think much of it, in fact it's normal for Kammy to cook. But something is off. Then I realize . . .

"Your hair!"

Kammy grins, patting the edges of her tight 'fro, somewhat lopsided and in desperate need of moisture.

"You like it?" she asks, a slight uncertainty in her eyes.

"I do," I say with extra enthusiasm. "So . . . no more wigs?"

"No. It doesn't feel natural. Wearing hair that's been on someone else's head. Gross. Do you know that they drug women and scalp them before they harvest their hair?"

"I . . . I didn't know that."

She shakes her head. "You have to do your research, girl. It's a sick industry."

Out the corner of my eye, Devonte watches proudly from Vanessa's doorway.

"She's right. Why would you abandon your culture, your beautiful features, to look like the ancestors of the people who kidnapped, raped, slaughtered our people?" he says, rubbing my arm. "Glad you're home."

A warmth builds in my chest, and I ignore it, wiggling away from his touch.

"So, Vanessa texted and said that you were making dinner?" I ask, trying to keep it casual.

He backs into the kitchen, and I join Kammy on the sofa.

"A while ago, I spent the summer in Cuba studying, learning about different healing herbs and foods we must eat to live. You must feed your mind and body with nutrients, only way the soul will grow."

That makes a lot of sense.

"It's time you stop eating the white man's food and adopt a vegan diet. Strictly clean. The food you eat is filled with chemicals and pollutants that even affect your cycles. Think about all the toxins that you digest that line your uterus, swallowed by your unborn children. Then they come into the world, sickly, degenerates. Even years after you stop eating it."

He walks out of the kitchen with a steaming pot.

"Every day you're going to drink this tea. It's not like the other tea. It's a different type of detoxification."

Devonte pours brown liquid out of the pot into our school mugs and passes one to each of us.

"This will replace two meals every day."

The tea tastes exactly like dirt. Like he went to the backyard, dug up some roots, threw them in hot water with a splash of lemon.

"What kind of tea is this?" I ask.

He scoffs with a smirk. "You ask as if you don't trust me. Have I steered you wrong yet?"

I remain silent. He gives me a look, shaking his head as if he finished scolding a silly child.

Loren sips the tea, trying to fight the bitterness, but Vanessa seems not to mind the taste at all.

Kammy stares into her cup with a frown. "Wait, so tonight, all we're gonna have is tea?"

He nods.

Kammy's face crumples. "But . . . I'm hungry."

"There are other things to fill your appetite. Knowledge of self is first."

"Can't I just make some mashed potatoes or fries with this?" Kammy asks, almost begging.

"Fries huh? I bet you had lots of fries at that Rec Center, right? Hanging out with your friends."

We nod, not wanting to lie.

"Well, all fries are dipped in oil made of pig sweat. Do you know what pigs are made out of? Pigs are made of rat, cat, and dog. It's not a real animal. It was made in a lab, used with scraps they gave slaves. That's why they tell the Black man not to eat pork. Swine is not for kings or queens."

"They talk a lot about this in the Bible," Vanessa confirms. "It's the parts white Christians edit out. So they can keep feeding us bacon."

Don't white people eat bacon? I think, but don't say it out loud.

"Discipline today, harvest tomorrow," Devonte says. "That's the motto. If you don't practice and focus on your health today, you'll regret it tomorrow. You'll regret it today if you keep eating the crap the man serves you."

I glance over at Loren.

"Hey, maybe you should be careful with this," I whisper, trying not to draw too much attention.

Loren hesitates, eyes flickering over to Devonte. He waves a hand.

"I've taken her into account. Loren doesn't have a disease. She has a DIS-ease. Meaning that her body is not at ease with how she's been treating it."

I blink and look at Loren. Now is her chance to step up. She said she would keep on top of her health, so there would be no more fainting spells.

But she only shrugs. "I think this could really help. I've heard of people going vegan and curing themselves of all kinds of things, even cancer. It's worth a try."

* * *

"How can you be pure of heart if you are holding on to materialistic possessions. Things made by the white man."

Loren watches Devonte comb through her closet taking designer items like belts and purses and throwing them into a black garbage bag. I didn't have items worth throwing away.

"What are you going to do with this stuff?" she asks, arms crossed.

"Sell them. Use the money to pay me back for all the training I've been giving you."

Loren frowns. "But you said—"

Devonte stands tall, frustration bleeding through.

"I've been cooking and cleaning, and teaching you queens for weeks. Don't you think you owe me something? People pay thousands for my counsel. Nothing in this world is free. Haven't you learned that? Don't you want to work in entertainment? This is how it works."

Loren fidgets, biting her lip.

He sucks his teeth, stomping out of her room and into Kammy's.

Kammy sits on her desk, holding a Gucci purse close to her chest. She takes a deep breath.

"It's just . . . my dad gave me this bag," she admits, sheepishly. "He saved up for it. It was a graduation gift."

Devonte crosses the room. He cups her cheek with a soft smile.

"The same father who used to come into your room at night? The same father who let your pastor do the same?"

My mouth drops as Loren gasps.

Kammy's face falls, looking around at us nervously.

"Ah, so Kammy hasn't been telling you what we've been discovering during our sessions. The memories that I've helped unblock because they were so traumatic."

Kammy hiccups a small whimper, hands shaking as she clutches the bag tighter.

"But it's my favorite bag," she pleads.

Devonte narrows his eyes. His silence is distinctly loud, making everyone in the room afraid to move or breathe.

"Are you a sheep?" he asks.

Kammy shakes her head with a sniff. "No."

"No? You sure about that? 'Cause if you want your purse, then you should be a sheep and follow behind everyone else."

Kammy shuts her eyes tight, shaking her head.

"Well, if you want to be a sheep, then be a sheep!"

Devonte storms into the kitchen, snatches the fridge door, grabbing a half-open can of corn.

"Here! Eat like a sheep," he barks, tossing the corn across the floor. "Get down there and eat like a sheep!"

We stand in silence. Devonte clicks his tongue. "Woman, don't make me repeat myself. Get on the floor NOW!"

Kammy jumps, fresh tears springing. Then slowly, she sinks down to all fours, nibbling at the dirty corn-scattered on the linoleum. I can't remember the last time the floors had been washed. I hold back a gag.

Devonte steps over her like she is a dog in his way, snatches the purse, and drops it in his bag.

As dawn enters my room, I stare at the photo album on my computer, having more questions than answers. I slam the computer shut, resisting the urge to throw it against the wall.

This isn't what I thought it would be like at all, Kevin. . . .

In the five stages of grief, anger is the most destructive. Anger makes you take your pain out on anything moving, place blame on anyone, even the person who's gone. But everyone knows anger is just a mask over sharp sadness that makes you desperate to hold on to things, people, friends. Memories of loss make you never want to experience them again.

It's fascinating, the way grief lives in your body, like weeds planted in your lungs that keep growing back no matter how many times you try ripping them out. You can taste the hint of it every time you take a deep breath.

I wonder what Mom is up to. I haven't heard anything from my parents in weeks. Has their anger subsided? How could they just cut off their only child? What would they think of Devonte? Would they understand?

Maybe I should call her? After a shower.

I walk out of the room and trip over the body lying across my door, landing hard on my knees with a yelp.

I roll over, as the body stirs. "What are you doing?"

Legacy jumps to his feet. "Oh, uh. Devonte said I should

keep watch. Keep our women safe."

I rub the tender spot on my hip, knowing I'll be bruised by tomorrow.

"Fine, but you don't have to sleep on the damn floor," I snap.

Legacy looks sheepish. "Um, the couch is taken."

I glance over and there's Kareem lying across the love seat, his bare feet dangling, but his eyes are wide open, staring at the ceiling.

Legacy helps me up.

"Please don't tell him I fell asleep," he begs. Him clearly being Devonte.

"I won't. But Legacy, you should go home. Take a shower, change."

He stuffs his hands in his pockets. "I . . . live here now."

I shake myself awake. "What?"

"Yeah, me and Kareem. We're gonna be a real family."

After class, I head to the Malcolm Center for my Wednesday afternoon shift. I promised Nick I would help with the spring budget, to see where money can be allocated for different programming.

I walk into the office and find Nick behind his desk, alone, hand gripping his hair.

"Did you know about this?" he snaps, eyes blazing.

I stop in my tracks. "Huh?"

Nick swats at his laptop in my direction. On the screen is an email. . . .

OPEN LETTER TO THE KAPPA FRATERNITY:

To Whom It May Concern:

My name is Kareem X, as my slave name is no longer valid. I am a junior at Frazier University, and I am writing this letter to inform you that I am renouncing and denouncing my membership with Kappa Kappa Psi.

This organization is practicing occult witchcraft in the form of Christianity, which is exactly how slave masters controlled our enslaved ancestors. Through idolatry, manipulation, and mandatory worshiping of white gods at satanic shrines, when we all know God is a Black man. I refuse to bow to anything but our true king.

Further, I must also highlight the white infiltration that has also taken place. For a Black organization to allow our enemy to be a part of our society is a disgrace that I can no longer ignore. The enemy is clearly working among and through our sacred societies. You must stay woke and vigilant, brothers. . . .

Nick yanks back his laptop, stabbing the screen. "He goes on to write in DETAIL about our sacred rituals and ceremonies. Things no one outside of a Kappa man should know! Everyone has seen it!"

The letter was from Kareem but it screams Devonte.

My stomach grows tight. "I swear, I didn't know anything about this."

"Kareem moved out in the middle of the night. No one has seen him."

I think of him on the sofa. The haunted look in his eyes, as if he was lost in his own head, searching for an exit.

"I've seen him hanging out with your roommate a lot. Vanessa?"

"Uh, yes. He is her boyfriend."

"So who's that other guy?" he asks. "The one with the locs?"

I swallow. "That's . . . her brother."

Nick bristles. "Her brother? Does he go here? He looks kinda old."

"What? No, he doesn't. He's the healthiest man I know!"

I hear myself say the words, but I still can't believe they came out of my mouth. Nick's eyes widen.

"He's family," I go on to explain, trying to clean up my mess. "He's just visiting. Doesn't your family visit you?"

Nick blanches, neck growing red. "That's not the point! Jordyn, reading this letter . . . this doesn't sound like Kareem at all. It sounds like he's been brainwashed. And I have a feeling that brother of Vanessa is up to it. Look at the way he lurks around campus, around you."

"He's not lurking. He's welcomed. And it's fine, I—"

"He's a grown man hanging around campus with a bunch of college students! Doesn't he have a job? A home? Women his own age to be with!"

"What, are you jealous that someone of his stature would want to spend his time with us?"

"Stature? I don't even know the guy. And you don't either!"

That's not true, I want to scream in his face. Instead, I rub my throbbing temple.

"Look, can we focus and get back to work. I don't know anything about Kareem or your organization, but I guess he had his reasons."

"Fine. Sure thing," he snaps. "Wouldn't want you to miss curfew."

Is he really taking his anger out on me?

He pushes the computer my way, inadvertently opening a page he was clearly reading on the university website.

"Trustee? You want to be a student trustee?"

Nick closes the page quick and clears his throat, avoiding my gaze.

I nod, impressed. "Nick, that's actually a perfect position for you."

He raises an eyebrow. "You really think so?"

"Yeah! All your programming is geared toward making positive change for students. Look how you're obsessing over this budget, trying to squeeze water from a rock. And the town halls after the riots. You could really be a voice for students in a major way. It's a good look."

Nick stares at me blankly for a long moment then clears his throat. "Let's . . . get back to work."

I roll my eyes and slump into my seat. We work for about two hours in silence before Nick stands, stretches, and heads for the kitchenette. He returns with a small bowl that smells like heaven.

"What's that?" I gasp, nearly drooling.

Nick glances at his hands, walks back to the kitchen, and grabs another spoon.

"Here. Eat."

I stare down into what looks like a stew with sausages, shrimp, kidney beans mixed in a red sauce on top of a bed of fluffy white rice. My stomach cries out but I still hesitate.

"Um, no thanks."

"Look, just take a bite. It's fine."

"No."

"You'll like it. Just try it."

"No thanks."

"Just a little taste."

"I said no! And what is that, pork sausage? Rat, cat, and dog. And white rice is full of toxins! Shrimp are nothing but bottom feeders. Don't you know that!"

The words come tumbling out before I can stop them.

Nick blinks, shell-shocked. "Wait, what did you say?"

"I . . . I . . ." I'm about to lie when my phone pings.

Vanessa: Come home now. Devonte has an idea!

TWELVE

AS WE ALL gather in the suite, Devonte holds up a printed aerial photo of a plot of land, with a large clearing and giant trees next to a pond the shape of a bitten cookie.

"This is a piece of property I own, down in Virginia," he announces. "I'm going to build us a sanctuary. A place where people like us, free thinkers, believers, the divine . . . will thrive!"

The crowd nods excitedly, passing around the photo, approving of its beauty. When did he buy this land? How long has he had it?

"The only way to live is to make our own way. We'll farm our own food, build our own homes. Teach our children, 'cause as Malcolm X once said, 'Only a fool would let his enemy teach his children!'"

The room, full of familiar faces and more, nod and grunt with affirming snaps in the air.

"Look at you. Attending a college named after a white man," he says, shaking his head. "Board members, white men.

Government handouts, white men. You pay thousands of dollars to attend a school, pouring money back into white men's hands, listening to your parents rather than listening to the cries of our communities. The white man has been manipulating you, making you doubt your roots, your own Blackness. They're trying to rewrite history to make them look like angels rather than demons. Don't let them miseducate you any longer. Aren't you tired of them getting all the good jobs, stealing all the money, taking credit for the land your ancestors built, tired of them buying Grandma's house, tired of them putting your uncles, cousins, brothers in prison? Tired of them killing us in the streets like dogs?"

A murmur takes over the room.

"Bob Marley said, 'Emancipate yourselves from mental slavery, none but ourselves can free our minds' and . . . Ohhhh." He rubs his chin, a smile spreading. "Yes, that's what we will call it."

"Call what?" Kammy asks, hanging on to his every word.

"Our new home. We'll call it Emancipation!"

Vanessa claps her hands.

"It's perfect," she breathes. "People will pilgrimage from all over. Our own mecca."

Devonte looks at his sister with such pride. "We'll start work on it during the new year. But we need materials, tools, supplies. . . . That's why, brothers and sisters, it's time that you start giving toward the cause. The more we raise, the more brothers and sisters we save."

He looks at me and smiles. Kammy notices, her grin slowly fading.

"This is it, young stars. This is how we change the world. There is a storm coming. I can feel it, can't you? The change. Will you help me?"

"Yes!" the room shouts.

"Will you protect me, cover me from those that will try to kill this dream?"

"Yes!"

"Then, let us all be free!"

The room feels charged on raw energy. The picture of utopia sharpening, full of color and crystal clear sound. How addicting it is to be a part of something that's more than you.

Devonte sat us down and made us write a list of ten people we can ask for money. He then wrote the perfect script to use when calling our parents and loved ones.

I stare down at the words, struggling to figure a way out of this. No matter what, I cannot call my parents. I cannot let them in on this life. I cannot let them know what I'm up to.

Since Vanessa has no family, Loren goes first.

"Hey Ma," Loren starts nervous, the call on speakerphone.

"Hey baby girl! We been trying to call you for days. You can't call nobody back."

"Oh been busy with school."

"So busy you can't call your ma! And your sisters been asking about you. What's going on? How's school?"

Devonte gives her a stern look. Loren swallows.

"Um, Ma. I need some money."

"Oh Lord, for what now?"

"It's the only way for me to stay in school. They miscalculated something."

"How much do you need?"

Loren braces herself before mumbling, "Ten thousand."

"Ten thousand? Girl, are you crazy? See, that's why I told you to go to school in state, at least they would've given you some money. I ain't got that type of cash lying around."

"Ma, I'm the only one who's gone away to college. Can't you and Daddy borrow it from Grandma. Or . . . something. Please, Mom. I owe these people money and they ain't gonna let up."

Loren's mom sighs. "Let me talk to your father. Guess we can figure something out."

After Loren wraps up her call victoriously, Devonte scribbles out more notes.

"Jordyn, you're next," he says.

I sit there, stunned. The fact that Loren could call her parents and ask them for money without suffering the third degree, ridicule, and admonishment . . . the fact that her parents love her so much they'd give her anything, the shirt off their backs if she wanted, while I am unsure my parents will even pick up the phone . . . makes my heart shatter.

I grip the script in my hand, shaking.

Devonte touches my wrist and coos the soft words "What's wrong, Queen?"

The tears I've been holding back come bursting through.

"I can't ask them. I just can't!" I sob but quickly straighten, realizing I still have a job to do. "But . . . I want to go with you to Emancipation."

Devonte wipes the tears away with his thumbs. "I believe you. But everything in this world has a cost."

"I've already given you everything that I have." I shake my head. "My parents hate me. They won't understand what we're trying to do. They don't have Black pride like we do."

He takes me in for a moment. "You have three credit cards, right?"

I swallow. I never told anyone that.

"Yes," I breathe. "But they're under my parents' account."

He tips up my chin with his index finger. "Are you your own woman?"

"What do you mean?"

"Seems like everything you do, you must have your parents' help with. Sounds like you ain't an independent thinker, a free spirit. Maybe you're not ready to be enlightened."

"I am! You know I am."

"Then why can't you open your own credit cards?"

The question is so simple yet feels pivotal.

"My . . . own? Well, I mean I can. It's just . . . I never have."

"Then it's time for you to cut that umbilical cord and make

decisions for yourself." He shyly looks down at his palms. "Unless you're not ready to be with us."

Vanessa, Loren, and Kammy stare with curiosity.

Principle number three: Arouse in the other person an eager want.

I don't want to blow this moment so I dig deeper. "But . . . how will I pay for them?"

"You won't need to pay, Queen. They can't do anything if you don't have the money to pay it back. They can't arrest you. You're a student. All they'll do is send letter after letter, call after call. And we will tell them the truth: that their earthly laws no longer apply to you. It can be complex, that's why I'm here to guide you through it."

For the briefest moment, Loren seems bewildered. Maybe the same questions that are running through her mind are running through mine.

Vanessa, standing over us, nods. "Remember how I was telling you Devonte was good with finances? He has a stock portfolio and stuff. He paid for my car in cash."

I don't remember her saying that at all.

I wait for someone to ask the obvious question: If he has money, why does he need ours? But no one utters a word.

"Wow," Kammy says. "Maybe you can help us get cars."

Devonte doesn't take his eyes off me, even with Kammy raining compliments. It's a stare down that I have no plans on winning.

"All you have to do is take your credit cards to the ATM and make a withdrawal," he says, his voice reassuring. "In fact, since this is the first time you're doing this, I'll take you myself."

"Right now?"

"Yes. Also, can't let you walk around with money. Like I told you, I'm here to protect you. But before we go, let's fill out an application."

I look down at my palms. "I've never applied for a credit card before. What if they reject me?"

"It's not like school, Queen. They won't reject you."

Devonte helps me fill out the paperwork online. Within thirty minutes, I receive an automatic approval.

"Five thousand. Not bad," he mumbles. "We'll wait for the card to arrive before withdrawing the amount."

"But won't I have to pay this back eventually? And what about credit scores, stuff like that."

"Sister, you will be paid in gold and riches. Once we accomplish what we need to, banks will forgive."

"Really?"

"It's just a matter of filling out the right paperwork. Trust me, I know how the system works. They're trying to scare you, but you're strong. You have a lion's heart. You can face anything."

THIRTEEN

A GROUP OF seven girls I've never see before sit in the living room, drinking Devonte's tea, eating up his words like starving kittens.

"Low-vibrational foods are those foods that are lacking life-force energy. Foods that don't transfer energy and inject life into men, which is your sole purpose. Fasting is a part of our cleansing, our detox, our way to enlightenment, our door to emancipation."

I don't know where he met them. He just showed up with them and said, "Kammy, fix some tea."

He goes on to talk about men and women, and our roles, and what the white man has done to the nuclear family.

"You should dress modestly . . . like Jordyn," he says, pointing to me. "She doesn't walk around campus with her skin out and yet she is gorgeous."

Heads turn and I lower my gaze, face steaming hot.

When we wrap up, I head for the bathroom, eyes landing on his black soap, raw shea butter, and wooden beard brush. He threw away all our toothpaste and hair products, replacing them with organic ones. So swept up in his tailwind that I didn't realize he just about moved in without any sign of leaving.

In the shower, something else occurs to me—I didn't immediately recognize the look in Kammy's eyes when he called me gorgeous. Then it hits me.

It's jealousy.

I swipe the thought away and change into my pj's. All I need is a good night's sleep. In my room, I find my phone sitting on the desk, face down. I grip it tight, a lump snowballing in my throat.

Because I know with unwavering certainty that I left it on my bed.

I haven't been to the library in weeks, but I decide to finish my Ethics paper, now two days late. Late papers are penalized one-third of a letter grade for each day, so if it's not perfect, I could end up with a D. I've never had anything less than a B in my life and even that grade I challenged. Because I wasn't going to bring a B home to my parents. Not when their expectations of me sat somewhere next to Pluto.

At times I wonder, if they didn't have such lofty goals for me, would our lives be any different? Would Kevin still be alive? Would he be here, at Frazier U, rather than me?

I stop short on the first floor, spotting Nick at a table, books spread out.

I bump my hip into his seat. "Surprised to see you here."

Nick doesn't look up. "This is usually where people study for midterms."

With not many free tables left, I sit across from him and

take out my iPad and computer.

"You're roommates with Kammy, right?"

"Yeah. Why, how'd you know her?"

"I'm TA-ing one of her classes." He shakes his head. "That girl is as sharp as a bowling ball."

I snort and throw hands over my face.

He chuckles. "Did you just snort like Miss Piggy?"

I laugh louder and someone says "Shhhhh" and we fall silent, him mouthing the word "sorry" to anyone nearby. It feels good to laugh. Almost unnatural.

When I think about it, Nick is actually a great catch. Funny, flirty, super smart, and cute. It would be a shame to let that go to waste.

"Hey, can I ask you a personal question?"

"Depends."

"Why don't you have a girlfriend?"

He shrugs. "Don't want one. That simple."

"You ever had one?"

Nick pauses, his smile slowly fading. "Yeah."

"You don't think that's a sin against God not to take a woman?"

He frowns. "A what?"

Stunned by my own word vomit, I fumble with my computer.

"Nothing," I squeak, with a nervous laugh. "That was silly, never mind."

Nick doesn't seem convinced and on the brink of asking his own personal questions of me, which I can't answer. I need a distraction.

Principle number four: Become genuinely interested in other people.

I scan his setup and notice a bright painting on a textbook—*Slavery to Liberation: The African American Experience.*

"Why do you have this?" I ask, tapping the cover.

He looks at me as if I'm asking a dumb question. "It's for Afro-American Studies II."

"YOU'RE taking Afro-American Studies?"

He laughs. "Worse. It's my minor."

"Seriously? Laying it on kinda thick, don't you think? We see you love Black people, you don't have to overdo it."

He rolls his eyes. "It's a university requirement. You can't graduate without taking one Afro studies course. I'm hooked on history, so I decided to make it my minor. Plus, you can't fight for injustice without having an intimate knowledge of the history of how we got here."

I'm impressed, but I refuse to admit it.

"Okay. So what do you know about the Willie Lynch papers?"

"Pff. That's a myth."

I purse my lips. "Of course YOU would say that."

He looks at me for a moment, studying, his smile slowly fading. "Wait, are you being serious or are you joking? Why are you asking about the Willie Lynch papers?"

Don't tell him. He'll just try to gaslight you. That's what they all do.

I stack my books, stuffing my computer back in my bag, and shoot up to my feet.

"Forget it! It's not important. I don't even know why I brought it up."

I rush out of the library, still thinking about the course requirement I didn't even know existed. But who needs to take a class on Black history when I have a man, right at home, who's allegedly teaching me everything I need to know about being Black?

"Where have you been?"

Devonte sounds more angry than concerned. The living room is once again filled with people. People I don't know. The suite is burning hot. Too many bodies and smells makes my stomach cramp. Or maybe it's the lack of food.

Kammy is passing around tea, wearing a long brown skirt, her hair wrapped in a cream scarf. She looks exhausted, aging overnight, her smile straining.

"Well," Devonte snaps. "Where have you been?"

"The library," I say meekly, checking the time. Still an hour before curfew.

"We need you here," he spits, shaking a stack of papers in his hand. "I told you that."

Loren and Vanessa are on the sofa, folding pamphlets, laughing with one another. They look so relaxed, natural, at ease. As if this all were completely normal. So why doesn't it feel that way for me yet? When is the moment where it'll finally sink in, like it sinks in for others enough that the lingering doubt will leave?

Because this isn't normal. And you of all people know that.

I shake the thought, temporarily embolden. "I have a paper to finish."

Devonte snarls in disgust. "How can you talk about papers when—"

There's a knock on the door. Devonte rolls his eyes.

"Come in," he barks.

The door opens and in walks Nick.

There's a brief moment of stilted silence, where everyone freezes and my body goes numb. The room stares at him. He gives an awkward wave.

"Nick?" I gasp. "What are you doing here?"

"Hey. You left this at the library."

He hands me my iPad. In my rush to leave, I must have forgotten it.

"Oh. I . . . thanks," I mumble, clutching it to my chest.

"No problem," he says softly.

Nick takes a long look around the room. Everyone stares back, their eyes hard, cold, unwelcoming.

I want to shove him out of the suite, give him a running head start. The need to protect him returning with full force. But suddenly, shame blossoms. Here is my peer, seeing my suite, my chaotic living situation in full view that I didn't realize until now, I didn't want anyone to ever see. It's like company popping over and finding out you're a hoarder.

Nick is neither oblivious nor afraid. He stands tall. He locks eyes with Kareem in the corner of the room, his lips tightening.

"Y'all have a good night," Nick mutters, gripping hold of the door.

He gives me a look before walking out that says one thing: he's worried.

The door slams behind him. Devonte slowly rising to his feet. The unimaginable gall of Nick's presence making his hands shake in rage.

"You see?" he hisses, pointing at the door. "You see how they think they own EVERYTHING, that they can walk into a Black man's house without permission?!"

He takes two strides in my direction. Terror floods my body as I flinch, ducking, expecting his open hand to come down across my face.

Devonte snatches the iPad away, giving me a cold, unblinking glare. Then he straightens, pushing back his locs before rejoining the group in the living room. Vanessa and Kammy stare at me cowering on the floor, faces expressionless.

"Jordyn, I want those new pamphlets done tonight," Devonte hisses without looking at me. "Now, where were we?"

Trembling, it takes me a few moments to move, realizing what I just did—I was bracing myself for a hit. And in some alternative universe, I would have said I deserved it. I deserved to be smacked because I was studying with my white classmate instead of focusing on the mission. I deserved it. . . . My mouth goes dry.

I walk into the bathroom and retch up the meager contents in my stomach.

FOURTEEN

PIGS IN THE blanket, bacon-wrapped shrimp . . . the ballroom smells like an all-you-can-eat buffet.

I am both disgusted yet desperate as I add lemon to my water to keep me from fainting. I'm lightheaded, my stomach pinching from hunger.

FUSA is holding a small mixer in the Malcolm Center for Frazier board members. I volunteered to collect tickets while the executive board members float around the room, charming their members, encouraging involvement and promises of more donations.

The black cocktail dress is hanging off my shoulders, a bit wrinkled since I had to sneak it out in my book bag and change in the Rec Center bathroom. I've lost weight since I've been here. I also haven't worn this dress since . . . Kevin. Just the thought of him in that casket makes the room spin.

I'm here, Kevin. Failing, but I'm here.

I haven't turned in my paper and I more than likely will be

on academic probation by the end of the semester. How could I waste time studying for school when I'm studying for life?

So, what keeps me coming back to student government? Probably because it's all I have, separate from everyone else. It can't be touched, and it keeps me somewhat grounded in reality.

In the ballroom, Nick is wooing a few men in power suits. He doesn't look too bad in a white button-down and gray slacks. He even tied his hair back in a small man bun.

I sway on my feet, my belly howling.

"Girl, is that your stomach?" Brianna asks from the ticket table. "You can take a break and get something to eat. That thing is loud!"

She shakes her head and I'm too desperate for food to turn down the offer. I rush into the ballroom, straight to the platters, most of them untouched as waiters walk around with appetizers and mocktails.

The moment I walk in, Nick spots me, but doesn't acknowledge. He goes on chatting with the adults.

I pick up a small plate and pile it with grapes, strawberries, and a few chunks of cheese. Maybe I should sneak plates back for Loren and Kammy. Vanessa doesn't seem to mind our new diet. Probably used to it.

I catch a whiff of his scent before a hand squeezes around my forearm. My plate of cheese and grapes falls on the floor, scattering away, as I'm yanked and dragged into the hallway.

Devonte. He's out of place in his jeans and T-shirt. His locs aren't even tied back. He leans inches from my face, nails digging into my arms. How did he know I was here? Who told him?

"This isn't a party," I whimper, scrambling to explain. "It's a mixer for the board members. No one's even drinking!"

Devonte grumbles. "After all I've done. All I sacrificed . . . for YOU. Do you think I'm stupid?"

"Devonte . . . it isn't what you think. This is for student government."

"Don't you think what we're doing, what we're trying to accomplish, is more important than this shit? Don't you—"

"Hey, hi. I don't believe we've met, formally."

Devonte drops my arm, stepping back. I'm too in shock to fully realize that Nick has slid in between us.

"I'm Nick. School of Arts and Sciences president."

Devonte scowls at his extended hand in disgust. He doesn't take it. Doesn't even answer him.

"Okayyyy," Nick says, with a chuckle. "So, are you a student here? What's your major? We have all kinds of alum in there."

Devonte narrows his eyes at him before switching his glare to me. Nick is nothing but an invisible wall.

"Uh, Jordyn. You think you can help me with the gift bags? I don't want to have security help with them instead. They're just LOOKING for something to do."

Devonte heard the inflammatory word: *security*. He may have security at the dorm wrapped around his finger, but not here on the main campus. He stares at me with a smug smile and shakes his head.

"See you later," he hisses.

We watch him stroll off in the same lazy, unbothered pace he always walks, bouncing down the steps.

Once he's out of sight, Nick turns to me, eyes flaring. "What the hell was that about?"

"Nothing!" I insist, my voice squeaking, lip quivering.

"Nothing? What was he doing grabbing you like that? In front of everyone? Did he hurt you?"

For a change, I can't fight back the tears from the humiliation. My eyes swell, and I bite my lips to hold in a sob.

Nick straightens and quickly springs into action, leading me down the stairs and into the back FUSA office. He closes the door, so we're alone, and offers me a box of tissues. I plop on the desk, hot tears dripping into my lap.

Nick faces me, hands in his pockets, his expression softening.

"Jordyn," he begins. "If you're in trouble . . . if he's abusing you . . ."

I wave him off. "He's not my boyfriend. I'm not in an abusive relationship."

"You sure? Because, Jordyn . . . I've seen guys like this. It doesn't . . . end well."

Why does it feel like he's begging me to believe him?

"What do you mean, 'guys like this'?"

"Older guys . . . who are trying to take advantage of . . . younger girls."

I sniff and in an instant, my defenses go up.

"You mean young STUPID girls, right?"

His mouth gapes. "No, I don't think you're stupid at all. Anyone could be taken advantage of!"

I slam down the tissue box. "Seriously . . . can we NOT do this? I'm fine."

"You're not FINE! This isn't FINE!"

I hold up a hand with a sharp nod, closing my eyes to regain composure. "Nick, I need you to mind your own business. Everything is under control. I can handle this myself."

Nick is struggling with the words. "Jordyn, this is . . . fucked up. You know it is."

He's right. But I can't let him know that. So much more is at stake, and I can't risk him involving himself.

"Good night, Nick. I'll see you tomorrow."

I run out of the Malcolm Center, heading back to the dorm, letting the tears fall.

Music thumps out of Vanessa's room as I run into the suite, heading straight into the bathroom. Tears mixing with the little makeup I wore have created a sad drip painting down my face.

I have to quit FUSA. I can't risk another run-in and public embarrassment.

Outside the thin bathroom door are more strangers, sitting among Devonte's other fans in our tiny living room. With all these people, why did Devonte have to come and find me tonight? Doesn't he have others to worry about? Where are Kammy and Loren?

As I toss my tissue in the trash, I spot medicine bottles and tiny jars at the bottom of the bin. My heart sinks. I grab them and burst out of the bathroom.

The suite smells of sweat and incense. The heat of so many bodies stuffed in one place makes it sweltering. Devonte said it would be good for us. The humidity and sauna-like conditions will detox our pores of chemicals.

Kareem is squeezed on the sofa, as the others, none that I recognize, argue over Devonte's talking points. He looks different. His hair has grown wild, face gaunt, and ashy. I have a hard time tearing my eyes away as I knock on Loren's door.

She swings it open with a smile. Legacy is lying on her bed, reading one of the books Devonte expects us to memorize.

"Hey girl! Where you been?" Loren says, beaming.

I hold up the vials of insulin. "Isn't this yours?"

Loren glances at my hand, her smile faltering.

"Yeah. What about it?"

"You're just going to throw it away," I snap, shaking her prescription bottles. "Don't you need them?"

"Not anymore." She sighs. "They don't make medicine with Black women in mind, so I'm gonna go organic."

"Huh?"

She crosses her arms. "When they make medicine, they test it on WHITE lab rats, not black ones. So, how do we know if this stuff really works on us?"

I stand there, waiting for the punch line to her joke. When it doesn't come, I hear the tinkling of broken glass as my facade crashes around me.

What the fuck am I doing?

"Loren, this is fucking medicine! Science that's been proven for decades."

"Proven by who? We're just supposed to believe whatever they say. That's like the police policing themselves."

"You can get really sick! You can die!"

Legacy sits up, worry in his eyes.

"How do you know the medicine isn't MAKING me sick?" Loren shoots back. "Or sicker than I already am? We don't know anything about what they do in those labs and what these vaccines and medications are doing to our bodies. So I, at least, have to try a different way. A safer, healthier way of living. People have been curing themselves with diet and herbs for centuries."

I don't have to ask where she's getting this nonsense from.

I shake my head. "This is dangerous."

"Not as dangerous as those pills," Loren spits, and walks back into her room, slamming the door shut.

I turn back to the living room, almost forgetting we had an audience.

Vanessa stares from her threshold, worry in her eyes.

"Jordyn, maybe we—"

I don't wait for her to finish. I walk into my room and slam the door.

This time, Devonte has gone too far.

FIFTEEN

RAIN PUMMELS THE windows of the Malcolm Center, thunder rumbling as if it's right over our heads. A deafening sound.

Loren, Kammy, and I sit in the café with limp pieces of salad on our plates, waiting out the passing storm. Loren's eyes are sunken, and Kammy's face is pale, lips chapped. Devonte said the herbs he mixes in our teas should help increase our energy but some days I can barely make it up the hill to class.

I look at the girls across the table with trembling fingers. I've been building up the courage all day to have the conversation. I know what I have to do, I'm just not sure if I'm ready to do it. Rather than being an outlier, for the first time in my life, I have friends, a real clique I belong to. And these girls wanted to be my friends, from day one with no hesitation. I never experienced that kind of love and instant loyalty. Yet it's starting to feel like we're a family of Black dolls propped up, collected, manipulated, and I can't seem to stand the idea of cutting the strings that bind us to our puppet master.

Because then I will be alone.

"Hey," I start, "um, don't you think that it's maybe time for Devonte to, like, hold his meetings in his apartment?"

Loren frowns. "What do you mean?"

"I mean, he's been with us for a while now. And our suite is really small. So, I don't know, maybe it's time for him to, like . . . leave?"

I pose the concern as a question, using our limited space as an excuse rather than the conditions Devonte has us under. But Loren and Kammy stare blank-faced before sharing a quick nervous glance with each other.

Finally, Kammy speaks first. "No, I don't think so. I think it's fine."

"Yeah, and he's helping us," Loren agrees. "It's easier when he's close by."

Loren stretches across the table with a grin. "He says this summer he's going to introduce me to Jay-Z's publicist. I can maybe get an internship at his label back in New York."

"That's . . . amazing," I say, trying to sound genuine, falling flat.

"And he's helping me work out my issues with my family," Kammy adds. "He's not really bothering us, right? He said he just has to stay close because we still have a lot of deprogramming to do."

I swallow, needing a different approach. I can't come on too strong. But I have to find a way to lure them away from him before it's too late.

"But . . . like, all the food stuff. The late-night sessions and meetings. It's just . . . a lot. No other students are going through this."

"Girl, other students are blind," Kammy scoffs. "They don't see the world for what it is. He's helping us open our third eye so that we won't be taken advantage of."

"But . . . he's not even a student."

"He's a student of life," Kammy counters. "He doesn't need a degree to help us. Who even needs a degree, period?"

Outside, the rain is thick, an ocean dumping on our campus. We're spiraling down a whirlpool to the bottom of the sea and no one knows it.

"He's inviting people to live with us," I say, unable to hold back my outrage. "Without even asking if it's okay!"

"Well, it's important that we stick together," Kammy counters. "A united front against the white agenda."

"He's the best professor we could ever get," Loren adds. "He's teaching us about real life. About the culture. I wouldn't know half the stuff he's been schooling us on because everyone wants to whitewash history."

"Does that mean we have to suffer while we learn?" I ask, leaning back in my seat. Of all people, I thought Loren would be at least sensible about this.

Loren looks at Kammy, something passing between them, and my stomach caves in. A secret. We're not supposed to have secrets. Kammy crosses her arms.

"Jordyn, he's been cleaning and cooking and mentoring us for free after he saved our lives, and you want to just kick him out? That's cold-blooded."

"Come on, Jordyn," Loren says, more lighthearted. "He was in prison! Do you know what kind of conditions he had to live through? They had him in solitary confinement. Black men kill themselves every day after going through stuff like that. We can't just ghost him."

I hold my breath until knives stab through my lungs from the inside out and I'm ready to flip a table.

"Yeah," I hiss, hands rolling into fists. "Trust me. I know."

Loren sits back, as if sensing the danger brewing inside me.

"Well, I don't know why you're complaining," Kammy mumbles bitterly with a neck roll. "He treats you better than the rest of us. He's taken it easy on you."

This comment catches even Loren by surprise.

"He does not," I snap, losing patience. Didn't she see him about to smack me the other night? "And I'm not the one getting extra sessions like you."

Kammy's eyes toggle between us, guilt setting in. She sighs, her shoulders slumping.

"I'm sorry. I didn't mean that. I'm just . . . not myself. And I'm really hungry."

"Me too," Loren admits.

"But the truth. I think we're in love," Kammy says, a bashful smile taking over her face. "Real love. Deep twin soul flame love. I don't want to lose that connection. Not when this is the only thing that makes me feel closer to God."

Loren doesn't look surprised by Kammy's revelation, which means they've been talking about it behind my back. I wince, feeling the familiar sting of being left out in the cold without even knowing it.

"You're right. I'm sorry. Guess I'm just being hangry."

Loren grins, placing a hand on my arm. Her fingers are like ice chips.

"We in this together, girl! Besides, Devonte's good for our cred. Look how many people we got up in our spot now. Everyone knows who we are and trying to be down!"

I nod, realizing that it may be too late to save them. But maybe it's time to save myself.

"Hi, is Ms. Rogers available?"

I wait at the front desk of the Student Housing office, located in the Frazier Administration building. The secretary returns, and a plump woman with dark chestnut skin in a teal sheath dress follows, her salt-and-pepper hair shaved close to the scalp.

"Hello sweetheart, how can I help you?" she says, her large orange earrings dangling.

I extend my hand. "Hi, I'm Jordyn Monroe. Can we talk . . . in private?"

Ms. Rogers blanches then quickly glances at the secretary before righting herself.

"Oh. Hi. Yes, this way."

I hesitate before following her into her office, unnerved by her response. She shuts the door behind us and sits at a giant oak desk, fumbling with a cup of Frazier pens by the monitor. The cabinet behind her holds a dozen framed pictures from over the years at various school functions. She's probably been working here for decades.

"How can I help you?" she asks, folding her hands, feigning confidence.

"I was just wondering if there are any other dorm rooms available."

She blinks a dozen times in two seconds, glancing over my shoulder, as if making sure the door is closed tight.

"Is there something wrong with your current room?" she asks.

This part will be tricky. Trying not to raise any alarm bells or red flags. Nothing that could get back to the girls.

"No, no. I was just . . . checking to see if I have options."

"Options?"

"Yeah. Options. Just in case."

She stares at me for a moment, as if trying to figure me out. Then turns to her computer, pecking at her keyboard.

"Well . . . all our dorms are at full capacity. Your dorm has a wait-list of about fifty or more. But rooms tend to open up by spring semester. Often students drop out due to financial reasons."

"Oh. Okay. Thanks."

"Are you . . . I mean, if there's an emergency or issue, we'll have to address it. But there will be an investigation. So do you think you want to change now, or do you think you can wait until spring?"

I nibble on my lip. On one hand, an investigation would be the quickest way to get rid of Devonte. But it would also cause friction when the girls find out it was me who raised the red flag. There must be another way to avoid that, to save them without them hating me.

"I think I can wait until spring," I say with a confident nod.

She gives me a polite smile and her nervousness sparks a question in me.

"Has anyone from my suite . . . been by to ask the same thing?"

She shakes her head. A little too fast. "No, not that I know of."

I can't tell if she's lying but I also can't let on I suspect she is.

I paste on a smile. "Spring semester. Got it. Thanks for your help."

She opens her mouth as if to ask something, but I'm already on my feet, rushing past the secretary, out into the main hallway, releasing the pent-up breath causing a fire in my lungs.

Outside the office, I lean against the wall, stomach queasy. This wasn't a part of the plan. Where did I go wrong? Did I make a mistake coming here?

"Jordyn?"

Shit!

I whirl around and Kerry is walking down the hall, waving. "Hey girl."

"Hey," I croak out, relieved it's not one of the girls. "What are you doing in here?"

She huffs. "Begging for more financial aid. Unless my mom can magically come up with some dough." She glances at the sign above the door, and frowns with a laugh. "What are you doing in here?"

I stare into Kerry's eyes, remembering her suspicions of Devonte from the very beginning, and can't hold it in any longer.

"You may be right about Devonte. He is creepy."

She wipes the smile off her face and steps closer. "What happened? Tell me."

I don't even know where to start.

"I just . . . got to get out of my room. He's been . . . lying to us about stuff."

Kerry nods, concern in her eyes, and I'm relieved to finally find someone who has seen Devonte for who he really is. Maybe she could help me convince the others.

She glances in both directions, as if worried we'll be overheard.

"Were they able to find you another room?"

"No," I groan. "There's nothing available until spring semester."

She holds my hand. "But what did you tell them? Did you tell them what was going on so that they'd move you?"

"No, not in so many words," I admit.

Kerry shakes her head. "This is serious, Jordyn. You gotta be careful. You can't fuck with your home life like that. Did you talk to the girls yet? You not about to leave them there, right?"

The thought of all the things the girls would go through, without me there, makes my stomach sink.

What if . . . what if . . . shit.

"Um, hey I have to go," I mumble in a daze, rushing toward the exit.

"But Jordyn, what happened!"

A whistle comes up my throat as I burst through the door, running across campus, just for the air to hit my skin, cool it down. Fresh air fixes everything. I stop by a bench, parked right outside the football stadium, to catch my breath, my thoughts scrambling. Am I doing the right thing?

"Hey! Jordyn!"

I freeze at my name. Nick comes jogging out of a building near the sports center.

"Hey! I've been calling you," he says, standing in front of me "Why haven't you answered your phone?"

"How'd you get my number?"

"The FUSA directory. Are you okay?" he asks, his face serious.

He's still thinking about the other night. I stifle my annoyance.

"Yes. I'm fine, I told you I—"

"Okay. Then, come with me."

"What?"

"Come. With. Me," he says, pulling at my arm.

Too exhausted to fight, I let him lead me away. We walk

across the Quad into Webber Hall.

"What are we doing? Where are we going?"

Nick turns to me. "You said something the other day that raised a red flag. Look, just . . . keep an open mind."

What is he talking about?

I follow Nick up two flights of stairs and down a busy stretch of classrooms until he stops at a door and knocks.

"Come in," a voice calls from the other side.

Inside is a cozy corner office, with windows facing the Quad. The only areas not stacked floor to ceiling with books, papers, and African art.

A tall, dark-skinned older man wearing a baby-blue button-down shirt under his red and green dashiki stands in the middle of the room, glasses and textbook in hand.

"Hey Dr. Barnes," Nick says.

"Nicolas!" he cheers, closing his book, giving me a curious glance. "To what do I owe the pleasure?"

"I want to introduce you to someone." Nick pushes me toward a wooden seat facing a mahogany desk. "This is the student I was telling you about."

His eyebrows shoot up. "Ohhh yes. Come in, young lady, have a seat."

I flash Nick a deadly glare and sit. Dr. Barnes's smile is almost infectious, eyes childlike.

"I received a letter from a student in my African American Studies 101 class," he says, holding up a printed email, about ten pages long. "Nick mentioned you might know this young lady. Ms. Kamara Young?"

I swallow. "Yes. She's my roommate."

"Mmm. Well, she sent a rather long letter, cc-ing deans and the provost, in an effort to correct what she considers a misunderstanding of historical events. She believes I am teaching a whitewashed version of Black history and demands my resignation. It was quite illuminating."

"Really?"

"Yes. Most of the letter read as a manifesto of sorts. An attempt to course-correct principles and foundations with propaganda." He points at the letter. "I've graded all of Ms. Young's papers so far. And I have reason to believe that this letter is not in her own words. But I am quite familiar with the rhetoric."

I sit back in my seat. Devonte had a hand in this letter. If he didn't write it himself, he funneled the script directly into her mouth.

"Nick has told me that you may have some questions about things you've been reading . . . or being told. Things he thought I could provide some clarity on."

I clear my throat, trying to ignore the sense of panic floating through my veins. Am I going to let this man, this brilliant professor, think the worst of me? That I'm just some girl who believes what she's told, that I'm gullible, fresh for the picking.

Well . . . I can at least ask a few clarifying questions.

"Have you ever heard of the Lynch papers?" I ask.

He smiles. "Yes. I've heard of them."

"What do you think?"

He shrugs. "They are not without merit. But in recent years they've been exposed as a hoax. See, stories, typically passed down through our ancestors, are large brushstrokes on a canvas. It's a scholar's job to investigate and add context details. Could someone have given a speech that taught slave masters how to control their slaves with brainwashing-type tactics? Absolutely. But the speech they are referencing does not correlate with the time and date in which it was supposedly given. Imagine reading a speech given by President Obama and it's dated 1777."

I glance at Nick, who doesn't meet my eye. Embarrassment and humiliation mix a toxic cocktail through my system, and I explode.

"Okay. Well, what about vaccines sent to poison and control the Black population? Or food that has toxins in it. Or the chemtrails!"

Nick shifts beside me, crossing his arms tight over his chest. I breathe in deep, waiting for him to scold the side of me that knows that none of this makes sense. But he just looks sad. Is that pity?

Dr. Barnes stares at me, his smile never wavering.

"Ah yes. The chemtrails. I've heard of this. Why wouldn't you believe that they are spraying pesticides in the sky? No one believed that Italian mobs were targeting Black communities with crack and now live in expensive mansions paid for with the blood of our people. It sounds just as crazy yet only one of those stories is true."

He leans forward, folding his hands on the desk.

"You know, I have my own theory. I believe that conspiracy theories have done an equal amount of damage as racism has to our Black communities. From enslavement until now, we, above most others, have earned the right to be suspicious of white people's intentions after our history with one another. But our paranoia has rendered us frozen in our own imaginings. When you uproot and strip humans of their culture, you leave them vulnerable prey, easy to attack with stories rooted in believable truths. All it takes is to add a bit of fiction into the narrative you want a person to follow for it to be gospel. It doesn't mean we're gullible people. It means our collective generational trauma has us questioning everything. My honest advice is to continue the practice of skepticism with a critical eye. For example, if someone says they have a source or an example, tell them to provide three more. The ancestors gave us sharp instincts for a reason."

I lower my eyes. Kevin always said I didn't have the best instincts.

"I'm not saying that we should trust recklessly," Dr. Barnes continues. "But our rightful mistrust does not give license to forgo common sense and practicality. Ignoring science to our own detriment based on irrational principles. That doesn't protect us. That gives the people who planted these conspiracy theorists in our communities, these covert terrorists, these snakes in the grass . . . exactly what they want. To eradicate us from the inside out."

"Hey, you okay?" Nick asks.

Nick and I walk out of Webber Hall in silence, ambling over to a free bench next to a cluster of trees, marked with different fraternity and sorority symbols.

"That was . . . a lot," I admit, still processing. "What made you think I needed to talk to him?"

"Rat, cat, and dog," he says. "I heard that before. I didn't know . . . well, what that guy has been telling you."

Why can't he just mind his business? "Nick, I told you I—"

"Yeah, I know what you said, but I know what I *saw*." He takes a deep breath. "Look, I've been asking around about that guy. Everyone says he gives them the creeps. He's been trying to seduce other students to his cult."

The word cuts like a sharp knife up my chest but I breathe in and lean into the blade.

"Cult?" I parrot with a chuckle. "Who called it a cult?"

"Well, isn't it kinda obvious?"

Obvious to everyone except the ones in it, I think to say but hold my tongue. Because I can't give this theory oxygen. It needs to die so my dreams can go on living. But the thought of my friends being suckered into something so heinous so quickly gives me whiplash.

Friends? You're a part of it too.

That's when I spot her. Leaning against a tree, watching me. She would be just another shadow in the crowd except I recognize her face. I've seen her in our suite. But she's not just watching, she's on the phone. . . . She's on the phone with him!

She'll tell him what she saw, that I was on a bench, talking to the white boy who boldly walked into our dorm, into Devonte's home, like he had a right. Hot dread swells up my belly as I stare back at her in horror.

"Jordyn?" Nick asks, frowning. "What's wrong?"

"Hey, I have to go," I cough out and jump off the bench.

"What?"

"I just . . . I just have to go."

Nick is on his feet. "What, no, Jordyn. This is serious. Come back!"

I don't answer him as I bolt, mind and heart racing with nowhere to go.

SIXTEEN

FRAZIER HAS A gorgeous campus. Especially at dusk.

I stroll through the Quad under a red-orange sky, making a point to take in the architecture of every building, the various monuments, intricate iron gates leading to the Quad, and the walkway made of bricks etched with the names of famous alum. I've been making my way around campus for hours, trying to come up with an excuse to avoid the punishment to come.

Everything is falling apart quicker than I ever imagined it would.

On the Quad, clusters of friends giggle on benches, debating music, sports, and celebrities. Things the girls and I used to talk about. Those few euphoric weeks when it was just us. All I ever wanted. A belonging, a clique.

And before the girls, all I had was Kevin . . . then I was alone.

Loneliness has a way of holding a mirror up, showing the emptiness of your life that you're too ashamed to admit that you're ashamed of, despite it not being your fault.

Back in high school, I remember watching students making prom plans, going to basketball games, and voting for homecoming king and queen thinking . . . how could the world keep spinning now that Kevin is gone? Did anyone even feel the earth come to a halt when he left us? Hear life come crashing down all around us? I did. I felt every ounce of the change happening that I could never return to normal. There weren't many people that wanted to stay in my orbit or wanted me in theirs after that.

Well . . . there was one.

I take out my phone and he answers on the fourth ring.

"Yeah," he spits.

"Hey Jack," I mumble, and it feels good to hear his voice, despite his abrasiveness. "You busy?"

"What's up? I'm in the middle of something."

I remind myself that he wouldn't have answered if he didn't care.

"I just wanted to say again . . . I'm sorry. For how things ended. It wasn't fair to you."

There's a long moment of silence before I hear him take a deep breath.

"Jordyn . . . what the hell happened? Everyone thought I should break up with you. But I didn't. I stood by you. And then you just . . . ditched me for some Black school no one's ever heard of."

I shake my head as if he can see me. "You mean you and your

family never heard of. Lots of people know Frazier. It's one of the most prestigious HBCUs in the country."

"HB-what? You're even talking crazy now, Jordyn. If you wanted to just be around some Black guys, you could've just said that. It's just . . . I put my neck out being with you and this is the thanks I get?"

"Wowww," I say with a chuckle. "You wanted a cookie for being with a Black girl? Well. Guess I'm glad I called."

"It wasn't even like that and you know it! Don't make this a race thing."

I cough out a laugh. "Then what was it like?"

"You stopped being you after . . . you know. And I get it, I guess. But that was two years ago. When are you going to move on and stop being so pissed!"

I clutch the phone, fingers burning hot enough to melt the case. "It wasn't some long illness he was diagnosed with. He wasn't sitting in hospice waiting to die and I had time to prepare. He was snatched from us and you expect me to just get over it!"

Jack huffs, his voice cold.

"Jordyn, this plan of yours . . . is freaking crazy. And you're acting like he was murdered when he was the murderer!"

Blood boiling, I stare at the phone and press End with a shaky hand, resisting the urge to slam it on the ground. I can't snap. I need to stay in control.

A street lantern pops on over my head. The dusk sky begins fading to night as a chilly breeze wraps around my neck. Whatever

I thought this semester was going to be like didn't matter anymore.

I take a deep breath and head for the Rock.

Kareem opens the door like a bouncer at a nightclub, nodding but not meeting my eye.

In the living room are my suite mates, sitting among more of Devonte's fans. Followers? I don't know what to call them. Loren and Kammy are on the sofa, hands folded, their eyes cast down, faces composed yet solemn. Next to them is our RA, Shante. I'm not the least surprised Devonte's seduced her. Vanessa stands next to her brother, hands on her hips.

And standing on the opposite side of Devonte . . . is Kerry. The sight of her smug smile makes my stomach drop to my feet.

"Heard you've had a busy day," Vanessa says, words dripping in sarcasm. "Trips to Student Housing. Hanging out with that white guy?"

Kareem leans against the suite door, arms crossed.

Hands trembling, I clear my throat and try to regain control. "I think this is a . . . I mean you got it all wrong."

"Where you been? What, you stopped by the police station too?" Vanessa snaps, stepping closer. "You seem like the type."

"N-n-n-nooo," I stutter. "I would never."

"How could you do this to me? To us?" she yells, pointing to Devonte. "He's my BROTHER! The only real family I got! And you go behind my back and rat us out?"

"I wasn't trying to get him, I mean you, in trouble," I say, feeling myself babbling. "It's just . . . it's been really intense, and I was thinking that maybe—"

"After everything he's done for you, for US, for Black people, you try to get him kicked out?"

Shante stands now, crossing the room to position herself in front of my bedroom door.

"THEN you go yapping to that white boy about us," Vanessa continues. "You know what he's gonna do, right? What they always do!"

"No, it wasn't like that! That's not what, I mean, that isn't what . . ."

Kerry stares at me, her eyes cold. No signs of the same concerned girl I spilled my guts out to just a few hours ago. Behind me, the girl who had spotted Nick and me talking leans against the stove, shaking her head.

The room goes quiet, everyone turning to Devonte. He clasps his hands together, then motions around the room.

"So, you're not happy with us? Your family?"

My brain scrolls through the principles of *How to Win Friends* and can't think of one that could salvage this situation. There's no use in trying to reason with Vanessa. But I could maybe still reach Loren and Kammy.

I turn to them with pleading hands. "I tried talking to you guys about how I was feeling. I wasn't trying to move out. I wasn't trying to LEAVE you. I was just—"

"I asked you a question," Devonte says, voice just above a whisper. But I know him. This is all a show. Acting as if he's wounded when he's really rage contained in skin. Everyone there is more concerned about his feelings than mine when they have no clue what's lurking.

Unsure of what to do, I utter the only thing I can think of. "I . . . I . . . I'm sorry."

He shakes his head. "I thought you were smarter than the others, sis. I thought you knew better. You know you belong with us. Don't you want to be a part of our family?"

One part of me screams YES! Yes, I've always wanted to belong to something. But the other side of me, the side that knows better, can't utter those words. Even to save myself in the moment.

Vanessa shakes her head. "I thought we were sisters."

"We are," I cry, aiming my words at Loren and Kammy, but they don't stir.

Devonte purses his lips as if he's contemplating what to do. The room hangs with bated breath.

"I think I understand what's happening here," he states matter-of-factly, turning to his audience. "See, families fight. They have disagreements, fights, then they heal, they become stronger. But before healing can occur, there must be consequences for disloyalty. And you have to accept those consequences to be cleansed and move on."

There is a charge in the air. Something unsaid but understood by everyone but me. I can feel the girl in the kitchen shift, inching closer. I look to my left and right, and it suddenly dawns on me that I'm surrounded.

Consequences?

A gasp escapes me as I back away, shaking my head. "No."

"Pain makes you remember to never make the same mistake twice," Devonte states, stuffing his hands in his pockets. "Pain is the only way you learn."

Panic surges through my veins. I wasn't prepared for violence. Talking, yelling, screaming . . . but violence? That's a category of life I have no knowledge of.

Neither did Kevin.

Devonte turns and nods at Kerry. Kerry steps toward me and with one swing, she lumps a fist into my belly.

I hunch over with an *oof* and slump down to my knees, wheezing air through the throbbing ache. I roll to my side, glancing at Loren and Kammy. They won't meet my eye, which makes me think back on what they said at lunch.

"He's taken it easy on you." Have they been through worse?

Devonte nods at Kerry. "Again."

"No," I whimper and try to scoot away but Shante and Kareem box me in, the girl behind me pinning my shoulders. I scream, swatting at their hands as I watch Kerry charge toward us. My body becomes like a brick, so weighted down with fear that I can't move. And just before Kerry can reach her arm back for another blow, the door bursts open. A large dark-skinned man barrels in, shoving Kareem aside like a bowling pin. He stands over me, short locs swaying in front of his hard eyes. Kerry reels back into Vanessa. Shante holds both hands up in surrender, shaking her head.

"I didn't touch her!"

I glance up at my savior and he's not a man at all, but a boy my age with a chubby baby face, except he's the size of a small car.

Within seconds, Nick and two of his line brothers rush in. He takes one look at me, eyes flaring, and races across the room.

"Shit, are you okay?" he whispers, helping me to my feet. I wobble, blood rushing to my head. He gives me a once-over, pushing the hair out of my face, cupping my cheek to check for damage. The only time I've ever seen him this frazzled was the morning he woke up in my room.

I can't form words so I nod in response.

It takes Nick a moment to process, as if he didn't believe me, pulling me closer to his chest. But with one blink, his hands roll into fists as he scans the room, locking eyes with Kareem.

"What are you doing here?" Vanessa barks. Loren and Kammy are up on their feet, watching the scene unfold, unsure of what to do but also curious.

"I'm here for her," Nick hisses, his arms shaking as he steadies me. Or maybe I'm the one shaking.

She scoffs. "I bet. Get the fuck out my room!"

"She lives here too," Nick spits back. "The rest of you don't!"

"Yo, you gave up your brothers, to lay hands on a female?"

the big guy says to Kareem. "Sucker-ass Negro."

Kareem doesn't speak, only glancing at Devonte, as if waiting for approval to attack. But Devonte holds up a hand.

"Brother, can we help you with something?" Devonte asks, always starting with poised kindness. He can't look out of sorts. It's not good for the image he's trying to portray.

"Ain't nothing you can help us with, old head," the frat brother says.

"Don't know what you're up to here," Nick warns. "But people are starting to talk so you probably should just leave while you got the chance."

Devonte doesn't even spare him a glance, strictly keeping his eyes on his frat.

"Brother, this is a private meeting, and you're not welcome."

"Man, this ain't your spot or even your campus! You may got these pussies whipped but that got nothing to do with us."

This time, Kareem doesn't wait for Devonte's command. He walks right into the frat brother's face.

"Who you talking to like that, bruh?" he shouts, finger pointing at the boy's temple.

The boys start shoving, voices growing loud. Nick backs me up, straight into the kitchen. We slam into the fridge and I shriek. Nick steps between them, breaking up the fight.

"Yo Kent! Calm down! It's not worth it!"

He storms back into the kitchen, scooping my book bag off the floor.

"Come on, let's go," he whispers, grabbing my hand, and pulls me toward the door.

"Hey! Where you going?" Devonte barks, losing his composure. The unhinged look in his eyes makes me freeze. Nick notices my hesitation, his gaze toggling between us. He pulls me closer.

"She's getting the fuck away from you," Nick snaps.

Devonte stares me down. "If you leave, you know you can't come back from this."

My tongue feels heavy in my mouth, too heavy to move.

"She doesn't want to!" Nick retorts, swinging the door open. We fly into the hallway, Nick's friends in tow. I sniff the air, free of oils and incense as one fact jumps above the rest.

I can't come back?

We file out of Kent's car in front of the Kappa house. Nick grabs my hand, and without one word, he leads me into the house and up the stairs. He quickly ushers me into a bedroom on the second floor and turns on the light.

My heart hasn't stopped racing. Adrenaline surges through every limb, throwing me off my equilibrium. Or maybe it's not adrenaline. Maybe it's pure terror. The kind that can kill someone.

"Sit," Nick orders, motions to a swivel chair, and I do what I'm told. He opens a mini fridge and offers me a bottle of water. "Here, drink this. You might be in shock or something. Sorry it's not sparkling."

I take a few sips, glancing around. His room is rather large and neat. The made bed sits flush against the window. Next to it, a small desk with a hutch, housing several civil rights autobiographies, and a dresser that mostly features his fraternity paraphernalia.

"Are you okay?" he asks, and I realize he's bending in front of me, searching my face.

"I think so," I mumble.

"I heard you scream," he whispers to the floor. "From down the hall. It was . . . Did he touch you?"

I did? I don't remember making a sound. I stare at his ghostly face, the skin on his knuckles stretched and pinched white.

"No. He didn't," I say, knowing he could have. The thought sends shivers down my arms. I try to take a sip of water, but my hands are trembling. Shock? Maybe that's why I feel so numb.

"I need some tea," I mumble, my throat burning. Maybe I was screaming.

Nick scoffs, standing up straight. "This isn't Starbucks."

His smart-ass-ness helps me out of the fog. "I'd settle for Dunkin'."

Slowly, my senses start to percolate, regaining some feeling in my body, noting my keys and wallet stabbing me through my jeans.

"You should stay here tonight," Nick says, as if trying the words out for the first time. "You can sleep in my bed, I'll take the floor. Tomorrow, you should report this to Housing."

I blink up at the suggestion. "No! I mean, I don't need to report it. I just need to wait until he . . . cools down."

"Cools down? You need to get him out of your suite! Or move out!"

Everything he's saying makes complete sense, but I still can't bring myself to do it.

"Move out? But . . . I don't want to leave my friends."

He scoffs. "Some friends. They let him treat you like that?"

They were in shock, I tell myself. Like me.

I take a look at myself in the floor mirror near his closet. I walked out of the suite with nothing. No clothes, no books, not even my . . .

I shoot up to my feet, flying toward his door. "Oh God! I need to go back! My laptop!"

Nick stands in front of me. "Whoa, whoa! We can't go back. Not right now. We almost didn't walk out of there."

I gnaw on my bottom lip. If they open that laptop . . . they'll know everything. I can't let that happen.

"Please, Nick! I really need it," I beg. "My whole life is on it!"

He shakes his head. "If we go back there tonight . . . something is going to happen. Fighting on campus can lead to a whole slew of problems that we can't have." Nick studies my face and huffs. "Look, I'll send someone with you tomorrow to grab some things but you're not going anywhere tonight. Your room door is locked, right?"

I nod.

"So don't worry about it. And if they break in and mess with your stuff, you can file a police report and sue. You have to start thinking like a lawyer, Bambi."

I nod again, shuffling to the bed in a daze. It all happened so fast. One minute we were a happy family and the next . . . I'm talking of moving.

Not yet. I'm not ready to give up yet.

I need time to think, regroup, and plan. But I can't do it in the suite. I look around Nick's room as an idea pops into my head. An outrageously stupid idea. So mortifyingly ridiculous I have trouble saying it out loud.

"Um, can I stay here . . . for a little while?"

Nick blinks in surprise. "You mean . . . oh. Uhhhh . . ."

"I can't go back there. Not right now. I need to talk to Housing first. See what they can do."

"They'll just kick him out."

"But they would have to prove that he's overstayed his welcome. Prove he is actually living there. That may take some time. And you know everything moves slow around here."

Nick seems torn. He stuffs his hands in his pockets. "Yeah but . . . don't you know . . . anyone else? This isn't exactly a Holiday Inn."

That's the worst part, I don't know anyone else. And I definitely don't have the funds for a hotel. It kills me to ask Nick this, but I really don't have any other options.

"Please," I beg. "I promise I won't be any trouble. I'll sleep on the floor."

Nick rakes his fingers through his hair, letting out a puff

of wind. It wasn't a hell no. He probably needs extra incentive.

"I promise to help you with your trustee campaign. Even be your campaign manager. Twenty-four-seven, whatever you need. And judging by who you're going against, you can use all the help you can get, white boy."

Nick stops fidgeting, letting my words sink in deeper. He knows a white student going against a Black student at an HBCU, the odds are stacked against him. He needs a solid team to help him rally the votes. And I'm willing to do it for free.

"Okay. You got a deal. But only for two weeks."

"Thank you," I breathe, the tension in my shoulders easing just a smidge.

He nods then walks over to his dresser. He tosses me a T-shirt and basketball shorts.

"Bathroom is down the hall on your right."

I roll the clothes into a ball under my chin. They smell like him.

"Why did you come? I mean . . . how did you know something was wrong?"

Nick stares at me a moment then shifts away. "The look in your eye. It was . . . familiar."

I swallow and turn on my heels. "I hate sparkling water, by the way."

Despite being in a strange bed, I fall into a deep sleep within minutes of hitting his pillow. Until I hear shouting.

"NO! NO!"

My eyes crack open, zeroing in on the shadowy shapes the streetlights outside have cast on the ceiling of Nick's room.

"NO!"

I roll over and see Nick on the floor, tossing, fighting the air, like he is clawing out of quicksand.

"Nick?" I jump out of bed and shake his shoulder. "Nick, wake up!"

Nick pops up, flinging his arms. I duck, for the second time in twenty-four hours, with a shriek and turn on the light.

Nick scans the room, looking for an assailant, his breath ragged, pupils dilated. Sweat trickles down his panicked stricken face.

"Whhh-what happened?" he rasps.

"You were dreaming. Or having a nightmare."

"I . . . shit," he mutters, rubbing his eyes.

"Are you okay?" I ask, standing a few feet away, trying to steady myself from the jarring wake-up call.

"I haven't had a nightmare in a while," he mumbles, more to himself than me. He turns off the light and slinks back down to the floor. I lie in bed, wrapping the blanket around me, and watch him sleep.

SEVENTEEN

I WAKE UP with a throbbing headache and Nick nowhere in sight. I must have passed out just before dawn. I take in his room and feel a rush of cold hit my skin, wishing it was all a dream. That I was back in my room, back with the girls, where I felt like I belonged.

On the desk is a black thermos and a handwritten note.

Here's your tea. Meet me at Malcolm after class.

Class. Our midterm. Shit.

I click open the lid and take a sip. Black tea with a little sugar. Tastes awful.

I slip on my clothes from yesterday, struggling to decide what to do first. Go to the dorm and grab my stuff or go to Housing and report Devonte? Either idea makes my stomach tense. I don't want the girls to get in trouble. But I also can't fail this midterm. Most of all, I need my computer.

Dorm it is.

I open the door and cup my mouth to keep from screaming.

"Who are you?"

A guy is sitting against the wall across from the door, fighting to stay awake. His head jerks up and he rushes to his feet.

"Kwame." He's rail thin with a deep voice. "Nick sent me."

"Sent you?"

"Yeah. Supposed to take you back to your dorm."

Nick sent me an escort. That's . . . nice of him.

"Are you a Kappa?" He's not wearing any colors.

"Prospect," he mumbles to the floor.

That means he's trying to be a Kappa. One way to earn a spot is by doing favors. I sigh, grab Nick's hoodie off the hook, flipping it over my hair.

"Well, let's go."

Kwame and I take the bus back to campus and walk up to Rockland Hall. I keep my head down, hoping to avoid eye contact. Hoping not to run into anyone. But the lobby is hectic as students head to morning classes. Loren and Kammy have class, so they should already be gone. The only person that could be left is Devonte.

In the elevator, I steel myself. If he's home, what do I say? What could he say? Would he apologize? Could I forgive him?

I grip my keys as we walk down the hall. Kwame puts his hand out.

"Let me."

I look at him, unable to hold back an impressed smile. He's

brave. Or has no idea what we're about to walk into. We turn the corner, heading to the familiar last door on the left, my stomach and shoulders tightening with every step.

Kwame unlocks the door and steps in first. I take a hesitant step after him and am met with silence.

The living room is empty.

The unusual sight leaves me momentarily stunned. I pick up my chin and head for my bedroom. The door is still locked, the room as I left it. I rush to my desk and find my laptop still stored safely in the desk drawer. I breathe out with relief, quickly grab my duffel bag out of the closet, throwing some clothes, shoes, toiletries, and a flat iron in. The suite may be empty but not for long.

Once I'm packed up, Kwame grabs the bag and heaves it on his shoulder.

"Let's go," he says, walking out, all business-like.

I take one final look at our suite, thinking of all our nights here, laughing, joking, learning. A warmth suddenly comes over me. The memories flooding back. I was a part of something beautiful. And now . . . I'm on the outside, cold and alone. I promised myself I would never feel this way again.

Was all this a mistake?

As we board the elevator, Kwame looks at me. "Nick said something about you needing to go to Student Housing."

A knot forms in my throat the size of quarters.

Not yet. Not yet. Not yet.

"Uh yeah, I'll go later. I gotta get to class. Midterm."

* * *

I go through the motions of school in a hazy daze, carrying my life in a duffel bag, exhausted and destitute, the events of last night still replaying in my head, mostly with different scenarios. What if Nick hadn't of come when he did? How far would the consequences have gone? How was I not prepared for that? How could I have been so stupid?

Stupid is the word that keeps playing on repeat.

Nick and I make plans to meet at the FUSA office. He has meetings until late. Not wanting to be in the frat house without him, I sit in the conference room, making a pathetic attempt to catch up on my assignments. I'm sure academic probation is waiting for me around the corner. If someone were paying attention to my transcript, from high school until now, they'd know something was going on.

As I sit shifting through my notes, I can feel eyes on me. Every time I look up, I'm met with curious stares before they flicker away followed by whispers. Maybe they're friends with Devonte. Maybe they know what happened. I sink lower in my seat, my thoughts going dark.

What am I going to do, Kevin?

"Hey," Nick says appearing at the conference room door in his frat jacket, and I sit up quick.

"Hey!"

He notices his sweatshirt with a raised eyebrow. "Did you go by Housing?"

"Didn't have a chance. Midterms." A believable lie.

He nods. "Okay."

He grabs my duffel bag, hoisting it over his shoulder, and we head out. We jump on the bus toward the Kappa house in silence as I try to make sense of the sadness and confusion, rising above my anger. Here I am again at school, an outsider with no friends.

How did it happen so fast? How did our friendship evaporate like snow? What kind of spell did Devonte cast while I wasn't around? Maybe that's it. Maybe I shouldn't have joined FUSA or taken fewer classes. I should have stayed close. Then, it wouldn't have been me against them. It would've been us against him.

A few Kappas are in the living room, playing music, watching football with beers, some dressed in nothing but their boxers. They give me a curious once-over as I follow Nick upstairs, snickers trailing behind us.

Nick drops my bag in the corner of his room.

"I'll be back," he announces.

I sit at his desk, taking out my laptop, itching to open up my photo album, just to ground myself with the familiarity. But I can't risk Nick seeing. Not that I think he would judge me, I just don't know him that well.

That's when I let out a delirious laugh. I've moved into a complete stranger's place, in a frat house, in a city miles away from anyone who really knows me. My plans have gone so far left they almost seem right. But I'm not homeless. I still have a little time to turn this around.

I take out my books and start studying. An hour later, Nick returns with a steaming bowl in his hands.

He shoves it in my face. "Eat."

I push the bowl away. "What is that?"

"Does it matter? Eat."

The sharp, ragged knife of hunger twists.

"I can't eat that," I croak, holding back a gag.

"You can't or you won't? I saw that kitchen. I can tell you haven't eaten in days."

"I'm fine," I say. "I'll just take some tea."

He screws up his face in disgust. "Tea? Look, just take a bite."

I glare at him. "We've been here before, you know. You can't force me to eat something I don't want to."

He stoops to my level. "I'd rather force you than watch you waste away. So what will it take for you to eat something that I've made specifically for you?"

Floored, I glance down at the bowl again.

He made this . . . for me?

A knock at the door makes me jump.

"HANG ON!" Nick shouts, placing the bowl on his desk and shoving me toward the bed. "Shhh . . . lay down. Stay quiet."

"Seriously?"

"Just do it," he hisses and covers me with blankets.

"One second," he calls at the door, ripping off his shirt. I snap my eyes closed but I can still see his tan ripped body behind my lids. Nick steps out, having a mumbling conversation behind closed doors while a shiver runs down my arms at the idea of how much Devonte's influence has penetrated.

Nick walks back in, turns off the light, and slides into bed next to me. His hand grazes mine and he flinches. I stiffen as we lie in silence, listening to the cars drive by.

"You're not allowed to have girls over here?" I whisper.

He scoffs. "We're not monks, of course we can have girls in our rooms."

"Then, what's the deal?"

"It's . . . complicated."

"I'm pretty smart."

Nick shifts but keeps his distance.

"Having a girl here, once or twice, is cool," he starts in a measured voice. "But after that, in order to stay here, overnight, you'd need to be my girlfriend. So . . . I told them you are."

The fact takes a moment to process. "Seriously? You didn't want to run that by me first?"

"You rather me tell them about the creepy cult in your dorm and get everyone kicked out?" he snaps. "And don't think for one second I bought that bullshit story that you didn't have time to go to Housing. You're just scared."

I swallow the acid on my tongue. Because he's right. I am scared. For the plan to work . . . I need more time.

I pull the blanket up to my chin. "So why are we in bed together?"

Nick shifts again, this time nervously. "Sometimes . . . we go in each other's rooms without knocking. And it would look weird if my girlfriend was sleeping on the floor or vice versa."

I sigh, holding back a delirious smile. "Thanks. For everything."

Nick flips on his back, staring at the ceiling.

"Okay. I have a confession to make."

I sigh. What else could go wrong. "What is it?"

"I can't sleep without the TV on."

I turn to look at him. "Seriously?"

He squirms a bit.

"That's why I had a nightmare last night."

"So why didn't you turn it on?"

"I didn't want to disturb you. After the night you had, it didn't seem right."

Hmmm . . . that was pretty considerate. "Okay. So . . . turn on the TV."

He jumps up, grabbing the remote, opening Netflix.

"What do you want to watch?" he asks.

"I have a choice?"

"If you're going to be here, we need to decide on a show together. The last thing I want to hear is you complaining about anything I'm watching."

"Well in that case, can I have some tea too?"

"Tea?" He raises an eyebrow.

"Yeah. I can't sleep without it."

He rolls his eyes. "Fine. I'll boil water, you find us a show."

After about fifteen minutes, Nick returns with some Earl Grey and honey while I cue up *Love Island*.

"A reality show? I'd rather mop the ocean."

I shrug. "The internet said it's good and the internet is never wrong."

He blows out some pent-up air. "Fine. Let's give it a try."

We're about thirty minutes in when I huff.

"Okay, this is horrible," I say, reaching for the remote. "Let's find something else."

He snatches it back. "No way. We're not quitters, Bambi. We must persevere."

And so we hate-watch three episodes, before falling asleep.

EIGHTEEN

IN THE COLD light of day, I can now see that the Kappa house is ancient. Old sticky mahogany floors, decrepit light fixtures and kitchen cabinets that hang off their rusted hinges, the furniture, most broken in some way, picked up off the corner or from a grandma's thrift store, and the entire place smells like spilled beer.

But it's not my dorm. And that strangely feels like both a good and a bad thing.

Nick's already left for class, and it's too awkward hanging at the frat house without him, so I dress quick and leave for the day.

With no morning classes, I head to the FUSA office, hoping I can hang there until lunch. But when I walk in, I see Mercy and Brianna at the front desk.

"Hey girl," Brianna says.

"Hey," I return weakly. I should abort my mission, but I don't want them to think I'm scared of them. They aren't the ones I should be scared of. I cross the room to the empty desk and lay out my notebook and iPad.

From the corner of my eye, I see Mercy nod over to me with a smirk and Brianna strolls my way.

"So you and Nick, huh," she says, teasingly. "Heard you two made it official. I knew all that flirting was going to lead somewhere."

"I wasn't flirting with—I mean, yeah I guess," I mumble, already hating the way this rumor has two left feet as it runs around campus.

"I can't believe you got White Boy Nick to settle down."

"Yeah girl, what kind of magic you put on him?" Mercy asks from her desk, her tone icy.

"I . . . guess the kind of magic he likes," I say with a strained smile, hoping my subtle bashfulness will keep them from asking more questions.

Brianna giggles. "I knew those rumors about him were bullshit. Well, guess we'll see you at the party!"

"Party?"

"Yeah, the Kappas' party on Saturday," Mercy says.

"Oh. Yeah. Right, I forgot!"

Mercy raises an eyebrow as if she wasn't buying my act just as Brianna gasps.

"Oh shit," she says, staring down at her phone, and begins reading. "'DC police to be indicted in the shooting of an unarmed man.'"

"About fucking time," Mercy grumbles.

I open my phone to the same alert. The autopsy report ruled his death a homicide. And though this is great news, the question becomes: Even if charged, will they actually be convicted? Will they actually spend any time in jail?

I watch Mercy and Brianna chat about it, Nick and my love affair quickly forgotten.

How many times have events like this happened and I had no one to talk to, no one to commiserate with, left holding my feelings in like a poorly made dam? Now all I want to do is be with the girls to talk about the news. I want the camaraderie, the sense of belonging in the midst of trials. I don't want to be an outsider. I did that far too much in high school.

Well, at least when Kevin wasn't around.

After forcing myself to eat some wheat crackers in the cafeteria for lunch, I sort through my Ethics notes, homeless in every way possible. No friends, no dorm-room family, and my real family is barely speaking to me. The only thing that I can claim is a fake boyfriend, and even that will eventually meet its expiration date. But I have to keep going. Even if I decide to leave at the end of the semester, my transcript will follow and haunt me. I need to keep up with my classes, bang out the perfect midterms and finals.

I look at the time, grab my notes, and head for the door. I have ten minutes to get to Constitution and Law. Grades are lowered with every absence, and I already have three.

As soon as I step outside and turn the corner, I see the girls, standing in front of the Malcolm Center. A burst of instant joy swells in my chest.

"Hey!" I shout, waving wildly. I can't help myself.

Loren spots me first, but the brief expression of relief on her face is washed away with a scowl. All three of them are almost dressed identical—long corduroy skirts, bell sleeve shirts, makeup-less faces. But Loren has the most drastic of changes—her braids cut off almost to the scalp. I try to keep my mouth closed and not gawk.

"Hey guys, what's up?" I ask, hoping to start small.

The girls look at each other, eyebrows raised, lips pursed. My body tenses, the scene all too familiar, bringing me right back to high school. The cold shoulders, the awkward silence.

"You heard about those cops," I say. "It's all over the news."

Kammy rolls her eyes. Her hair is wrapped in a purple scarf. Vanessa is glowing and gorgeous as usual.

Desperate, I try again. "Sooo . . . I heard about this party happening at the Kappa frat house this weekend. You should come!"

"I don't want to be seen anywhere with you, Bed Wench," Vanessa snaps, her voice so sharp it cuts.

"My sister is right," Loren breathes, her face stoic. "It's bad enough that white boy goes to this school, now he's taking good-quality Black women away from our brothers."

"You are a disgrace to your race," Kammy hisses, visibly shaking in anger.

I dig my nails into my palms to keep from crying, their acid-covered words burning with each syllable.

Principle number ten: The only way to get the best of an argument is to avoid it.

I breathe through the pain. "I'm sorry . . . I just needed some time to think. Vanessa, honestly, your brother kind of scared me."

She scoffs. "Of course. A Black man defends himself and all of a sudden, he's scary. You weren't shook when you were eating up all the food he cooked for us. So did you already run to Student Housing to snitch?"

"N-n-no! I would never. Like you said, he's your brother."

"He's so much more than that," Kammy corrects me. "He's like . . . a prophet. He's here to enlighten us. He's done everything for us. Everything! And this is how you treat him?"

I'm almost too stunned to speak.

"He was going to hurt me! What was I supposed to do?"

"He didn't touch you," Vanessa snaps. "He helped you find your calling, to be a writer. And that ache of loneliness you always felt, he purged you of that."

I reel back in shock. He told her. Of course he did.

The air begins to feel hot and suffocating, even with the fall breeze.

"Okay. I'm sorry. I was confused, I guess. But . . . we're just college kids."

Loren waves around at the Quad. "This college . . . none of this is real. All you're doing is pouring money back into the white man's pockets when you could be with us, helping to free our people. Really free."

"If that's the case, then why stay here on campus?" I shoot back. "Why keep going to classes?"

Loren opens her mouth then closes it. She doesn't have an answer to that. Even as she processes the question, you can tell her resolve is faltering. Maybe she's still in there, the real Loren. The one who can tread through the bullshit.

Vanessa quickly jumps in.

"We stay here so we can talk to as many of US as we can. At least we're trying to make a change. Where is your loyalty to your own people? Your self-respect?"

"You know what I think," Kammy says, crossing her arms. "I think Devonte is right about you. You and that white man are gonna try to get Devonte sent back to prison."

"What? That's . . . no, I wouldn't."

Vanessa rolls her eyes. "Come on, y'all. She chose her destiny, let her live it. With the pigs in toxic waste!"

Loren gives me one last long look and starts to walk away. One by one their backs turn. My heart starts racing. I want to cling to them, grasp hold and scream, *Don't go back to that room!* I also don't want to be alone again. *Please don't leave me*, I'm ready to scream but instead blurt out something far worse.

"I still want to go to Emancipation with you!"

Loren and Kammy hit an invisible wall before spinning around, wide-eyed. I gasp, surprising my own self.

Vanessa frowns, seeming unconvinced. Desperate, I keep talking.

"Your brother is so smart, and I was just . . . scared. But I want to be with you guys. We were friends before your brother, right? Sisters. Family! I don't want out of the family."

Vanessa crosses her arms. "Yeah? Prove it."

I swallow, thinking of the only thing that will get Devonte's attention.

"I have some more money."

Bargaining. It's the most pathetic of the five stages of grief. It's the stage that you will do anything, give anything, to have life back the way it was, if you're not busy trying to find meaning for your pain. Screaming up to the sky with one question: Why? What did I do wrong to deserve this?

Nick texts to meet him in the lobby of the Malcolm Center at six p.m., directly in the middle of student rush hour. I stand by the statue of Malcolm X, overanalyzing every detail of the convo I had with the girls. Do I want to go to Emancipation? No! But do I still want to be with my friends? Absolutely. If telling them this lie will keep the lines of communication open, maybe I'll have a chance at saving them.

That's if I can. The way they looked and spoke, they seem to have changed overnight. How could so much happen while I've been gone?

Or maybe they've been doing a lot more without me that I don't know about.

Why am I so easy to be left out and behind? Why am I never anyone's favorite friend that they can't live without? Why am I—

"Hi, baby."

I whirl around to the familiar voice. Baby??

Nick swoops in, giving me a quick closed-mouth kiss on the lips. The shock of his touch, his scent, overwhelms me so that I almost fall into him. He keeps both hands locked around my waist to balance me.

"Hey?" I croak out. "What are you—"

"Remember, we have DATE night tonight," he says, a little louder than necessary.

I stare back dumbstruck but manage to play along.

"Oh. Right. Date night. Sorry. I almost forgot."

"It's alright." He slips his hand into mine with a light squeeze as he leads me down to the Rec Center. Music plays out of loudspeakers in the back. It's Wet Up Wednesday. A day most of the fraternities and sororities take over Malcolm Center in droves. I've only been in here a handful of times but never on a Wednesday.

We walk through the Rec hand in hand, Nick stopping every few feet to say hi to someone, giving high fives and sharing quick jokes. I nod nervously, playing along, remaining mute behind him.

He leads me to a booth and places an order at the counter. The entire Rec Center seems to be staring at us, whispering and giggling.

"Sooo, this is what you'd call a date?" I ask as he returns with a tray.

Nick drowns his fries in ketchup like a real psychopath, licking some off his fingers.

"It's about visibility. Optics," he whispers. "We need to look like a legit couple to make it believable."

This is both hilarious and sad at the same time. But as I glance around the Rec, it's clear that the mere sight of Nick and me sitting together is giving people plenty to talk about. He slides the basket of fries over, hinting at us to share. I stare down at the plate, my stomach churning.

"All fries are dipped in oil made of pig sweat."

I breathe through my nose to keep myself from throwing up across the table. I know it can't be true, what he said about pigs. But he had the research in hand. What if he's right? What if corporations silence whistleblowers and we're just poisoning ourselves?

"You're quiet."

Lost in my own thoughts, I refocus on Nick, eyes locked on my face. Today his hair is long enough to pull back in a messy man bun; wearing a gray hoodie and jeans that sit on his hips.

"Yeah, so?"

He chuckles. "So, you should kind of look like you like my company."

"You want me to hold your hand or something?"

He grimaces. "Whoa, slow down, girl. Buy me dinner first. I'm not a piece of meat."

I can't help but laugh. "Alright, what do you suggest?"

"We could, you know, talk."

"Talk? And you'll be honest with me?"

"I'd never lie," he quips, popping a fry in his mouth.

Up for the challenge, I straighten.

"Okay. What made you want to go to Frazier?"

He smirks. "They have a good prelaw program and an excellent law school."

"Right, but seriously, why Frazier? You know what kind of school this is."

He raises his eyebrow. "Yeah. A good one."

I roll my eyes. "Fine. Be obtuse."

"I'm not; you're just dancing around the questions you want to ask instead of being direct. I think you mean to say, why am I attending a predominantly Black university rather than a PWI."

"Exactly."

"Because . . . it's a good school." He gives me a Hollywood-type smile. "Why are you here?"

"I don't need a reason," I scoff. "I actually belong here."

"Ha! You sure about that?"

I narrow my eyes. "What does that mean?"

He waves a fry around like a pointer. "I can smell Ivy League all over you. This wasn't your first choice. Probably wasn't even your fifth. What changed your mind to come here?"

I lick my lips, hunger almost making me blurt out the truth. Almost.

"For once in my life, I wanted to know how it would feel to not be the other."

Nick's expression softens. He takes me in, as if he understands. But how could he possibly?

"Anyways, enough about me," I say with a bright smile. "Why don't you have a girlfriend?"

He rolls his eyes, clearly sick of the question. "Because I don't need one."

"Have you ever had a girlfriend?"

"Does it matter?" he snaps. I lean back, satisfied. Clearly I've struck a nerve. I'll come back to that later.

"Okay. Where are you from?"

He stuffs a chicken tender in his mouth. "The south."

"When's your birthday?"

"I'm a Libra. And no, I don't know the time and location."

"Christian? Baptist? Jewish?"

He makes a cross over his chest. "I believe in God."

"What do your parents do?"

"Work."

I purse my lips, unamused. "Why are you always this vague? You act like I'm asking for your Social Security."

He leans forward. "You're not asking about me. You're asking about my makeup so you can judge me."

Judge him? I'm just asking simple questions. Then again, I can't really tell him about the real me either.

I raise my chin. "Do you usually bring girls to Rec?"

He blinks. "Uh, no. You're the first."

This is a surprise. Then again, I am his first official "girlfriend."

Another group of people pass by, fist-bumping Nick, giving me the curious once-over.

"You're pretty popular," I note, sipping my water.

He shrugs. "That's just 'cause I'm the unicorn on campus."

"A unicorn huh? Fancy."

"Well, even unicorns have issues. It's hard not fitting in."

"Cry me a river," I sing.

My phone buzzes. A text message in our group chat.

Vanessa: You better have that money tomorrow.

NINETEEN

ONLINE BANKING MAKES it easy to see just how broke you really are.

I consider calling my parents, asking for an advance on my allowance. Just something to hold me over the next few months of the semester. But then, they would probably smell that something is wrong and rip me out of the school. I don't want to go back home to judgmental stares and I-told-you-so speeches. I'll eat air before I grovel to them.

That is . . . if they don't see my monthly statement first.

According to my accounts, I am three hundred dollars short of maxing out my credit card. The card my parents gave me for emergencies. Any day now they'll call to ask if I'm going crazy and I need to come up with a reason before they drive here to find out for themselves.

At least that's what I think they'll do.

Kammy: Devonte wants to know where's the money you promised.

Me: I'm working on it.

Vanessa: The movement doesn't have time to wait on you.

Me: Please. Can we talk.

Silence. No response.

I reread my messages. If I give what I have left to Devonte, I won't have much left to live on. But at least maybe the girls will talk to me, be my friends again.

But what if Devonte doesn't? What if he changes his mind, moves the goalpost? What if I'm too late?

I tap my calendar on my iPad. "Okay. So we have two town halls planned in the spring, all confirmed. I've already sent invitations to community leaders. We need to schedule a door-to-door canvassing in the junior and senior dorms."

Nick chomps on an apple in his swivel chair. "Why not the freshman dorms first? They seem easy."

"Juniors and seniors will care more about what's going on with the school than freshmen. Some freshmen don't even know what a trustee does. Which leads me to my next idea: we need a social media campaign. Videos, badges, the works. I know someone on the AV team in Malcolm Center that can do the shoot for free and I'll write up the script."

"Well, I would want to pay them for their work," he says.

"That's . . . nice of you." Nick doesn't act like he has fat pockets, but he also doesn't seem like a broke college kid either, which once again has me wondering about his home life.

"Um. In the meantime, I've drafted some slogans and a letter of intention. Hopefully your frat brothers can help with the petitions. I can put together a volunteer sheet."

Nick leans over, his arm rubbing against mine, when I notice a familiar scent.

"Is that baby powder?"

He considers me for a moment with a smirk then nods in approval. "This is good."

Nick and I mostly hang in his room, going over possible campaign strategies, or just sitting in silence studying. His frat brothers, who still snicker or stare every time I walk by, are downstairs watching the football game, TV volume on a thousand.

"You don't want to watch the game with the bros?" I say, brushing my hair down.

Nick looks at me from his desk and frowns. "What are you doing?"

Nick is good at deflecting by asking his own question rather than answering any of mine.

"Wrapping my hair."

"You can't just stuff it in a bonnet?"

I chuckle. "No. I need to wrap it to keep it straight. My mom taught me this trick. And what do you know about bonnets?"

"I've seen a few," he says, giving me a wink, and I gag with a laugh.

"Anyways, I gotta be cute. Heard we're having a party on Saturday."

Nick raises an eyebrow. "We are?"

I laugh. "Glad you're in the know."

Nick shrugs. "The guys come up with any excuse to throw a party. But it'll be good for people to see us together. Appearances."

"Yeah, right," I say. One thing about Nick, he's all about optics. I tie a scarf around my wrap and once done, my underarms are damp.

"Ugh," I groan, fanning myself. "Why is it always so damn hot in here all the time? I'm going to sweat out my hair."

"Why don't you get braids if you're always so worried about your hair getting wet?"

I bite my lip. Mom never allowed me to get braids. Thought it looked too . . . Black.

"Or you can just lower the temp."

"Eh. No can do. The boiler is old. We can only set it to hell or the Ice Age."

"Seriously?"

He shrugs. "I don't mind it. Look."

He presses his fingers to my neck and I swat them away. "Ah! You're freezing, you vampire!"

Nick laughs. "Why don't you just take off your hoodie. Or should I say MY hoodie."

I yank off his hoodie and I'm down to my leggings and a white camisole. Nick's eyes flare for a brief second. He clears his throat, fidgeting with some books on his desk.

Cheers downstairs almost shake the ceiling.

"How do you sleep in this house?" I ask, watching the plaster crumble.

He repacks his book bag. "I don't know. How did you sleep in that dorm?"

I think on it, remembering how most nights I slept fine. Except for the strange noises at my door.

Nick turns to me with a wince. "Oh. Too soon?"

"A bit."

"Okay. Game's almost done so we might as well get ready for bed. I'm not going to lie, I've been thinking about *Love Island* all day. People really sign up for this fully knowing the world is going to watch them make fools of themselves."

I sit crisscross. "I bet you'd be a fan favorite if you signed up."

Nick grabs the remote, flipping to the series.

"You've seen those bros. They are not the sharpest tools in the shed."

I cackle, falling back on the bed. "OMG, you're such a little old Black lady!"

"Yeah right, Ms. 'I need my night night tea.' Such a grandma!"

"That's funny," I say, fighting a yawn. "My brother used to call me Grandma too."

"Thought you were an only child?"

I feel a brick smack me in the face and stop breathing.

Shit.

"I . . . I . . . huh?"

Nick's lazy smile starts to fade. "You just said you had a brother."

There's no lie I can tell to wiggle out of this. Only thing left to do is to downplay it.

"Oh. Uh, yeah. He, uh, died . . . a while ago."

"Damn," he mumbles, shaking his head at the floor. He glances at the TV and clicks on an episode.

How the hell did I let that slip? I'm too comfortable around him. I need to refocus.

Nick says nothing else. Which makes me wonder why. Usually, when you say someone close to you died, people always want to know the gory details, watch you squirm as you explain, your grief on display like a torture porn.

We watch two episodes in silence until he finally speaks.

"Are you okay?"

It isn't until he speaks that I notice the tightness in my chest.

"Talking about my brother . . . is hard," I admit.

He rakes his fingers through his hair, staring off in the distance. "Yeah. I get it."

I cock my head, seeing him. Really seeing him. And then it hits me. He's been through the five stages of grief. We can all sense it about each other in some way.

"You've lost someone, haven't you?"

Nick doesn't flinch. He's cool as a cucumber as he stands, grabbing a fresh T-shirt out of his closet. He rips off his shirt as if I'm not sitting there watching him undress. I look away, unable to erase the image of his abs and the cute little freckles on his arms.

"Let's go to bed," he mumbles. "I'm tired."

I shake my head. "Why don't you want people to know anything about you?"

"'Cause it's not important. Who I am, right now, is more important than my past."

"Not to Black people. Our history is our everything. It explains how we are the way we are today. That's why so many people are trying to erase it. Don't be like those people, Nick."

Nick mulls this over.

"You're not a bad guy, Nick," I say, softly. "And not just because you're an alien on campus."

"Alien, huh? I kind of like that."

I snap my fingers. "You know what!? For your campaign, you should lean into your differentness, instead of shying away from it."

He smirks. "That's not a bad idea. You're kinda smart, Bambi. One sec. Don't start another ep without me!"

Nick leaves the room, and I laugh, realizing this has been the most TV I've watched since coming to Frazier. Back home, shows were my lifeline. While most of my classmates were living their lives, I spent endless hours on series, both old and new. Even rewatching the ones I had finished . . . when Kevin was still alive. So it's nice to be back in my safe space . . . with Nick this time. Even if it's just temporary.

My phone buzzes and I scramble to grab it. A text message but from an unknown number.

You can't hide with that white boy forever.

My lungs sting, the sweat under my arms pooling. They know exactly where I am.

I reach across the bed and peek out the blinds. The street is empty except for the parked cars, the road clear. But I sense someone is watching, waiting. . . .

"Everything okay?"

I spin around to Nick, standing in his flannel pants with a gray T-shirt, holding a cup of tea.

Clearing the fear out of my throat, I paste on a fake smile, slide over on the mattress, and pat the empty space between us. Nick rolls his eyes and laughs.

I shouldn't be here without Nick or his escort, but I'm fresh out of clean clothes and the Kappa house laundry room smells too funky for me to even consider stepping into.

Knowing the girls' schedules by heart, I have a small window when the suite should be empty. The question is whether Devonte is there alone or not. Or maybe the boys. Or some of his other followers.

But I have to take the risk.

I scurry through the lobby, keeping my head down, straight to the mailroom. I open my box and a stack of letters fall out. The official kind, from credit card companies. I gather them up in my bag and book it to the elevators.

I put an ear to the suite door. No music, no voices.

No Devonte.

I step in and stop short at the sight of my room door ajar, the lock broken. Pulse throbbing, I slowly enter.

The room has been ransacked, a tornado spiraling through twice. Nothing appears to be missing. Just clothes torn, books and sheets tossed. I set the mattress right and slump on my bed.

They were looking for something. . . . What did they find?

Without thinking, I dig into my bag and open the first letter, congratulating me on opening a new credit card. A credit card that I never applied for. There are two more letters like it. The next letter is a statement, confirming cash withdrawals.

Credit card companies charge a higher rate for a cash advance than regular charges. The longer the debt stays on my account, the higher it will become. Within a few months, my credit will be ruined. I won't be able to get an apartment, a car, a home. . . .

The suite door slams shut. I gasp, spinning around.

"What are you doing here?" Kammy yells.

I try to think of the best way to defend myself but my thoughts are cut off at the sight of her arm.

"OMG, Kammy, are you okay? Are those bruises?"

Kammy notices her sweater has dropped off her shoulder and

quickly gathers it up before storming off to her room.

"Kammy, please talk to me," I beg, following. Her room smells just like Devonte. Kammy's face is slimmer, the sparkle is missing out of her bright eyes.

"You don't look so good."

She whips around. "You need to stay out of my business! You're not one of us anymore."

"Kammy . . . I'm still your friend, I still care about you. And I think you know, deep down, that this isn't right."

Kammy stands in the middle of her room, scratching at her head wrap.

"You know, Devonte been talking about you. Feels like that's all he talks about. You really hurt him."

"I hurt him?" I scoff.

"Yeah! Devonte needs us. He's the path to true Black enlightenment. He has a plan for the advancement of our people. And you just . . . abandon him?"

"Kammy. He's been lying to us about everything. About the chemtrails, pork, toxins in food. I have proof that—"

"You're gonna believe some white man before you believe your own people? Do you even hear yourself?"

"No, do YOU hear yourself? You really think this one guy, this ex-con, has all the answers? Think, Kammy! Why does he need a bunch of college students to carry out his plan? And why does he need our money to do it?"

Kammy breathes in deep, rubbing her forehead.

"Once we open Emancipation, people are going to learn the truth. They are going to BEG to get in. When this country falls apart, and civil war breaks out, we'll be ready."

I sigh. It's no use. She's already gone. My phone buzzes with a text.

Nick: Hey. Where are you?

"You know, I'm no longer a virgin."

I glance up at her defiant chin pointing to the ceiling.

"Kammy. No . . . why?"

She crosses her legs, fidgeting with her fingers.

"It's a part of my healing," she says. "He says he has the perfect man for me to be with, once we're at Emancipation."

I shake my head. "You didn't have to have sex with him to heal anything."

"Yes, I did," she says, her voice cracking. "You don't know what it's like having PTSD."

"Do you?" I challenged. "Do you even know what was broken that he had to fix?"

For a moment, the real Kammy emerges, her eyes widening, the hysterical bravado erased.

She blinks. "What?"

"Do you really think what Devonte told you happened with your family really happened the way he said it did? How does he know? He wasn't there. But you were."

Kammy steps back, tears filling her eyes. "How could you be so cruel? My family abused me!"

"Kammy," I start, then think of another way. "If I could bring you proof that Devonte is lying to us, would you consider hearing me about other things too?"

Kammy mulls this over then rolls her eyes. "Fine. Whatever. Bring me your proof. Then we'll talk."

"Okay," I say, grabbing a few things and heading for the door.

"Have you . . . seen Legacy?" Kammy asks.

"No. Why?"

She swallows. "No reason. You should go."

TWENTY

IT'S COMICAL WATCHING the Kappas prep for one of their parties. They slowly take turns loading liquor, cups, and bags of ice into the house, pushing their rickety furniture against walls, and setting up the DJ equipment. Nick is good for keeping things relatively organized. I offer to help and they put me on cleaning duty. Which I guess is warranted. Around eight p.m. people start trickling in, mostly other Kappas who don't live in the house. By ten, the living room is packed.

I stand in the corner, empty cup in hand, tinkering with my phone, looking out of place, making it painfully obvious that I'm there with no one. Being alone with no friends should be a familiar feeling by now. But at a party, the longing can't be ignored. I had something special once, the shadow of it still lingering in my hand. But if I can convince Kammy, then Loren, of who Devonte really is . . . we can have all of that again.

"Hey Jordyn."

I almost jump out of my skin until I see Neveah standing beside me.

"Hey! I haven't seen you in a while."

"Girl, working homecoming was a full-time job!" She shakes her head, laughing. "But it was fun! I definitely want to do it again next year. And you stopped coming to our study group."

"Oh. Yeah. Things just been . . . crazy."

"Well, you better pop back in before finals," she says with a grin. "Okay, question! Have you thought about running for office next year?"

I cough up a laugh. "You mean, like an official position?"

"Yeah! I heard you're good with budgets. You should run for treasurer!"

"Really? I don't know if anyone would vote for me."

"Why not! Folks know you. Anyway, girl, think about it. I'mma go find my man!"

"Okay. Uh . . . thanks!"

Neveah waves, heading deeper into the house. Butterflies tickle my insides. She thinks I'm good enough to run for office? That people know me? I hope she isn't just making small talk . . . because I would love to be an officer.

That's if I'm still here next year. . . .

Across the room, I see Nick making his way through the crowd, his eyes locked on me. And for a moment, I forget that he's not my real boyfriend, that he's not really into me. But the way his eyes are peeling off my top, it's hard to keep track of the truth.

"Hey you," he says.

Nick threads his fingers through mine and pulls me close.

"Hey you," I mumble.

He sniffs my neck and I shiver, a smile creeping across his face. This feels too natural. Too organic. Too damn good.

"You look really pretty," he whispers.

I chuckle, glancing down at my plain jeans and simple black shirt.

"Uhhh . . . are you drunk?"

He shakes his head. "A little. I've cut back since that whole drugging fiasco."

I almost forgot about that. If that cup was meant for me, what would've happened if I drank it? What would have happened if I was unconscious in the suite?

"Hey," Nick says, studying my face, and sobers up. "You okay?"

"Yeah. Just . . . tired."

He nods, pulling me closer. "Want to call it a night?"

"But you're having a party."

He shrugs. "It's fine. Besides, it'll look like we're hooking up. That we can't get enough of each other. Plays well into the story."

Is that what's happening right now? We're just playing?

I blink and manage to say, "Uh, yeah. Right. Good idea."

Someone needs to drill it into my head that this is all a charade. But what happens when the charade is over? How exactly do we plan on going back to the way things were. And how am I going to—

"POLICE! NOBODY MOVE!"

Nick's eyes flare as he spins around, pushing me behind him. I let out a laugh. I always wondered why the police haven't shown up to break up parties the Kappas threw.

But as I look at the door, I realize this wasn't just two officers checking out a noise complaint. It's an army of plainclothes, wearing bulletproof vests, guns drawn, storming in the house. Chaos erupts. Nick never lets go of my hand.

"Yo, what's going on?" one of Nick's frat brothers shouts. "Neighbors call or something?"

"We have a warrant," the cocky officer sings, waving a piece of paper around in the air.

"For what?" Nick snaps, snatching the paper, and I read over his shoulder.

"Distribution of controlled substances."

Drugs?

"What the fuck?" one of the frat brothers barks, while the others put their hands up, slowly dropping to the floor. An automatic response to cops that Nick doesn't have.

"Wait, hang on!" Nick shouts, trying to stop the unnecessary pat downs. "Where are you getting this intel from? You can't search without probable cause."

The cop smirks at Nick, slapping the warrant against his chest. "We got an anonymous tip."

My stomach hits the floor.

Devonte.

TWENTY-ONE

THERE'S LOTS OF yelling coming from the first floor.

I pace in Nick's room, turned inside out after the police investigation, resisting the urge to run downstairs after all the times he's saved me. But I don't think my presence is going to ease tensions when I'm the one that's started all this.

Of course, the police found drugs in the frat house, but just weed. Nothing as damning as what they expected or what was anonymously reported. The police only arrested one person. But that's enough to cause a fraternity uproar. The frat brothers are downstairs shouting at one another. I listen for Nick's voice in the fray, a voice of reason, but he's silent.

Devonte did this. If not him directly, one of his people made the phony call. They know I'm here and are doing anything to smoke me out until I come crawling back. But to bring Nick into this, his frat . . . I don't want anyone else to be hurt because of me. Enough is enough.

I whip out my phone.

Me: Kammy, we need to talk. Tomorrow.

I stuff the proof I need to show Kammy in my book bag. Pages of documents disproving about 90 percent of what Devonte has told us. If this isn't enough to make her come to her senses, I'll pull out the big guns. Then I'll head to Student Housing.

Nick enters the room, face blanched, shoulders sagging. I jump to my feet.

"Are you okay?"

He takes a deep breath. "Put on your shoes. We're going out."

"I'll have a cheeseburger deluxe, medium rare with sweet potato fries. And a Coke."

Nick passes his sticky menu back to the waitress before she turns her attention to me. I lick my lips, sitting up straighter.

"I'll, um, have the sprout salad. Water with lemon, no ice."

The waitress seems unfazed by our polar-opposite orders, collecting my menu and heading back to the kitchen of a Georgetown pub to rush in our orders before it closes at two a.m.

"Medium rare?" I gag, cleaning my utensils with a paper napkin. "Why don't you just eat it raw out of the package, you animal."

The corner of his lips pull up to a smirk. "This place has the best burgers in the city. I could've grabbed some grass outside and thrown it on a plate if you wanted a salad."

Nick and I sit in a booth in the far back of the pub, away from the sticky-surfaced bar full of drunken white college students. Frazier can make you forget that Washington, DC, is not only home to politics but at least four other universities. It's like the whole world disappears the moment you step on campus, entering a Black utopia.

"So," I say, rubbing my arms. "Your brothers are blaming you for the raid?"

He twists a straw wrapper between his fingers. "You and me both, yep."

I wince. "Seriously?"

"Oh they know you're the problem. No one would dare set up the frat except crazy people. And your bunch are the only crazy people on campus."

"So what happens now?"

He shrugs. "You're my girlfriend, so they're not gonna kick you out. They're just . . . letting off some steam. I may get my ass whooped later though."

"Nick!"

He waves a hand. "It's fine. I can take getting yelled at. I've been getting yelled at all my life."

I raise an eyebrow. "You never told me . . . What did your parents think when you said you were going to Frazier U?"

He sighs. "They didn't give a shit."

My mouth forms an "oh" as I fidget with the silverware.

He rolls his eyes. "I'm what you call an 'oops' baby. My parents had me when they were just shy of fifty."

"Whoa."

"Yeah. They were ready to enter that sweet empty-nester stage in their life. Then I come along and ruin their plans. Needless to say, we are not close."

"Empty nester? So they had kids before you?"

He nods. "Two boys and a girl. Then me."

Interesting. I don't imagine Nick with siblings. Then again, he doesn't give me only-child vibes. More loner.

The waitress appears with two shots of brown-yellow liquor. "Drinks on the house!"

I start to argue but Nick takes the shot and holds it up to me. "What are we toasting to?"

I join him. "I guess . . . to not having drugs in the frat house?"

Nick barks out a laugh.

We knock back our shots on three, the liquor smooth, tasting like honey.

"So other than you," Nick says, "and your brother . . . did your parents have any more kids or plan to?"

"No. It was just us. A boy and a girl, that's all they wanted."

Nick folds his hands. "What . . . happened to your brother?"

I don't know why I tell him. Maybe the last week and the alcohol has made me weak to the point that I blurt out the truth.

"He killed himself."

Nick straightens. I have his full attention.

"He was two years older than me," I continue. "But we were best friends. Everyone loved him. Voted most likely to succeed in high school. Then he went to college and things . . . changed. College changed him. Which everyone said it would . . . but this was different. There were no warning signs that he was in trouble. It just didn't make sense. It still doesn't."

I wait, expecting the typical "I'm so sorry" or "That must have been so hard, prayers to your family," the regular clichéd crap. Nick just listens. That leaves some space to be myself.

"He left a letter in his sloppy handwriting," I say with a bitter laugh, wiping a betraying tear away. "Asking us to go on, to live without him. God, suicide is so fucking selfish."

Nick frowns. "Selfish?"

The waitress returns, refilling our waters. Once she's gone, Nick shifts in his seat, leaning forward. He stares at my hand on the table, as if considering reaching for it, then changes his mind.

"I don't think the people who commit suicide are intentionally being selfish or thoughtless. I think they're too blinded by the pain of living to be rational and think things through. They don't mean to hurt you. They don't even mean to hurt themselves."

You don't understand, he left me! He didn't think about what would happen to me! I want to scream back but don't because I know it sounds ridiculous.

"When my parents went to get his body . . . and all his stuff from his dorm . . . it just sat in the garage for weeks, collecting dust. When I finally opened a box, I found a Frazier mug. He had gotten accepted for a transfer. The last time I saw him, he talked about wishing he had gone to an HBCU. Wishing that for once, he could just be free and accepted in a school without all the bullshit that comes with being a token Black guy."

"So that's the real reason why you came to Frazier, isn't it?"

I shrug. "Something like that."

"Damn," he mumbles. "But also cool, that you're honoring him this way."

I wouldn't use the words *honoring him* but I'll take the compliment.

"He talked so much about how if we went to Frazier that we wouldn't be the outsiders anymore. That we would belong. But our parents were against it in every way possible. They weren't big on Black history. My mom even found African art to be tacky. So yeah, I guess I am honoring him. But I would've rather he be alive, so we could complain about our parents, school, and *Mad Men* again . . . together."

The waitress appears with another two shots. "Looks like it's your lucky night!"

I grab the shot, taking it back before Nick can even touch his. Nick sips his slow, eyes never leaving my face.

I click my tongue. "You lost someone, haven't you?"

Nick stares at me but doesn't say a word. Just like the last time I asked him. No response is response enough.

I lean forward. "You ever hear of the five stages of grief?"

He frowns. "Yeah. What is it, denial, anger, bargaining, depression, and acceptance?"

"Yeah. But there's one more I came up with. I call it the boomerang. Every time you go through the stages of grief, and you think you're finally okay, something triggers a memory, and you go through those stages all over again."

He lets out a laugh. "When does it end?"

"Honestly, you never stop grieving. You just learn to coexist with it. Some days grief is sitting in your kitchen in front of the fridge looking for something to eat, then some days it's sleeping in your bed, and other days it's standing in your backyard, waiting to be let in from the cold. It's like living with a feral street cat. There some days, missing the next."

He nods. "I hate cats. I'm a dog person."

I laugh. "I'm not surprised. We all deal with our pets in our own ways."

The waitress arrives with our food. I watch Nick grab his ketchup and drown his fries with a smile. It felt somewhat good talking about Kevin. Mom and Dad never wanted to talk about him because his death meant a flaw in their parenting. And they spent too much of their lives being perfect to be reminded of such a blemish on their record. They still haven't called once. Meanwhile, Nick has been walking through fire, all for me.

"Nick, I don't want to get you in trouble with your brothers. I can figure something out."

"You're not moving back into that place," he says without looking up. "Not until that guy is gone, and honestly, I don't trust you around the rest of those girls either."

I watch him take a bite out of his burger and smile.

"Thanks, Nick. I really don't know what I would have done without you."

He places a handful of fries on my plate.

"Tell me one thing. That night you took me home from the party . . . why'd you do it?"

"Honestly," I say with a wince. "Someone wanted you to give the girls a peep show."

He laughs and when I don't join him his smile drops.

"No. NOO! Are you . . . Damn! No way!"

The waitress appears with another two shots of brown liquor.

"Bartender said you make a cute couple," she says, placing them on the table. "Drinks on the house."

We glance over at the bartender, a pale woman with long black hair.

"We are a cute couple," I agree, holding up the shot.

Nick stares at me, a glint in his eyes. He chuckles to himself, twirling the shot glass around.

"What?"

He shakes his head. "Nothing. Cheers. To us. The cute couple."

The lights are still on in the frat house and we walk back close to four in the morning, freezing in our too-thin jackets. We sat in that booth talking for hours about randomness, and, if I'm honest, I could have sat there until daylight.

"So you really think I should run for treasurer? Seriously?"

"Absolutely! You got all the chops. You caught things our current treasurer couldn't. We need people like you in office."

I smile up at him. It's nice feeling needed, being seen.

Nick opens the door for me and we step straight into an ambush.

"So what's this I'm hearing about you're fucking some guy in your dorm?" Kent shouts, stalking up to me.

I reel back. "Huh?"

The room is full of Kappas, most that don't even live in the house. Nick looks around, clearly stunned by their presence.

"Bitch, is you cheating on our boy?" he shouts louder.

Nick steps in front of me. "Whoa whoa whoa. You need to fall back, right now! Where is this coming from?"

"Word is your girl likes having trains run on her by them hotep bros!"

"Where'd you get that from?" I snap.

"I ain't revealing my sources," he says, cockily. "But she's been seen sneaking back into her dorm. I'm just saying, if she's for the streets, she should be in the streets and not up in our spot. And I'm not trying to hear some shit about her cheating on you and we take all this heat!"

"I'm not cheating on him. I don't know what you're talking about," I say. I can't believe I have to defend such a stupid lie.

"Oh for real? Tell me you weren't in the Rock two days ago? Don't make me break out the pictures."

Pictures? Of what?

My mouth opens and closes. "I . . . I went there to get my mail. That's it!"

Nick looks at me but stays silent.

"So are y'all really a couple or nah?" someone asks.

"What kind of question is that?" Nick snaps. "She's my girlfriend! We're in a relationship. She's even coming home with me for Thanksgiving to meet my parents. This is the real deal."

The men whisper to one another.

"All I'm saying, dawg, is that if she's in some trouble, you could just tell us. But she can't hide out here and fuck our shit up."

"Hey man," Nick shouts. "If you want US to go, then just say that."

The brothers stand quiet. Kent ice grills them all.

"Bitch better be worth it," he snaps, knocking over a lamp.

Nick grabs my hand, leading me up to the room, shutting the door behind us. He rips off his coat, throwing it at the wall, and runs both hands through his hair, panting. I watch the torn look on his face, the encounter cracking him open and feel a twinge of guilt. Because if he knew the real me, I can't imagine him keeping up with this lie.

Heart racing, I walk over and tackle him with a hug.

"Nick, I . . . I don't want you lying for me," I whisper.

Nick's hug is stiff at first, but then he melts, his arms scooping under my armpits, chin resting on my head. His cool silky fingers glide up my forearm, twisting into my fallen spaghetti strap. He slides the strap up slow, returning it to my shoulder. His dark pink lips part as if he wants to say something, but he just stares without even a hint of a smile.

Heatstroke, I reason to myself. The shots mixed with this boiling room. Because the thoughts racing through my head feel almost like lust.

And I like it.

He pulls away slightly, running his fingers through my hair, pinky grazing my neck. Then he blinks, collecting himself, and clears his throat.

"I'm . . . gonna go make you some tea."

He rushes out of the room, leaving me aching for his warmth in the blazing hot room.

TWENTY-TWO

Me: Kammy where are you?

FOR THE LAST three days, I've tried calling Kammy several times. But there's been no word from her. I consider waiting outside the dorm, but I'm afraid someone will spot me and give Kammy a heads-up. Or worse, someone sees us talking and reports back to Devonte. I don't want her to suffer consequences like I almost did. This conversation needs to be an ambush.

I wait for Nick in front of Webber Hall to finish with classes. After the party, things went pretty much back to normal, and we fell into a comfortable routine.

I see him walking across the Quad from the Malcolm Center, his face in a tight knot. But as soon as he spots me, he lights up and my heart flutters. Despite everything I'm facing, Nick is the small dose of happiness I never imagined I would have again.

"Hey you," he says as he approaches.

"Hey you."

He gathers me up in a hug that feels so real. And after living with Devonte all those weeks, sometimes I don't know what's real and what's fake anymore.

"How was your day?" he asks, as we head for the bus stop.

"Not bad," I say.

"Ready to go home?" he asks. "'Cause, and I cannot believe I'm saying this out loud . . . I've been dying to watch the next episode of *Love Island.*"

We take the bus, chatting the whole way about our favorite contestants and looking up the audition requirements.

"You'll need to get a tan. But I mean, it's a $100K prize. Why not go for it?" I insist.

"So I can go on there and look like Boo Boo the Fool? I don't think so."

"Not Boo Boo the Fool!" I laugh so hard I snort, making Nick laugh just as hard.

"Okay, do you think Kordell and Serena are gonna win?" I ask, as we hop off the bus two blocks from the frat house.

"No! They are the worst!"

"But they're the cutest couple," I whine.

"I thought that title went to us," he says with a wink.

I can't stop the stupid silly grin from spreading across my face.

Is he flirting?

"You know, you're really good at this whole fake boyfriend thing," I say, trying to divert for my own sanity. "It's like you've had experience. You should reconsider your stance."

"Thanks, but no thanks."

I shrug, feigning confidence. "Suit yourself. But you know, I won't be around for much longer to hate-watch *Love Island* with. You'll have to find yourself another accomplice."

A shadow of disappointment crosses his face. "This is true."

I measure his tone, unable to get a reading, and slow to a stop. "What is it?"

Nick sighs and faces me. "It's just hitting me that once you're gone . . . I won't have to admit that this . . ." He swings our hands. ". . . is slowly becoming the best part of my day."

I grin. "Well, I guess you'll live."

He smiles, pulling me closer. "Or maybe not."

I stare up into his eyes, daring myself just to imagine what a real kiss would feel like from him. And just as I think of stealing one for myself, I hear my name.

"Jordyn?"

The sound of her voice stops me in my tracks. I spin around and gasp.

"Mom!"

Standing beside their parked black Mercedes is Mom and Dad. I immediately drop Nick's hand. How much did they see?

Dad looks from Nick to me and then turns back to Mom.

"Oh so THIS," Dad barks, waving at us. "This is where our money is going and not YALE?"

I'm almost too stunned to speak. "What—what are you doing here?"

"We came to visit our daughter," Dad snaps. "Except she's not where we thought she'd be. Where we're paying for her to be."

Nick clears his throat, stepping forward, offering his hand. "Um, hello Mr. and Mrs. Monroe. My name is—"

"Son, not now," my dad says, holding out his palm. "We're talking to our daughter. Stay out of this!"

Nick's eyebrows shoot up. He steps back, giving me an apologetic look. At least he tried.

"How did you know I was here?" I ask. How the hell did they find me?

"Your roommate Vanessa called," Mom says, holding the strap of her Chanel handbag.

My heart stops beating. I could collapse right then and there. "You . . . you talked to Vanessa?"

The shock renders me lifeless. How did she get their number? *Does she know? What does she know?*

"What did she say?"

Puzzled by my reaction, Nick frowns.

"Doesn't matter," Mom snaps, outraged. "We've seen all we need to!"

"We're paying for a dorm," Dad says, "while you're shacked up with some boy in a goddamn frat house!"

"No, it's not like that," I shout.

"Wait, sir, if I could help explain," Nick starts but my dad flashes him a sinister look. A look I know too well.

"Didn't I say we weren't talking to you?" Dad barks, his voice becoming louder.

Emboldened, Nick steps up. "But sir, you're not even listening.

There's a reason why your daughter—"

"Nick, forget it," I say, stopping him. "He doesn't care."

"Oh I care," Dad says with a haughty laugh. "If not I wouldn't be here."

Mom huffs, seemingly disgusted by the entire conversation. "Jordyn, get your things," she says. "We're taking you home."

"Home? It's the middle of the semester!"

"No, not to Connecticut! Back to your dorm."

TWENTY-THREE

"THERE YOU ARE!" Vanessa sings. "Welcome home! We've been so worried about you."

Vanessa and Loren are standing in the living room, fresh-faced and wide-eyed. They even have their old clothes on, playing jazz music. The suite is tidied up. Doesn't look like anyone but us have been living in it.

No Devonte in sight.

"Hi! You must be Vanessa," Mom says, her tone cheery. "Thank you so much for contacting us."

The sight of them hugging, sharing girly giggles, makes my hands roll into fists, itching to attack, hearing nothing but a pulse in my ear, steaming in anger.

How. Fucking. Dare. She!

"Don't worry. We'll take real good care of her," Vanessa insists.

Dad drops my bags in the middle of the suite, breaking me from my trance.

"Which room is yours?" he says, his tone curt.

I point to the door and he busts in.

"Why is the lock broken?" he asks.

"Oh, my bad! We did that," Vanessa says. "We thought she may have been in there. Decided to do our own wellness check."

Mom and Dad share a nervous look, the first time they almost seem human, before slowly stepping into my room.

The room is back in order. The bed is even made.

Mom looks around and I sense the judgment leaking out of her. Or maybe it's disappointment, knowing that this was supposed to be our interior design moment together.

We catch eyes and she sighs before turning away.

"It's small in here," Dad notes. "And it smells."

Out in the courtyard, Dad finally loses his composure. "Do you know what you look like? What people are saying about you? Living with some horny frat boys, being passed around like a whore!"

"Troy, lower your voice," Mom growls, glancing around. She's not disagreeing with him. She's more worried about appearances.

Dad points in my face. "You may have swindled your way into this ridiculous plan of yours . . . rejecting YALE for this ghetto mess. But I'll be damned if you sully our name, our reputation, being some slut about campus."

I bite my lips to keep myself from crying but the tears are too strong. An ocean of shame and frustration falls out my eyes.

"Now, you are going to stay in this dorm. I don't want to

hear one word about you sleeping anywhere else but the bed we're paying for. Do I make myself clear? If not, no more Frazier. Got it?"

I nod, keeping my eyes to the ground.

Dad looks at Mom then storms back to the car without even saying goodbye.

Mom lingers, taking me in, eyes stuck on my hair, now a frizzy mess.

"You look too thin," she says, softly. "We are paying for a meal plan, you know."

I sigh. "I know."

"And . . . there are counselors here. Mental health professionals. The agreement with Dr. Burke was that if you feel—"

"I know, Mom! Please." I beg for her silence. I don't want to hear any more about doctors.

She eyes me down. "Whatever this is, Jordyn . . . I hope it's worth it. Because I don't understand this one bit."

It is, I want to tell her but stay silent.

She huffs, digging in her bag, taking out a wad of money and slipping it into my hand. "Just . . . at least buy yourself some curtains, for God's sake."

Back in the suite, Vanessa and Loren are sitting on the sofa, drinking tea and chatting as if they didn't shatter my world. I walk in, my movements stiff, and face them. Deep, guttural rage wraps around my bones like a candy cane.

"Why?" It's all I can muster.

Vanessa sighs as if to say, "Silly child." Just like her brother would.

"Because we're your sisters," she says, a smile spreading across her face.

"We did it to save you from yourself," Loren adds. "That white boy has been brainwashing you."

I chuckle, pointing at my chest. "I'm not the one being brainwashed!"

"Devonte said you would say that," Vanessa says. "We all told him to give up on you. That you don't want to be saved. But he said he could never give up on a Black woman. So he's saving you once again."

"I don't owe him shit," I snap. "Where is he anyway? And where's Kammy?"

"Where they need to be," Loren says.

"Fuck you," I say, seething as I head for the suite door.

Vanessa frowns. "I know you're mad but . . . this was the only way! Just . . . don't make me have to call your mother again. Please. This is for your own good."

I blink before giving her a nasty glare, changing directions, and storm into my room.

TWENTY-FOUR

I HOVER OVER the toilet with a finger down my throat but nothing comes up. Didn't I eat today? What if I can't make it come back up? What if it's already a part of me?

What would Dr. Bunch say about these thoughts?

The question around my nutritionist makes me pause. I swallow down the panic, staring into the mirror.

"Pull it together," I berate myself with a slap, wiping the drool off my chin and slipping on Nick's sweatshirt. It still smells like him.

Tea, then bed.

I yank the bathroom door open to a room full of people, Devonte at the center of it all.

"Time is a construct. It has no meaning in this world until humans gave it a meaning."

The crowd grunts in response, girls snapping their fingers.

We catch eyes, his face poised. I haven't seen him since the last time I was here. The night of my intended consequence.

His voice is so smooth and hypnotizing. My body floods with emotions, starved for his attention, his reverence, yet equally terrified and disoriented and filled with rage by his presence. Killing him would be too easy.

I walk toward the kitchen, but Kerry is in the threshold, blocking my path, pretending she doesn't see me.

I sigh. "Excuse me, I need to get to the sink."

"Kitchen's closed," she says, checking her nails.

"What?"

"You want to use the kitchen? You have to ask for permission."

"This is my suite!" I snap.

Kerry raises an eyebrow. "Is it?"

Blood boiling, I turn to the living room.

"Why bring me back if you don't want me here!" I shout.

Devonte acts as if he doesn't hear me as he continues speaking to the women gathered around him.

"Menstruation is an abnormal condition for Black women. You weren't meant to hemorrhage the same time every month. Menstruation is a product of enslavement. Enslavement altered our DNA so that we would align with white man's religion, which practices witchcraft and blood sacrificing. That's the white man trying to control you."

The women in the group nod, beguiled by his intellectual prowess.

"Then," he continues. "They take even further steps by providing you products full of toxins to stick inside yourself.

Planting seeds of diseases, infections. Think of all the females you know with cervical cancers, fibroids, fertility issues, transferring diseases to their unborn children.

"But it's been proven that Black females on a holistic diet of natural foods do not menstruate. Your cells regenerate and become of pure African blood. It all goes back to low-vibrational food, Queens. You have to remember that—"

"That is literally not true," I say, plainly. The room turns to me. "Menstruation is a part of a woman's human anatomy."

Devonte grins, holding up a printed article. "There are research studies done on African females who do not have periods."

"Those studies were done on malnourished African women in war-torn countries," I shoot back. "Malnourishment, just like other stressors, can have a direct effect on your menstrual cycle length and time. That's been proven with studies done on women all over the world. Not just Africans."

A silence falls. Devonte's smile wavers, the muscle in his jaw ticks. It feels good, beating him at his own warped game.

He stretches slowly toward his cup of tea on the table.

"I heard," he begins, "that you allowed the Kappas to run sexual acts on you almost every night. That's how you were able to stay in their home."

"That's a fucking lie."

"It's the reason why I insisted on saving her," he says to the women gathered by his feet. "Did you know every time a man enters you, he leaves a piece of his energy? Our sister here is walking around with the DNA of the white man she let penetrate her. His DNA can infect her unborn seed, leading to more babies carrying their diseased bloodline."

"I haven't been with anyone!" I shout.

He sips his tea. "Anyone except that white boy."

"You leave him out of this," I hiss.

There's a hint of a smile on his lips, but his eyes are hard, neck tight.

"Hey! Watch how you talk to him!" a girl says.

"Just like you to jump to a white man's defense," another girl adds.

Nothing could be further from the truth. But how do I prove that when they're looking up to Devonte like he's a god?

Loren sighs, opening a book in her lap.

I groan, throwing up my hands, and storm off, passing Kammy's closed door. She still hasn't come out of her room. Usually, she'd be front and center at these types of meetings. Then it occurs to me, I haven't seen her in the last few days.

Where the hell is Kammy?

Behind my closed door, I can hear the girls talking. . . .

"I knew homegirl was a 'ho," a girl whispers.

"They say there's a video of her in an orgy. Nasty work."

"That's why she doesn't have an Instagram or nothing. 'Cause she used to be a slut at her high school too. Trying to reinvent herself here."

I wish I could cry, shed some sobbing tears into someone's

chest, let out my pent-up anger. How could my dad say those things . . . and Mom, just going along with it. As usual.

I look up at my computer and take a few deep breaths. It could be worse. My parents could've ripped me from school. They didn't even ask about the credit cards so I guess they haven't noticed yet.

They also could've talked about Kevin. . . .

Is the door locked? What if they come in here while I'm asleep? What would they do to me? I drag my chair across the room and prop it up against the handle just as my phone buzzes.

Nick.

"Hey you," I say, my voice a touch shaky.

"Hey you. You okay?"

I sigh. "Not going to lie, I've been better."

"I know none of this is funny but . . . I can't believe they went and tattletaled to your mom!"

It was a strategic move I should have seen coming. They must have gotten her number out of my phone. Thankfully, there wasn't much else they could see or do. All the pictures and notes I care about are in a decoy app, protected with a password.

"Why didn't you tell your parents the truth about them and Devonte?" Nick asks.

I choose my words carefully.

"'Cause I didn't want to prove them right about this school. They didn't want me to come here in the first place."

Nick hisses out some air. "Damn."

"I know. I just . . . need to make it work."

"Until you get another place in the spring," he corrects me. "Where are you, exactly?"

"In my room. About to go to bed."

"You got your tea? Hair wrapped up and whatnot?"

My sad empty mug sits untouched on the desk.

"Um, yeah."

"Okay. Come to the window."

The window?

I peer down into the dark courtyard. "Okay?"

"Look for the flashing light."

Across the street, closest to the baseball field, a parked red car flashes its lights twice.

I let out a sharp gasp. "Seriously? You have a car!"

"Don't tell the whole world. I only break it out for special occasions."

"Aww, you think I'm special!"

"Let's not get carried away," he quips.

I strain to see his face in the darkness. "What are you doing here?"

"Checking on you, I guess."

"You could've just called," I counter.

"I am calling! From a very short distance."

A warmth builds inside me, chasing away the terror. I step away from the window, worried he can see my blushing grin.

"You could just admit that you miss me."

Nick chuckles. "Don't have no problem admitting that now."

I twirl and plop on my bed. The sound of a loud crunch fills the room as something cracks beneath me.

What the hell?

I jump back to my feet, staring at the bed.

"Hey, you okay?" he asks.

I yank the comforter back and find my bed full of broken glass, the shards digging holes into my sheets. If I had just got in as is, I would've been pulling glass out of my feet and ankles, legs covered in bleeding cuts.

My throat goes dry. "Um, yeah. I'm okay."

"Okay, you go to sleep. I'll be out here for a little while longer. You know, in case you need anything."

I pick up a piece of the glass, holding it close to my face. "Night, Nick."

There's a turkey-themed dinner in the Malcolm Center today. The entire building smells like stuffing and candied yams. Some students have already started skipping classes, heading home early for the Thanksgiving holiday. I haven't bought a ticket home yet and my parents aren't exactly blowing up my line, eager to know my plans.

Truth is, I'd rather be here, stuck in my dorm, than stuck with them.

"A nasty 'ho," someone whispers behind me.

I turn around and recognize one of the girls from Devonte's meeting.

"'Ho," another whispers.

The words hit a nerve.

"She's been sleeping with everyone's boyfriend since she got here."

"Mmm-hmmm . . . legs always open."

It's been three days and the rumors about me being a slut have traveled at lightning speed. People avert their eyes or look straight on as I pass. How did I go from having a boyfriend to being a slut in a matter of weeks?

Is it that easy to destroy someone? To just make up a story and everyone believes it?

I toss my dinner and head to the FUSA office to clock in. Nick should be around. They were having a senate meeting tonight. I don't want to say that I miss him, but every time I make a cup of tea before bed, I find myself wishing he had made it instead.

As soon as I walk into the office, Nick is standing there, as if he was waiting, hands in his pockets.

"Hey you," I say.

"Hey," he mumbles. "Can we talk?"

The loaded silence in the office is unmistakable. Something's wrong.

"Umm sure?"

He motions to the door and I follow him into the hall.

"What's going on?" I ask. Why are we out here?

He sighs. "First, are you okay?"

"Uh, yeah, I guess." I roll my eyes. "Aside from the obvious. I'm sure you've heard the rumors."

"Yeahhhh. Just had a meeting with the other officers about it. That's why . . . we have to talk."

My stomach tightens. "Meeting? About what?"

I watch his face change, straining to say this next part.

"The executive board thinks that maybe it's not the best time for you to be . . . seen hanging around the office."

My mouth falls open. Is this a joke?

"I'm sorry, what?"

He squirms. "People are uncomfortable."

"I . . . And you just went with that?" I hiss. "Didn't bother to stand up for me?"

Nick blows out some nervous air. "It's not like I had much of a choice. I was outvoted."

"Seriously! They VOTED about me?" I let out a bitter laugh. "Well, thanks for being an ally!"

Nick runs his fingers through his hair, pity in his eyes. "Come on, Jordyn. That's not fair. I've been putting my neck out for you for weeks!"

"Only 'cause you're getting something in exchange."

"You know that's not the only reason," he hisses.

He's right. He has put his neck out for me and not just because of my campaign help. But the dog-piling mixed with frustration and guilt won't let me admit that.

"God! What was I thinking, trusting you," I snap. "I don't even know you!"

He crosses his arms. "You know more than most."

"Oh really?" I step closer. "Why don't you do girlfriends, Nick?"

Nick falters, his jaw going slack. "Jordyn . . . I . . ."

But I'm already walking away, back to Rock Hall, trying not to listen to the voice inside my head that's saying, you should have never trusted him.

'Cause that voice sounds just like Devonte.

The suite reeks of garbage. The fridge contains nothing but rotting fruit and vegetables. On the bottom of our oven lie the burnt carcasses of past meals that set off the smoke alarm whenever anyone turns on the broiler. Our bathroom is musty, with piss stains all over the seat. Without Kammy around . . . the place has gone to hell. The Kappa house was cleaner and that's saying a lot.

Out in the living room, there's laughter, music, joy. Devonte's voice a humming melody.

No one talks to me.

No one even looks at me.

I'm a ghost. A whore. A bed wench.

The day before Thanksgiving used to be one of my favorites. I'd help Mom with food shopping and prep while watching silly

Christmas comedies. Now, I'm stuck on the Amtrak home page, trying to bring myself to buy a ticket, but my fingers can't press a single key.

So I click through the photo album. It brings me ease, grounds me when I'm ready to fall apart.

In the five stages of grief, the depression stage is when the sadness is so consuming you lose the ability to function, overwhelmed by hopelessness. The simple act of breathing is so exhausting that you don't even want to function. You just want to sink. That's what I'm ready to do, sink into a hole and never come out.

My phone buzzes. Nick.

I don't want to talk to him but I haven't spoken a word out loud to anyone in twenty-four hours and I'm afraid if I don't use my voice, I'll lose it.

"Hey you," he says.

Tension in my shoulders fades. "Hey."

"I'm . . . just checking in. Are you okay?"

I try to think of the best combination of words that would eloquently describe how I'm feeling.

"I . . . don't know what I am right now."

"Have you eaten today?" he asks.

There he goes again. Caring. I suck my teeth. "What do you want, Nick?"

He sighs. "Jordyn. I'm sorry. You're right. I should've had your back. These rumors are stupid. It's just, with my position as president . . ."

I laugh bitterly. "Politics, I tell ya. Even on a college campus."

"Yeah, I guess so," he says with a chuckle. "Wait, are you still in your room?"

"Yeah."

"I thought you would be back in Connecticut by now."

I look at the photo album, my heart aching.

"I . . . don't want to go back and face my parents. I don't want to spend the next four days being chewed out. I'm not wanted here, I'm barely wanted there. I just don't feel like I fit in anywhere. God, the story of my life."

There's a brief silence on the line.

"Pack a bag. I'll be there in thirty minutes."

"Nick, I can't move back in with you. I—"

"Not moving back in. I'm taking you home."

Home? Does he mean home home?

I sit up straight. "Wait, seriously?"

TWENTY-FIVE

NICK WAS MOSTLY silent on the drive down to North Carolina. So I'm not sure what to expect. How does he plan to explain our relationship to his parents? Am I walking through the doors as his girlfriend or just a homeless friend needing a place to go? They must be okay with Black people to let their son go to Frazier so maybe it won't be a dinner filled with nonstop microaggressions. Like at Jack's house. I try to imagine what his mom looks like, what she'll cook for Thanksgiving dinner, and what silly dad jokes his father will say over his beer.

Nick pulls into a driveway just shy of two a.m. Even in the darkness, I can make out how enormous the place is. A modern rustic ranch-style home sitting on the bank of a river, the exterior made of cobbled limestone, wide windows throughout. There's even a fountain in the driveway.

"Um, where's the bathroom?" I whisper, as he opens the front door, not wanting to wake the whole house. Although

I'm somewhat disappointed that his parents didn't at least try to stay up to greet us.

"No need to whisper," he says, flicking on the foyer lights. "No one's here but us."

"No one? But . . ."

"Bathroom's this way," he says, his voice sharp as he walks down a hallway, flicking on lights as he goes. The air has a dampness to it, chill slithering into my bones. In the bathroom, I splash some cold water on my face, trying to organize my thoughts.

We're spending Thanksgiving here . . . alone?

I walk out into the living room, a creamsicle scene, with beige carpet, a giant U-shaped sofa, and a TV that looks more like a movie screen. The entire back wall is made of floor-to-ceiling windows that face the river. A tiny dock stretches out into the water.

Nick is at the thermostat, turning up the heat.

"Soooo . . . where is everybody?" I ask, rubbing my arms.

"My parents are spending Thanksgiving in Texas with my siblings."

He walks into the kitchen, inspecting the empty fridge.

"Why didn't you want to spend Thanksgiving with your family?"

He huffs. "It's the other way around. They didn't want to spend Thanksgiving with me."

"You and your little riddles," I groan. "Wish you'd tell me something real for once."

"Really?" He turns to me. "Okay. Why didn't you want to go home again?"

"You mean aside from my parents? Too many memories. Too many opportunities for them to try to convince me that going to Frazier is a bad idea. Not enough ways to avoid talking about it."

"Ditto," he says and makes his way up the carpeted stairs. I sigh and follow.

He opens a door down the hall and turns on a light.

"You're staying in here," he mumbles, not crossing the threshold.

I look around the massive room with a chapel ceiling and frown. "But this is your room. I can just take the guest room or the sofa."

"No, it's fine," he says, sullenly. "Guest rooms are being renovated. Besides, I don't sleep in there anymore anyways."

"Oh. Well, okay. Good night."

He opens his mouth to say something then closes it. "Good night."

The moment my eyes open, I sniff the dusty air, expecting the scent of sweet potato pies to float in the room. Mom loved waking up at five a.m. to start cooking. Her pies were always my favorite.

But since Kevin died, everything somewhat stopped with him. So I shouldn't have been surprised when I smelled nothing.

But the memories of honey ham and green bean casseroles haunt me. I text Mom and Dad.

Happy Thanksgiving!

I don't expect a reply. They didn't even check if I was coming home.

I slink out of bed, gazing around. Nick's room is like a time capsule. The robin's-egg-blue walls hold shelves with baseball trophies, awards, a high school diploma, and track medals. In his closet hang a few old sweaters and sports jerseys, all remnants of a life he left behind. I glance out the window that faces the driveway, sun sparkling off the water fountain, morning dew frosting the tips of grass in the front lawn.

Wonder why he didn't want to sleep in here?

I grab one of his sweaters and make my way downstairs.

Nick is in the kitchen, dressed in flannel pajamas and a Wu-Tang T-shirt, his hair all wet and jostled.

"Morning," Nick says in a raspy voice and places a mug in front of me. "It's mint."

"My favorite," I say, scooting into one of the barstools. "Thanks."

Nick nods, sipping a mug of coffee before staring out the windows at the water. Doesn't look like he's slept at all.

"Soooo, what are we going to do today?" I ask. "Do you want to cook? If we head out now, maybe we could find an open supermarket."

He shakes his head. "No, we're going to Anita's."

"Who's Anita?"

"You'll see."

Nick pulls up to a white one-level home surrounded by tall pine trees. A far smaller home, in comparison to his giant mansion. We climb out of the car, the weather a touch warmer than earlier. The screen door squeaks as it swings open and out pops a thin Black woman with graying hair, her smile shining bright.

"About time you showed up!"

Before he can respond, a gang of little kids run past her.

"Nicky!!!"

The kids wrestle him to the ground and he lets them attack him while tickling anyone he can get his hands on.

"Ohhhh! An ambush!" he laughs.

"Come on now, let him up! It's my turn," the woman says, pulling him up to his feet and wrapping him in a big hug. "Awww, welcome home, baby boy! You look good!"

"Hey Anita."

A tall guy about our age with dark skin wearing a durag runs outside.

"Aye, kid! You late! I was finna to head on over there to find ya and—" The guy notices me and frowns. "Uhhh . . . who dis?"

Nick steps beside me, smiling. "This is Jordyn."

The whole yard stands shell-shocked, wide eyes bouncing

from me to Nick and back.

I give a short awkward wave. "Uhhh, hi?"

Nick chuckles. "Jordyn, this is Anita, and my best friend, Richie."

Anita clears her throat, elbowing Richie, then smiles. "Welcome! Glad Nicky brought home one of his friends."

She steps forward and wraps me in a warm hug. A strong hug that could crack my back. I can't remember when I've been hugged like this. Maybe years.

"Chile, when's the last time you ate something?"

I let out a nervous laugh. "Well you know how school meals can be."

"Nicky was telling me last year, that's why I made sure he had the right pots and pans to get down if necessary. Well, come on. We just finished breakfast, but I saved you a little something."

Breakfast on Thanksgiving? I'm used to just drinking tea, maybe a little toast or a bagel.

Inside, her home is just as warm and cozy as she is, filled with a cacophony of voices. A few gentlemen sit on the leather sofa arguing about fishing routes, as the kids crowd around the TV, watching the Thanksgiving Day Parade. We cross the teal carpet, worn down with wear, and I notice a mahogany dining table with a lacy tablecloth and matching china cabinets, set with Sternos and chafing dishes, ready for a buffet-style dinner. The walls are covered with dozens of framed family photos. And that's when I spot Nick, a little white boy surrounded by a sea of Black kids—birthday parties, family reunions, fishing—growing as the years go by.

I look back for Nick, but he's still outside, whispering with a snickering Richie. I follow Anita to the back of the house, to an old spacious kitchen with yellow flowery wallpaper. There, a few women are focused on their Thanksgiving Day tasks: peeling potatoes, shredding cheese, and kneading dough. The entire place smells of a delicious turkey roasting in the oven.

Anita scoops scrambled eggs, bacon, potatoes onto a plate, topping it off with fresh biscuits from a cast-iron skillet. I struggle to hold the plate still in my trembling hands, hearing Devonte's voice . . .

"Rat, cat, and dog!"

Nick rushes into the kitchen, greeted by a chorus of "Hey Nicky!," and doesn't waste any time grabbing a plate and digging right in while standing and chatting with everyone.

"Eat, girl," Anita says, nudging the plate in my hand.

Not wanting to be rude, I take small nibbles. The eggs are soft and buttery, the biscuit fluffy. My mouth, not used to such rich food, aches as I chew slow.

Once Nick is done, he drops his plate in the sink, grabs an apron off the hook by the fridge, and joins the peeling crew, slipping right into the groove. I try to put away my dish but Anita catches me.

"You barely ate and you didn't touch your bacon."

"I . . . don't eat pork."

Nick looks up, watching me. I fidget under his gaze.

Someone behind me whispers to Nick, "She Muslim or something?"

I clear my throat, plastering on a giant smile. "Um, can I help? I'm pretty good at snapping green beans."

Anita frowns. "Green beans? What that for?"

"The . . . green bean casserole."

Beside us, the women snicker.

"Girl, that white people food! We don't eat that!"

"I tried to tell her," Nick says, and a woman swats his arm.

I laugh nervously. "It's pretty good! Don't knock it till you try it."

Richie bursts into the kitchen.

"Aye, come take a ride with me, kid. Heading to Trayvon's to grab the hooch."

Nick rips off his apron. "Be right back!"

I watch Nick and Richie play fight as they head out the door. He seems lighter here. Less serious.

Anita takes a pan of seasoned chicken legs out of the fridge. "Come on, girl. Let's get this going."

"Fried chicken?"

"You think that one turkey gonna feed all these people? You gotta have some chicken up in there too. No wonder you look like you're starving. Green beans, no chicken. Lawd."

Anita lays out some seasoned flour while whipping up an egg wash. She's tiny but I can tell there's a hidden strength deep in her bones.

"So, I take it this is Nick's second home."

She smiles. "Yep! We spent more time here than at his house."

"We?"

She chuckles. "Ahh, I see Nicky didn't tell you much of nothing, which is just like him. He shares things his way when he's ready." Anita takes out another skillet. "I was Nicky's nanny that just became so much more."

I smile, thinking back.

"What Black woman raised you?"

"His parents . . . well, they thought they were done having children so when Nicky came along, they didn't have much left in them to start all over again. His momma had no clue she was pregnant until she was close to seven months. Thought she was going through early menopause. So they hired me. At first it was only supposed to be a Monday through Friday thing but at some point they just left and wouldn't come back for weeks. Trips here and there. So I stopped going over to that big ole cold house and kept him here, with us. I even had to enroll him in school."

"The local school? Not private?"

"Mmm-hmmm. He wouldn't have it any other way."

She fires up the stove, grabbing a dented blue can out of the cupboards.

"Um . . . is that Crisco?"

She laughs. "Lawd, I know what you about to say and I don't give a damn. My grandma taught my mom who taught me everything she knows about cooking and this here is the truth! Can't make good chicken without it. I understand you young folks want to change things and that's why y'all's fried chicken is as soft as cotton balls!"

She passes me the can. "Here, drop a few spoonfuls in."

I grip the can, my skin flaring, stomach queasy.

"But . . . isn't this stuff kinda bad for you?" I whisper.

Anita nods, as if understanding something unsaid.

"Well," she says, softly. "I always like to say, food made with love can never be bad for you."

I smile, scooping another teaspoon into the pan, and it sizzles.

"So tell me, 'cause he won't . . . what's it like for him up there at Frazier?"

I chuckle. "You mean, what's it like for him being the only white boy at a Black college?"

She grins. "Ooo, I like you. You're sharp!"

I give a little bow. "He's very popular. And driven. And well respected. You did a good job with him."

She nods, her voice changing. "And . . . he's treating you good. You know, as his girlfriend?"

"Um, yeah. He's great!"

Anita nods, raising an eyebrow, and returns to her chicken.

After I fail at frying, Anita banishes me to the living room to watch TV with the kiddies. A movie just ends when Nick and Richie return. The sight of me makes them both bust out laughing.

"You got kicked out, huh," Richie says, cackling.

Nick smiles at me just as we hear Anita's voice.

"Come on now, Nicky, you gotta help me with this damn ziti. If you don't hurry up, we won't eat until Good Friday!"

"Be right back," he says, leaving Richie and me alone.

Richie narrows his eyes, dramatically combing through the beard that doesn't exist.

"Hmmm. You look like you got questions."

"You look like you got answers," I shoot back.

He swings his arms toward the front door. "Come on out and step into my office."

We walk to the end of the driveway, shooing away bees and late fall pollen floating in the air.

"Are you in school?" I ask.

He nods. "Oh yeah. Xavier. Full ride. Mom didn't play games about education."

Another HBCU. Of course. So much about Nick is making sense within just a few short hours of being here.

Richie stops and procures out of the dented mailbox what looks like a plastic bottle of water with the label rubbed off and two cups.

"THIS! This is old-fashioned moonshine. You don't look like the type that would know nothing about this. Try a little."

"Seriously? We haven't even had dinner yet."

He pours a little in a cup. "What them white folks say, 'It's five o'clock somewhere.'"

He hands me a cup and we cheer. I take a large sip and the warm liquid burns like acid down my throat. I cough up a gasp and hunch over, waving a hand at the fire in my mouth.

"What the fuck!"

Richie glances at the door laughing, patting my back. "Girl, what you doing sipping like that? I told you that was moonshine. Shit'll add hair to your chest."

I cough up a lung, the moonshine still stinging my tongue.

Richie looks back at the door, as if making sure no one is watching.

"So, what are y'all two up to?"

I stand up straight to meet his gaze. "What do you mean?"

He purses his lips, waving a cup at me. "You ain't his girl. I know my mans. So what kind of shenanigans y'all got going?"

I laugh. At least someone in this world knows Nick well. "He's . . . helping me through something."

Richie chuckles. "That's Nicky. Captain save a 'ho. Even to his demise. Ah damn, my bad. I didn't mean to call you a 'ho or nothing. I'm sure you're nice!"

I wave away the insult. "I'm used to it. How'd you know I wasn't his girlfriend?"

Richie's smile fades. "It's a long story."

"That ziti in there sounds like it's gonna take some time. So! What were his girlfriends like in high school?"

He shakes his head. "Girlfriends? Nah. He only had one."

"Okay. So what was she like?"

Richie pauses to look at the door again.

"Aight, I'm only telling you this 'cause you're here," he whispers. "He brought you here and put you in the middle of his shit. But, well hell I don't know. Maybe he did it on purpose. Maybe he's been trying to find a way to tell you 'cause he can't. He can't talk about it."

Damn. Do I really want to know?

Richie meets my eyes. "Her name was Ashley. And she was killed. Right in front of him."

"What?"

He looks at the door again. "Ashley had this crazy ex-boyfriend. Couldn't handle her moving on. Especially with Nick. They were good friends before they started dating. Nick convinced Ash to leave that abusive ass. And she did, but the man was obsessed with her. One night, he followed her over to Nicky's house and shot her in the driveway. Nick saw the whole thing."

"Oh God." Poor Nick.

"Yeah. Nick blames himself. Said he would never get that close to someone again. And you'll learn, when Nicky makes his mind up about something, he ain't changing it."

I nod, understanding so much about him now. So much we have in common.

Richie pours another splash of moonshine in my cup. "But I don't know. Maybe things have changed. You might be good for our boy. Or maybe you about to drag him into some shit again."

I swallow hard, thinking of Devonte.

"Hey!"

Nick is at the door, holding the screen open. "What are you two doing?"

"Talking about you," I shout.

"It better be good things," he shouts back. "Hey Rich, let me get some of that."

"Naw, playboy," Richie says, shaking his head as we walk toward the house. "It's too early. Don't need you laid out already."

"You trying to say I can't handle a little rotgut?"

"'Rotgut'?" Richie laughs then says to me, "I swear this guy is the oldest Black woman I know. Alright, man. But don't say I didn't warn you."

I notice that the night bugs scream louder in the country down south as I stand by, watching Richie drag a passed-out Nick out of the bed of his truck.

"What I tell you? Didn't I tell you!" Richie shouts, cackling.

We ate, drank, played cards, and ate some more. It was the most relaxing, stress-free Thanksgiving I have ever had. I could stay at Anita's forever.

Anita hops out of the front seat and takes my hand. "Come on, girl. You too."

"What? I—" But before I can spit out the word, I tumble forward. The earth begins spinning backward and forward. Damn Richie and that moonshine!

Anita and Richie deposit us on Nick's living room sofa.

"I'll drop your car off tomorrow with Uncle Pete," Richie says. "See you two later."

"Call us in the morning, Nicky," Anita says, kissing his forehead. "I can stop by and whip up some breakfast."

"My leftovers," I whimper, reaching for the unknown.

Anita laughs. "They're already in the fridge, baby girl."

I hear the front door close before the world fades to black. Then someone is shaking my shoulder.

"Hey," Nick utters. "It's time for bed. I can't sleep down here."

Barely coherent, I nod as we climb up the stairs on our hands and knees. The sight of us makes me giggle until I snort. Nick breaks down laughing, his face turning beet red. We reach the top and fall into each other.

Nick gives me a sloppy grin. "I want to sleep together like we always do."

"Okay," I mumble, swaying like a breeze hit me.

"I sleep better with you," he slurs.

"Okay," I say, and take his hand, leading him down the hall.

"Jordyn," he moans. "Wait . . . I . . ."

Then we're in his room, surrounded by his childhood. The sight of him in here reminds me of something. I turn to the window . . . looking out at the driveway.

"It happened here," I mutter. "You saw it happen right . . . here."

Nick follows my line of sight and whirls away, shutting his eyes. The action is too fast, and he stumbles forward.

"Jordyn . . ."

I step toward him, taking his hand.

"Nick, I . . ."

He brushes his thumb against my lips, the corner of his lip sliding into a silly drunken smirk.

"Shhhh . . ." He leans his forehead on mine. "Please."

"Talk to me," I beg. "Please."

Nick shakes his head, wobbling backward out of the room, releasing my hand.

"Tomorrow. I promise to tell you whatever you want. Trust me."

TWENTY-SIX

THE SUN SEEMS to beam directly into Nick's room.

A text dings. I lean up too quick, my head spinning. That damn moonshine.

Unknown number: Remember to stay strong this Black Friday. Do not fall victim to capitalism.

That's right. It is Black Friday. Usually, Mom and I would have big shopping plans at the outlets, then end the day at our favorite Italian restaurant with cheesecake. It was tradition. I wonder if she's thinking of me now. They didn't even call or return my text.

It must be Devonte sending these random texts. Mr. "I don't believe in phones" must have one after all. This is probably the longest I've gone without thinking of him in months. Most food I've had too.

Just the thought reminds me of our takeaway plates downstairs, calling my name. I lick my lips at just the thought of eating a slice of Anita's sweet corn bread with my morning tea.

I slip on Nick's sweatshirt and tiptoe downstairs. Nick is in the kitchen, facing the windows, mind so far away he doesn't hear me coming.

"Hey," I say, unsure of how to act around him. Especially after last night. "Are you . . . okay?"

He sips his coffee without looking up.

"Get dressed. Something you don't mind getting wet. There's something I want to show you."

Guess Nick is accustomed to moonshine. While he floats around the house, I'm still woozy and sluggish. Once dressed, we walk out into the backyard, heading for the river.

I didn't have many clothes to bring so I settled on some leggings and one of Nick's sweatshirts with Loren's sneakers. The sight of their laces makes my heart crack. I wonder what the girls are doing. It didn't seem like anyone was heading home for the holiday.

I put thoughts of them aside and refocus. "Okay, so where are we going?"

"Here," he says, pointing to the dock. At the end, bobbing in the water, is a purple-and-black Jet Ski. The moment I see it, I stop walking.

"We're going Jet Skiing?"

He shrugs like it's no big deal. "Yeah, come on, I want to show you something."

He grabs my wrist and tugs us forward.

"Uh, seriously? I can't get on that thing!"

"Oh come on, don't tell me you're afraid of water."

"No. It's just . . ." I cringe, embarrassed of my thought before saying it out loud. "I . . . really don't want my hair to get wet."

He rolls his eyes. "You're not going to fall in. Trust me, I'll be very careful," he says, as he slips a life jacket around my back, smirking as he tightens the straps.

Can I trust him? I'm not so sure. He's been so aloof. Sometimes, I don't even think I really know who he is and why he kept this part of himself a secret. But as he finishes strapping me in, eyes full of light and a touch of lust, I decide to be brave.

He pulls a scarf out of his back pocket.

"Just put your hair up in a bun, tie this around it."

I groan. "Okayyyy."

With my hair all done, we climb down onto the Jet Ski.

I press myself against his back and rope my arms around his stomach, squeezing my legs against him. The chemistry thickens around us. His head jerks up; he must be feeling it too.

He glances over his shoulder at me, cheeks reddening. Is he nervous?

"Wow," he mumbles, searching my face, and I want to kiss him. It was all I wanted to do since last night.

"Okay. Let's go," he says, easing away from the dock, towing out into the open water. "Hold on tight; once we get going, the water can be a little rocky. Be ready."

I squeeze him a little tighter.

"Careful," he chides. "You ready?"

Giggling, I nod.

The engine revs up and we take off, flying across the water, jumping over the small rip waves. He makes a quick turn in, spinning us around in a circle, and I shriek.

"Hold on!"

He revs the engine again and we sputter before taking off faster. I dig my face into his shoulder, staring at the passing houses lining the river, the thick trees, the lush woods, and the speedboats headed in the opposite direction. I feel myself springing back to life, the smell of the water, the wind hitting my face, holding tight to his hard stomach. We head south, going faster and faster over the rough waves. Suddenly he stops and we bob like a buoy. He glances over his shoulder, catching his breath, and grins.

"You okay?"

"Yes," I breathe.

Nick makes a sharp turn, heading toward the wooded riverbank. He slows to a creep, the engine silencing to a purr.

"Duck your head," he says.

"Huh?"

Then he drives straight into the brush. I thought we would crash right into the shore but I see a small opening, hidden in the thick vines you would never notice unless you were up close. He uses his arm to lift some branches out of the way and

I duck as we drive under. Once through, the water opens up to a beautiful cove. He drives to the middle of it and turns off the engine. We sit in silence, giving me a chance to take it all in. The sun dancing off the dark crisp water, beating on our shoulders, the lush tall trees hiding us away. A chilly breeze combs through Nick's hair.

"Wow, this is beauti—"

"Shhhhhh! Wait."

I listen to the birds chirping and insects buzzing around us. Nick scans the riverbank intensely, searching for something.

"Nick, what are we—"

"Shhh," he whispers then sits up straighter. "There! Over there, look."

He points to the trees in the distance. I squint, ears picking up rustling coming from the bushes until a small deer emerges from the wood, cautiously taking a step to drink some water. Nick looks over his shoulder with a triumphant grin.

"Bambi," he says, softly. "Not as beautiful as my Bambi."

I gush, burying my face in his back. He grips my hands, unhooking them from his stomach, then places them on either side of the Jet Ski.

"Hold still. Don't move."

Quickly, he hovers up and swings his leg around and sits back down so he is facing me. I grip the sides of the seat to keep steady. He grins with that charming all-American-boy smile and slides his hands around my waist, scooting me up onto his lap. I freeze, afraid of falling over, but he holds me tight. His palm cups my face, thumb gliding across my lips. He leans up, searching my eyes, as if waiting for permission, then falls into my lips.

The kiss is deep, purposeful, perfect. The kind of kiss that you never want to end.

He releases my lips with a smile.

"I've wanted to do that . . . for a long time," he breathes, still searching my face.

This is a different Nick. An overwhelming Nick. A sober Nick. Which feels so much better than the Nick I would've experienced last night. I bite my lip, holding in the urge to attack him. He smiles, then leans back on the Jet Ski handles.

"Okay, so you wanted to talk. Let's talk."

"What? Seriously," I gasp.

"You said you wanted to know everything. Well, now, here we are. Alone. And I'm giving you what you want."

I scoff, pointing over his head.

"You sure you don't mind Bambi knowing your business? I know how secretive you can be."

He shrugs. "Bambi's cool. Think she's too afraid to be my dinner."

"Do you really eat deer?"

"Hey, it's the other white meat."

"Gross."

He laughs. "How is eating Bambi gross but not cows?"

"Cows don't have first names."

He laughs, his hands gripping my back. "I love your ridiculous logic."

My laughter slowly dies down, bravery taking over. "Why didn't you want to tell me about Ashley?"

His eyes flicker away, arms tightening. "I didn't want to tell anyone. Talking about it . . . is re-traumatizing. It happened two years ago, and in a small town like this, you never forget it. No one lets you forget. I'm always 'the boy whose girlfriend got murdered in his front yard.' Or 'the boy whose rich parents let a Black family raise him.'"

"I know, says 'the girl whose brother killed himself in his dorm room.'"

He gives me a sympathetic smile. "But at Frazier, I thought I could just start over. Leave the past behind me."

"And never date again? You know that's not realistic."

He rubs a hand back and forth over his thigh.

"Remember when we talked about the five stages of grief? Sometimes I think I'm stuck in the bargaining phase. Like, if I stay alone, then maybe no one will ever get hurt again being with me and maybe I can finally forgive myself."

I shake my head. "That's not how it works."

"I know," he admits with a shrug. "But never kept me from trying."

That he does. He always tries. This moment seems too perfect for me to touch with my fears. I don't want it to. But I want to feel safe and loved. I want Nick but I'm afraid of losing him. I've lost so much already. The girls. Kevin. Can I chance losing Nick too?

"You think you could try another way . . . with me?"

He stares for a moment. Then without warning, he cups my cheek. An electric shock pulses through my body, the hairs on my arm skyrocketing and muscles below my stomach I didn't even know existed tightening. I meet his gaze forgetting how to breathe as the pad of his thumb rubs my collarbone.

He smiles. "I would like that . . . very much."

Nick is a good kisser.

We kissed on the Jet Ski, on the dock, against the back door, on the kitchen counter, by the stair banister. There's a desperation in his kiss, a ravenous hunger. Before I know what we are doing, we're kissing our way down the hallway, toward his room . . . toward his bed.

We stop in the middle of his room and I break away, just to catch my breath. But in that short second, his body locks stiff. He stares out his window and, in an instant, his eyes grow wide, pupils dilated, as if he was watching it happen all over again. He spins away with a stumble, holding the door frame to keep from falling. I step into the hall, into his line of sight, and rub his arms, consoling him.

"You're okay. You're okay."

He shakes his head, shutting his eyes tight. I've never seen him so pale and shaken. He tries to breathe through the panic, wheezing up air.

"What . . . happened?"

White-knuckling the door, he looks down at me, and I can see he's questioning himself but pushes through.

"Ashley and I had been friends since kindergarten. I always had a little crush on her. She didn't pay me the time of day. During our freshman year, she met this senior at our rival school. Eric. He was intense. Used to rough her up bad. I didn't know until one day, after school, I caught him slapping her.

"I convinced her to just leave him. To break up with him. And she did. But he didn't take it well. I said, he'll get the hint. He didn't. Stalked her at school, at work, even fucked up my car. Anita said that I should go to the police but . . . I didn't want to be some rich white kid reporting a Black guy. He just turned eighteen. An adult.

"One night, she was in her car, and he was following her. She called me and I told her to just come to my house. I was in my room when she pulled up, and as soon as she got out of the car, he shot her. The sound was so . . ." He shudders. "I thought he was just being a dick. But that look in his eye . . . I'll never forget it. I should have taken it seriously. I should have told her to drive straight to the police station, not to my house. If she did, maybe she would still be alive. My parents reminded me of that after the funeral."

I realize I've been holding a hand to my mouth, riveted. So

much about him makes sense now. I inch closer and hold his face between my palms.

"Nick. It's not your fault. You didn't kill her."

He takes a deep breath. "So that's it. That's my story. You know everything now. And now you know . . . why I can't do this."

I blink. "What?"

"I don't think I can do this, Jordyn. I can't go through something like that again. It almost killed me."

"But you just . . . you said . . . and today." I huff, with a stomp. "You can't keep on changing your mind like this. It isn't fair!"

Even as I say it, I know it's an unrealistic expectation to put on him. But how could he expect me to react any other way?

Nick's hands clench, his face a war of emotions. "Don't you know how freaked out I am, having feelings for you? I haven't felt like this in a long time. Don't you think I want to be with you?"

"You can if you really wanted," I snap.

He stabs at his chest. "What'd you want me to do? Just get over it? It's not that simple."

Hearing the words I said to Jack just a few weeks ago is like a splash of freezing cold water to the face.

I sigh, shoulders sagging. "I know. Believe me, no one knows you don't just get over it more than me."

His brows wrinkle as he stoops to eye level. "I'm not ready, Jordyn. I'm sorry."

My heart cracks once more with a loud clink, knowing there's nothing I can say to change his mind just like there's nothing anyone can say to change my mind about Kevin.

I step back with a nod. "Yeah. I understand."

TWENTY-SEVEN

THE ENTIRE RIDE back to DC feels like a slow march to my death. The dread a heavy wall inside my chest.

Nick and I stay silent for the most part. I'm not angry at him. A little confused but not upset. I'm too busy worrying about what waits for me back at the dorm. Will Devonte be there? What will they say? What will they do? What have they been doing all weekend? Why am I still worried about being left out?

As soon as Nick pulls in front of Rock Hall I steel myself.

Nick opens his mouth as if to say something, but I don't wait to hear the words. I slam the door behind me without taking a second glance back.

As soon as I turn the corner on my floor, I see a woman standing by the suite door.

"Hello?"

She gives me a once-over, her eyebrow arching up.

"You must be Jordyn."

"Yeah. How do you . . ."

"Kammy told me what you looked like. I'm Nina."

"Nina?"

"Her sister. So. Where is she? What boy got her so sick in the head that she wouldn't come home for Thanksgiving?"

I blink. "Uh, I have no clue. I'm just getting back from break."

Her lips purse. She steps back, nodding at the door. "Well, you gonna let me in or what?"

I jump, fumbling with the keys, and open the door. The suite is empty and somewhat tidy. Nina scans the room, unimpressed. She storms into the kitchen, yanking open the fridge.

"Ain't no food in here. Just some of this stuff that smells awful."

The tea. It looks fermented, lumps floating to the top. How long has everyone been gone?

"This kitchen is filthy," she mumbles. "Kammy would never . . . Which room is hers?"

I point and she marches over, swinging the door open.

"Why isn't it locked? Y'all don't lock your doors?" She steps into the room, her nose turning up. "It stinks in here. What's that? Body oils or something?"

I stand at the threshold watching her search through Kammy's belongings, shell-shocked.

"Did you try her cell?" I ask.

"Over a hundred times. We all have. Last time anyone heard from her was weeks ago, calling Mama, looking for money. But she didn't come home for Thanksgiving, didn't even call."

I glance at the bathroom, fighting the urge to throw up.

Nina shakes her head. "Thanksgiving is her favorite holiday. She wouldn't miss it. Not for nothing. Something's wrong. When's the last time you saw her?"

"I . . . uh . . . I'm not sure. I don't remember."

She huffs. "What d'you mean you don't remember? What was she doing? Who was she with? Do you know anything!"

I'm too blindsided to react to the accusation, still absorbing that the suite is really empty. Cleaned out like they were expecting someone to stop by. Where are they? Why didn't they tell me where they were going? Did they already leave for Emancipation . . . without me?

"Well?" Nina snaps.

I swallow. "Last time I saw Kammy, she was here . . . alone. But most of the time she was with our roommate . . . and her brother."

Nina purses her lips.

"Her brother, huh? You know she broke up with her man? Right after Halloween. That ain't like her either. She loved that boy. Even if he is dumb as rocks. He wanted to come here and check on her but we told him to wait until the holiday. That she'd be back and would get her mind right. All she needed was some time and prayer. Now I wish I hadn't waited." She tosses a book on the floor. "Why does her room look like this? Where's all her stuff?"

"What stuff?"

"Her designer bags, makeup, jewelry. Her wig!"

I look around. I hadn't noticed so much of her belongings were missing.

"Maybe she took it with her," I offer.

She rolls her neck. "How you roommates and you don't know where she is, what she doing, or nothing about her? She said y'all were close."

"I . . . I . . ."

Nina shakes her head and takes out her cell phone. "Something ain't right. I'm going to the police."

The police?

"No!" I exclaim. "I'm sure she's around and she's fine. Everyone loves Kammy!"

"Yeah and that's the problem," she snaps, walking out of her room. "She falls in love with everyone, thinking everyone is her damn friend. I told Mama she's too trusting to be going off to some college in some big city we ain't ever been to before."

My stomach ties in knots. Kammy sounds like the perfect victim.

Nina stands with arms crossed, expectantly. I have to play this smart. We don't need the police involved. That'll just complicate matters.

"Maybe she spent Thanksgiving with a friend," I offer.

"Which friend?" she snaps.

Tell her!

Telling her about Devonte may bring me more unwanted

attention, more rumors. But if Kammy is really missing, then she should know what's been happening here and what Devonte has done.

At that very moment, Loren hobbles into the suite. Her eyes toggle between us.

"Who are you?" she says to Nina, her voice scratchy.

Nina takes a step back, the sight of her languid movements startling.

"Uh, I'm Kammy's sister, Nina. Have you seen her?"

Loren takes a step forward, her sweater inching up enough for me to see a hospital band on her wrist.

Loren catches my gaze and straightens her sleeves with a shrug. "Yeah. She said she was taking the bus home for Thanksgiving."

"The bus?!" Nina exclaims, her eyes wide. "My sister would never catch the bus!"

Loren shrugs. "Maybe you don't know your sister like you thought."

The words make my mouth drop.

Nina narrows her eyes at us. She points a finger. "You're lying. You're both fucking lying!"

She slings her purse on her shoulder and storms out of the room. Loren watches and collapses against the wall, as if she can't hold herself up anymore.

I run to her side. "Loren! Are you okay?"

She snatches her hand away. "Get off me, Bed Wench."

I shoot up, stunned.

"Lo, come on! You're sick. When's the last time you ate something?"

Loren ignores me, limping into the living room. She doesn't have a bag on her. Did she stay here the entire holiday?

"Nina's going to go to the police," I say. "That's gonna bring some attention on us, on Devonte. He wouldn't want that, right?"

Loren nods in agreement.

"So where is Kammy?"

Loren slumps over to the love seat, eyes searching the floor, as if trying hard to remember.

"I don't know," she admits out loud. "Our Lord said she went to the bus station."

"Our Lord?"

"Devonte. That's what he wants us to call him. He's given up his earthly name for a title that fits his calling."

I bite my lip to keep from screaming. I would have never imagined Loren agreeing to uttering something so idiotic. Maybe I don't know her, just like Nina has proven that I don't know Kammy. Then again, they don't know me either.

Anxious for space, I head toward my room.

"How's Legacy?" she snaps at my back.

"Huh? How should I know."

She rolls her eyes. "Don't act all innocent. Our Lord said he saw you two together. How long have you been hooking up with him behind my back!"

"He's lying! I haven't seen Legacy since . . . since . . ."

Now that I think about it, I can't remember the last time I saw Legacy. The last time I even heard his name, Kammy was asking about him. Are they BOTH missing?

Suddenly, my throat constricts, a rubber band snapping around my tongue. I rush into the bathroom and heave up Anita's pie. But that still does nothing to tame my fear.

I have to get out of here.

TWENTY-EIGHT

EXAMS ARE COMING up. And if I don't ace every single one, I'll be one step closer to academic probation and two steps closer to being back in Connecticut. Despite all my strategies and explanations, my parents do not play when it comes to academics. So, I go old school, making flash cards and charts just to memorize terms. My parents aren't checking in, but they'll be sure to check my grades at the end of the semester. I want to show them that this school is just as academically challenging as Yale. But Devonte takes up so much space in my mind. The arguments I have with myself over him are not only time-consuming but humiliating.

I live in the library now, spending as little time as possible at the dorm.

Just as I'm making a dent in my flash card pile, Nick walks in. He's hard to miss.

We catch eyes and he stops gripping the strap of his messenger bag. It's been days since we last talked or seen each other. My mouth opens and shuts.

He's a stranger. Always has been.

I snap my computer closed, pack, and rush out of the library, brushing by him without a word. I'll finish up in my room.

There are two police cars parked in front of Rock Hall. I don't think much about it as I take the elevator up. But when I step off on my floor and head to the suite, I see officers walking in and out.

Oh no . . .

"What's going on?" I say in a panic, running inside. Our suite is once again filled with people, but none of them here to see Devonte.

There's a detective combing through my belongings. Another officer is carefully rummaging through Kammy's things. Another is in the living room. Another walks out of Vanessa's room.

"What are you doing?"

"Are you Jordyn Monroe?" the officer in my room asks.

"Yes! Is everything okay? Is someone hurt?"

"We're looking for Kamara Young. Have you seen or heard from her?"

My stomach tightens, heart racing. "No. But what does that have to do with my room?"

"Her family reported her missing. This was her last known whereabouts."

Nina. She finally went to the police. Where's Loren and Vanessa?

"We scanned through security footage of Rockland Hall for the last four weeks. There's footage of Kammy entering but no footage or record of her ever leaving the premises."

I turn toward the bathroom, ready to throw up.

"Is she . . . Do you think she's . . . Oh God!"

After I answer as many of the officer's questions as I can, I slink back down to the lobby like a zombie, half dead, half alive in misery. In the courtyard, I spot Vanessa and Loren, huddled together, wearing terrified expressions. As soon as they see me approaching, Vanessa reaches her hand out. I take it and we gather in a group hug, tears flowing. God, I've missed them. All the nastiness that's happened over the last few weeks doesn't matter anymore. We have something we can all agree on. Our love for Kammy.

"They can't find Kammy anywhere," Loren says, wiping her tears with the back of her hand. "What if something really happened to her?"

"This is all my fault," Vanessa cries. "I just assumed she was around, you know? I didn't think to check. I'm so stupid!"

"When's the last time you saw her?" I ask.

Vanessa shrugs. "Fuck, I can't remember."

"I haven't been feeling so good," Loren admits and starts crying again. "I guess I didn't even notice she was gone. Some sister I am."

I rub her arm. "Well, what did Devonte say to the police?"

Vanessa straightens, with a sniff. "He hasn't talked to them. It's not necessary."

"But . . . he lives with us. They were kind of a couple."

"No, they weren't," Vanessa says. "Kammy was just in love. Devonte isn't the type to settle down with anybody."

"Okay fine, whatever. But if anyone would know where she is or at least seen her last, it would be him."

Loren and Vanessa exchange a nervous glance. Sensing their apprehension, I try to reason with them.

"He could at least spread the word to the . . . family and help find her!"

Vanessa shakes her head. "We can't get him involved. You know this. Police are always looking for a reason to lock him up."

"Yeah," Loren scoffs. "How convenient they would be in our dorm the same time we're making plans for Emancipation."

Anger shoots through me. "Loren, Kammy is missing! Nothing convenient about that!"

Loren's face crumples with guilt.

"But Devonte is the next leader that will free a generation with truth and knowledge! We have to protect him."

"Oh, fuck this," I mutter, and head back inside. Vanessa grabs my arms, yoking me back with big pleading eyes.

"Jordyn, please. Don't do this. He needs us!"

I snatch my arm away and storm off, through the lobby and up the elevator, ready to come clean. What I should have done weeks ago. But when I walk into the suite, I find most of the officers are in my room, seemingly crowded around my closet.

The officer I spoke to before spots me by the door and whispers something to his colleague. He walks out into the hall, holding something in a clear evidence bag.

"Do you know who this belongs to?"

Inside it looks like a bright purple cloth with large dark rust-color stains on it. It hits me like a barbell to the face. That's Kammy's head scarf.

Are those bloodstains??

For a moment, I'm rendered speechless. The officer waits for me, expectantly.

"No," I whisper, my body going numb.

The officer reads my reaction, his tone curt. "Okay, how about this?"

He pulls out a Gucci bag. The one Kammy gave Devonte months ago. What is it doing in my closet?

"OMG! That's Kammy's," I say, instinctively grasping for it, and he raises it out of reach.

"Why would you have her things?"

My neck stiffens, mouth dry. "I don't . . . I don't know how they got in there."

The detective squares his shoulders. "Does anyone have a key to your room?"

"No . . . well, I . . . I don't know. Well, they all kind of do."

Even I can hear the uncertainty in my answers.

He nods. "Right. How about we take this conversation down to the station."

TWENTY-NINE

THEY QUESTION ME for over five hours. When was the last time you saw Kammy? Why were her items in your room? Do you know where she is? Over and over. Nothing about my story has changed. I had no idea, and I have no idea where she could be. Having lawyers as parents gives them enough cause to let me go.

But one thing is clear: someone is trying to frame me. And they're doing a pretty good job of it.

I didn't mention Devonte. Mentioning him would only have brought more heat to a situation I need to handle with minimal attention. Because if the police suspect that I have something to do with Kammy's disappearance, they won't be eager to help me if things go bad back in the dorm.

It's the bloodstains that make me sick to my stomach. I always knew Devonte was dangerous . . . but not on this level. Never like this.

And through the entire ordeal, no one has even asked about Legacy.

I walk out of the station close to midnight in a daze and spot his car parked across the street.

Nick.

He waves at me and I could burst into tears, I'm so happy to see him.

"Hey you," he says.

"Hey . . . you," I mumble.

We stare at one another, waiting for someone to make the first move. Finally, he reaches for my jacket and pulls me into him, gathering me the same tight way I love. As if he doesn't want to let go and I never want him to.

Nick pulls up in front of the Rock, shoving the gear in park. Outside, the dorm looks so normal. Just like the day I first moved in. No one would know what kind of insanity has been going on inside. Or maybe they do. Maybe everyone knows, and if so, why hasn't anyone tried to help? Why hasn't the university gotten involved?

"I . . . can't believe you want to come back here," Nick mutters, shaking his head. "I don't think this is a good idea."

I sigh and unbuckle my seat belt. "Thanks for the ride."

He grips my wrist. "Hey, I'm not leaving you alone!"

I snatch my hand back, trying to find some composure.

"Nick, I need a moment," I say. "Today has been . . . a lot."

"Yeah I know . . . but . . ."

"Nick," I hiss. "We can talk later."

I jump out of the car. I have zero energy left to give him or anyone.

The suite has been combed thoroughly. Every drawer emptied, cabinet opened, contents laid out. They even searched between the sofa cushions, dusting for fingerprints. This gives me pause. Devonte's prints should be in the system. They'll question him soon enough.

In my room, a foul stench permeates the air. The carpet has been sprayed, my towels and sheets taken.

They were looking for more blood. Kammy's blood.

The shivers set in, teeth chattering. I run into the bathroom and stop short at the message written on the mirror in red lipstick. Loren's red lipstick.

SNITCH!

I wretch up whatever's left in my stomach. The room spins. I slump over, taking my usual resting spot between the tub and toilet, with my head leaned back, face up to the sky. There's a ceiling tile out of place. They really looked everywhere for Kammy.

But Kammy's gone. Maybe forever.

I bite my fist, clenching my teeth, a sob reverberating back into me.

You're not a good friend.

It's gone too far. You need to stop this. Once and for all.

Kammy's missing, Loren's practically killing herself, and

I'm a person of interest in my roommate's disappearance . . . possible murder.

I pick up my cell and dial the number. This is the step I've been preparing for. All I'll do is leave an anonymous tip about Devonte. Then whatever happens after that . . . happens. But fingers can't be pointed at me. At least, I hope not.

"This is . . . Jo. Am I speaking with Arnold Woods?"

"Speaking," he says, slurping the end of a drink through a straw.

"You're Devonte Saunders's parole officer, right? I'm just calling to let you know that he's up to his scams again. Credit card stuff. I thought you should know."

There's silence over the phone for a moment. I check to see if I still have a connection.

"How'd you get this number?"

The question takes me off guard. "I . . . researched."

Over the line, a cup is slammed down, papers shuffling.

"You got a pen?" he asks, hastily. "Take down this number. You need to talk to Detective Andy Gates. Call him right now and tell him everything."

"Why? What's going on?"

"Just do it, you hear?"

I swallow and take down the number, afraid to ask any more questions. He doesn't say goodbye before ending the call. I dial Detective Gates, and it goes to voicemail. I'm nervous about leaving my number. What if he can track me down?

What if he finds out who I am?

"This is . . . Jo, I'm calling regarding Devonte Saunders. Can you please call me back?"

Something about the urgency in the parole officer's voice makes me uneasy. Something isn't adding up.

I fire up the laptop, putting his name in the search bar. Same things I found before come up. His hip-hop business dealings. His scam charges and subsequent prison sentences. But I keep digging, googling more. What did I miss?

I think of the detective and try both of their names in a newspaper archive site. Andy Gates + Devonte Saunders.

And there it is. A small article from over twenty years ago makes my heart plummet. Location and timeline works out with what I know about him. It makes sense why I couldn't find it before. He changed his name.

David Saunders . . . suspect in the murder of a nineteen-year-old college student.

I sprint out of the dorm, full speed toward the Communications building. Her class starts in ten minutes. I only need five minutes.

I spot Loren walking through the outdoor basketball courts, a shortcut some students use to avoid walking up the hill. Even from a distance, I can see that she's frail, wobbly. I fly right in front of her, out of breath.

Loren stops short, clutching her bag. Then her eyes go wide.

"What's wrong? Did they find her? Did they?"

I push the article in her line of sight. She scans the top line, her eyes narrowing.

"Where'd you get this?" she snaps, trying to grab my phone but I snatch it away.

"He was a suspect in a murder investigation," I explain, with rasping breaths. "A girl went MISSING and was eventually found, beaten to death. They didn't have enough evidence to prosecute him."

Even as I say this aloud, my chin trembles at the thought of what could have happened to Kammy.

Loren hesitates, nostrils flaring. "You know how they have fake news articles. What do we keep telling you? You have to do your research. That's not even his name!"

I grip her arm, noticing how fragile her wrist feels in my hand. "He CHANGED his name! This is REAL, Loren! There's a case number! You have to believe me. I wouldn't lie about this."

Loren wiggles out of my hold, glaring at me.

"Stop," she says, her voice cracking. "Jordyn. Just . . . stop."

I watch her walk off, realizing it's too late. She's gone. Just like Kammy.

We only have a few weeks of school left before fall semester is over. Spring can look one of two ways, depending on what happens with Kammy.

I glance at the chair propped up against the door to ensure it stays locked. But the strange chanting music thumping through the walls makes it feel like Devonte's meeting is happening in the middle of my room. How is he just able to carry on like normal? Why doesn't campus police do anything? He's probably in their ears as well. I look at Devonte through a terrifyingly different lens now, imagining those soft, gentle hands wrapping around my throat. Would he even break a sweat?

All I know is that I haven't slept in forty-eight hours since finding that article and I may not be able to hang on for much longer. But I can't leave Loren alone.

My phone buzzes. Nick.

"Hey."

"Hey? What's that sound?"

I scoff. "My roommates."

There's a brief pause. "I'm coming up."

"What? No! Don't."

But Nick's line is already dead. I stare at the chair propped up on my room door. Should I make a run for it, meet him halfway? I don't want him in here. I don't know what Devonte is capable of. People are missing. He could be next!

A pounding on the suite door makes me freeze. He must have already been on his way when he called.

The humming stops.

"Oh, you bold to be walking up in here again," Kareem says.

"Is Jordyn home?" Nick asks in a playful voice.

"No," he snaps. "But we can make another call to her parents for you."

I swing my door open, finding Nick and Kareem facing off. Nick raises an eyebrow, and slides right by him, walking into my room.

"You shouldn't be here," I snap, slamming my door shut.

He smiles at me. "Hey you."

I chuckle, unable to resist him.

"Hey you," I gush.

He holds up a plastic soup container. "Brought you some gumbo."

"Gumbo. Who made it?"

"Me, of course. Food is my love language."

I snort. "That makes entirely too much sense given you are a man of few words."

"You have to eat something," he insists. "You can't survive on twigs and berries."

"Everyone else eats twigs and berries and they're just fine."

He shakes his head. "If everyone jumped off the roof, would you jump too? You need some meat on your bones."

I giggle. "You know, these little proverbs sound funnier now knowing who raised you."

The corner of Nick's mouth tugs into a grin. "Yeah, yeah." He slips off his jacket and tosses it on the chair.

"What are you doing?"

"I'm staying." He gazes around the room. I did my best to put it back in order after the search but there are still traces of it on the walls, the dresser drawers crooked and out of place.

"No way. I'm already in enough trouble with you here."

"You're not in trouble with someone who doesn't belong here," he gripes.

"It's not about him. It's about . . . my new reputation," I say, grimacing. "I don't want it getting on you. You have a campaign to run! You've already done enough for me."

"I'm staying," he states, resolve in his eyes.

I open my mouth to argue but can't find the strength. Mentally, I'm all over the place.

"Fine. Take the floor."

He glances down and chuckles. "Aren't we past that?"

I sigh in defeat and scoot over on the bed. He holds up a finger and grabs the container of stew.

"First, eat five spoonfuls, then I'll leave you alone."

I snarl at the container then huff. "I'll only eat if you talk."

"About what?"

I narrow my eyes. "You know what."

Catching my meaning, he sighs and pulls a plastic spoon out.

"I can feed myself, sheesh." I grab the spoon and pop in a scoop. The spicy flavors take over my mouth, warmth entering my belly. He stares at my lips and I look up at him, expectantly.

"Oh! Right. Uh, first . . . I'm sorry for the way I acted during Thanksgiving. Well, after it. Thanksgiving Day was . . . amazing! Having you there with my family, my real family. It was fun."

He pauses, nodding at the gumbo. I eat another spoonful.

"It was . . . also a lot for me to take. Seeing you, in my room, at my house. You're right about the boomerang. Any time I talk about Ashley, it's like it comes up all over again. I can still hear the gunshots, like a never-ending echo. But it wasn't the shot that gave me nightmares. It was the silence that came right after it. It's why I have trouble sleeping without noise."

He tilts his head at the spoon and I eat another bite.

"I don't just want to be friends. I want to watch *Love Island* with you. I want to kiss you whenever I want. I want to kiss you now. But . . . I don't know if you'll forgive me for being an ass."

Those silly heart flutters. I feel them again and eat another spoonful.

"But whatever happens between us, I want to do everything in my power to make sure you're safe. Including using my school government perks and calling Student Housing myself to find you a new spot ASAP."

I hold the spoon midair. "Really? You'd do that?"

Nick kneels down eye level with me, hands gripping my knees.

"Jordyn, I'd do anything for you," he utters. "I just . . . can't lose someone I care about again. It would break me. And all this . . . really scares me."

Those bright, childlike eyes. I can lose myself in them forever. I free up my hand to push a piece of hair behind his ear.

"You're not going to lose me. I promise."

He gives me a silly grin. "And lastly, truth is . . . I'm having a hard time sleeping without you. It's weird."

"See? I'm useful."

His hands slide up to my waist. "So am I."

THIRTY

FUSA IS THROWING a holiday party in the ballroom for both students and staff. Nick has invited delegates and board members. Today, he plans to announce his intentions on running for trustee.

"Are you sure you want to show up to your party with the whore of the university?" I ask. "A potential murder suspect? A sexual deviant?"

"Shut up and don't be ridiculous," he says, fixing his silver tie in the hall mirror. He's wearing a charcoal-gray suit and a light blue button-down that brings out his eyes.

I chuckle, patting down my hair. It's not perfect but I've gotten better with the flat iron. It makes me think of Kammy. How she would have had this bone straight. How Loren would've had the perfect lipstick to go with the outfit Nick bought me—a green velvet maxi dress with bell sleeves and a slit that stops right at the top of my thigh.

"Nervous?" I ask.

"Yeah." He blows out some tense air. "But if I can face your dad then I can face anything."

I laugh. "Just remember your talking points."

His eyes widen. "You think that'll come up tonight?"

"The moment you say you're running, they're gonna ask why."

He gulps, pulling at his collar. "It feels like the frat house in here."

Giggling, I pull him close, fixing his tie the same way I used to see Mom fix Dad's before work.

"You look pretty." Nick smiles down at me proudly. "I'm glad you're here. I don't think I could do tonight without you."

What a coincidence. I don't think I could've survived this semester without him.

I stand on my tiptoes and just as I'm about to kiss his cheek, my phone buzzes. An unknown number. Maybe it's the detective finally calling me back.

"Hey, I have to take this," I say, rushing toward the door. "Be right back!"

"Okay, meet you in the ballroom!"

I nod and run out into the lobby to catch the call.

"Hello," I answer eagerly.

"Watch out! They're coming for you."

My back goes rod straight. "Loren? What's going on? Are you okay?"

"They're coming for you," she repeats. "Don't say I didn't warn you."

The line goes dead. A chill runs down my arms. I stand stock-still, looking out the glass doors. The night breeze flows through the trees on the Quad, kicking up fallen leaves that dance in an eerie circle. I can't explain it, but someone out there is watching. I can feel their eyes boring into my skin.

Tell Nick.

But tonight is his big night! He'll go into panic mode. Maybe I'll leave the party early, just in case Devonte comes and tries to cause a scene. Again. I take a deep breath and slide a hand down my hair to smooth the flyaways.

Someone passes by, clipping my shoulder like a hard body check. I stumble back in my heels, wincing an "Ow!"

The offending girl walks by without a second glance rushing downstairs, toward the Rec. It wasn't on purpose, I try to convince myself, rubbing my sore shoulder as my stomach begins to turn. Nausea mixing with nervousness.

I click down the hall, running into the nearest student bathroom next to the closed café. Every stall, thankfully, empty.

"Relax," I mumble to myself, in the first mirror. My trembling hands hold tight to the porcelain sink. When I can control my breathing, I wet my lips and pat my face dry. It's time to find Nick.

The door swings open and a group of girls file in. One by one, staring at me through the mirror. They have the same look in their eyes everyone has that follows Devonte. Cold, vacant, just the husk of someone that was once there. My lips begin to quiver.

The last one to walk in is Kerry. She smiles and locks the door behind her.

Consequences!

They make a small semicircle around me without uttering a word. My mouth goes dry. I can't move. Even if I could, move and run where? They have me surrounded.

Time ticks as I wait for my fate. Maybe this is just a bluff. A tactic to scare me. They wouldn't do anything to me in here, on the main campus, for everyone to see. That's when I notice one of them is holding a pair of scissors.

How far could my scream carry?

I don't have a chance to find out. The first girl steps up and slaps me across the cheek. The second girl clunks at my head, pain radiating down my neck, as the third girl shoves me into the wall. I try to keep my balance, to fight back, but it's impossible in heels. Another girl punches me right in the eye and I let out a scream that the first girl muffles with her hand. I bite and kick, but that only makes them hit my face harder.

Finally, the girl with the scissors approaches. I thrash and buck like a wild animal, desperately trying to cry out, imagining the blade slicing into my neck. But the other girls hold me steady as she chops clumps of hair off my head. Strands rain down my face and shoulders, blanketing the floor. I scream and scream, tears blinding me until Kerry shoves me hard into the stall door. My head bounces off the toilet and the entire world fades to black.

* * *

I cuddle the fluffy down comforter, the color matching my curtains, eyes locked on my sparkling canopy. Outside, it's pitch-dark, but the stars seem so bright, like twinkling diamonds. Living in the middle of nowhere helps. In the distance, dishes clink and water runs. I stretch out of bed, a furry rug tickling my toes. Kevin always teased me about having a dead polar bear in the middle of my room. Every few days we'd have text message meme wars about it. His always being the funniest.

For weeks I thought my phone was broke when he stopped texting, stopped answering my incessant calls and FaceTimes, until I realized he was avoiding me. College had separated us in ways I could not fathom.

I pad barefoot down the stairs and into the kitchen where I see him, dressed in that orange sweater I bought. We were so used to wearing gray and navy to school every day that any pop of color added to our wardrobe was welcomed.

Kevin stands over the sink, washing dishes. A tall, brown-skinned string bean, sprouting patches of a beard on his baby face, his hair long and clumpy. That should have been my first sign that something was wrong.

He looks up and gives me a small smile.

"Hey JoJo." His voice is so calm, so resolved. I didn't realize how much comfort it brought me until I heard it.

But I purse my lips, slipping into the leather barstool facing him. "You know Mom and Dad are gonna kill you when they get home, right?"

He shrugs, unimpressed. "I'll be gone before then. Tea?"

"Yes."

Kevin turns to the glass kettle already boiling.

"You know you could've just asked for the money. Why steal from them?"

He shrugs, setting two white mugs on the counter. "How much did I take?"

"You don't know?" I snap.

"No. I'm not sure," he admits without looking at me. He takes the oakwood tea box out of the cupboard. "You seem like in a mint kind of mood tonight, old lady."

Kevin was always good at guessing the type of tea I needed. Whether it was tea that felt like a hug, tea to cure a heartbreak, or tea to calm my frazzled nerves when I felt I had no one to talk to, no one to understand the pressure weighing me down.

He did, though, because he was under the same pressure.

I watch him dunk the bags in, where he'll let it steep for two to three minutes, then will add cream, then honey.

He knows me. He was the only person who knew me. I thought I knew him. Until he went to college.

"Kevin, are you on drugs?"

He chuckles. "No. High on life."

I smack the counter. "This is serious."

We lock eyes as he pours the steaming water into the mugs, a shadow crossing his face.

"No," he says, his voice deep. "This is a dream."

I swallow, watching the wall behind him ripple like a breeze teasing a smooth pond.

This is a dream, a snapped shot that plays on a loop in my nightmares. The last time I saw him. The last time he was alive. He came home in the middle of the night, talking nonstop about HBCUs. How they're a utopia for Black people, our very own mecca, wishing he had gone. Wishing he had done things differently, insisting that I do it instead. The craze in his eyes made me nervous. He had to be on drugs, that's the only explanation for the lunacy.

Now he stands in front of me, calmly fixing my tea.

"I thought you wanted me to go to Frazier."

"Yeah, I wanted you to go. But not like this," he says, leaning back against the stove. "I wanted you to go so that for once, just once, you could experience what it's like not being the other. Not always being the token Black girl in every class or activity. This might be the only chance in your life to experience that. I regret not taking my own chance. Regret not standing up to Mom and Dad like I should've."

I tie my fingers in knots, holding my breath.

"You left me," I mumble to the floor, tears swelling. "You were all I had."

"I know," he admits, sliding the mug across the counter. "But you have to let me go now. Or else."

I shake my head and take a sip of tea.

THIRTY-ONE

"LOOK AT YOUR face! Your hair! You're not fucking staying here!"

The cops were called after I was found unconscious. Thankfully, security footage picked up the faces of every girl that entered the bathroom and they were immediately arrested.

I limp into my room and touch my laptop on the desk, just to ground myself. I hated leaving it, even for one night.

"I have to stay here. For now."

Nick is furious. He hasn't changed since leaving the hospital this morning. There are dried bloodstains on his button-down. My blood.

"You're an adult. You don't have to listen to your parents. They would understand that you decided to stay with your boyfriend after being viciously attacked."

I laugh. "You don't know my parents."

At the hospital, I FaceTimed Mom. She stared at me for ten excruciating seconds before the tears started to flood, uttering,

"My God, Jordyn. Your hair . . ."

Mom went into lawyer mode, pulling strings and having detectives move expeditiously to make the necessary arrests. Even at the height of their calls, I could hear my dad mumble in the background, "This wouldn't have happened at Yale. Those are civilized people."

What they weren't aware of is that I'm still high on the person-of-interest list in connection with Kammy's disappearance. Being jumped in the bathroom and losing all my hair didn't win me any points or favors with the police.

Nick shakes his head. "Fuck a call. I'm going to Student Housing today! This has gone on long enough. I'm going to get you out of here."

He kisses my forehead. "I'll be back. Lock the door behind me, rest, and if anyone knocks, just call me. NO! Call 911. Just promise me you'll stay safe."

"I promise."

Nick hesitates, before running out the door, and I exhale, slinking down to my bed. On reflex, I touch my hair, forgetting most of it is gone, and it feels like I've gone with it.

This entire plan is off the rails. Devonte has so many people on campus in his pocket that I'm in serious danger. Anyone could throw me down the stairs, hit me with a car, or spread even more rumors that I can wind up in jail . . . it's all too much.

Her door creaks as it swings open and every muscle in my body clenches at the sound.

Loren stands at my threshold, hands folded. She's wearing a green head wrap, yellow top, and a long denim skirt. She takes in my injuries, my forced haircut, with dull lifeless eyes.

"I . . . came to see if you were alright," she says softly.

"Do I look alright?" I snap, seething.

She shakes her head. "I tried to warn you. You can't blame Devonte for this. You were running around saying he murdered some girl."

"He IS a murderer!" I jump up, the movement so painful, black spots blind my vision, and I grip a chair for balance. "And you don't see that him and his fucked-up sister are scamming you?"

Loren has a hard time facing me. "Devonte can be a little . . . extreme. Passionate. But he's not all the way wrong about the facts he's spitting."

A wry laugh escapes me. "Get the hell out of here."

Loren lunges forward.

"I'm serious," she shouts. "You gonna look around and say he's making up the statistic about the number of liquor stores we have in the hood compared to availability of fresh fruits and vegetables? Black maternal mortality rates? Police brutality? The damn cops who almost got us killed in that protest are already out on bail, still getting paid with our tax dollars!"

I don't answer her. There's no use in talking to her.

She sighs. "Girl, I know it's easier for you to just follow along. But that's not the life I want to live anymore. And you can't make me live a life I don't want to. People grow! People change! I've changed. I can't just turn my back and party and drink knowing there's innocent brothers in prison. Or that there's a food industry literally poisoning our communities. After everything our ancestors have been through, I can't sit and dishonor them by pretending I don't see what I'm seeing. Our people are in mental bondage and don't know it. If you want to pretend you don't see that, that's on you. But I ain't you. So just . . . stop."

She gives me a curt nod, storming out of the suite. And I don't realize I'm crying until the door slams shut.

I stare out the window at the Quad, the view spectacular. Students flow in and out of different halls, gathering around benches, holding hands, laughing under a bright beautiful sky. Not a care in the world.

"What kind of tea is this?" I ask, hands hugging a black-and-white African print mug with a gold handle.

"Turkish," Dr. Barnes says, sitting across from me with his own steaming cup. "A black tea, brewed slightly different than regular black. I picked some up on a trip to Istanbul. Although I do prefer their coffee better."

His office is like a museum, artifacts from countries all over the world adorning every spare inch of his walls, smelling of spices and wet wood.

"Seems like you travel a lot."

"Most of our well-known Black artists and intellectuals would tell you to spend as much time as you can out of this country, or you will lose yourself to it."

"But . . . this is home."

"Hm. That it is," he says, tickled by something unsaid.

I wiggle my jaw, the hinge still sore and swollen.

"You haven't asked me about my face yet," I mutter. "Or my hair. I guess you already know."

He nods. "How do you feel?"

"Right now? I feel . . . hopeless."

He raises a gray eyebrow. "Hopeless? Hm. Now that's an interesting choice of word. Go on."

I look outside again, wishing I could be one of those carefree students. But then I think of Loren's heated words and fight back tears.

"How do you go on living in a world that hates us? That we never get justice in. Why bother even trying? I mean, how could we sit here, enjoying our tea . . . or be out there laughing . . . when there's so much work to be done? How can you travel the world knowing what are people are going through here? How can you just pretend like everything is . . . fine?"

Dr. Barnes sets down his mug with a smirk. "My dear, I see you are at the crossroads that most students find themselves in at some point in their college life, when they've stepped out of their parents' protective bubble and into independence."

"Really?"

He wags a finger. "It's been proven that the road to Black liberation and consciousness will never be a single lane."

"What do you mean?"

He folds his hands. "Did you know that the late great James Baldwin spent a considerable amount of time abroad in places like Paris and Turkey? He said it best, 'To be a Negro in this country and to be relatively conscious is to be in a state of rage almost all the time.' So, oh yes, the state of this world makes me very angry. But I do not let anger dictate the road I travel on. I choose joy."

"Joy?" I scoff.

"Absolutely! To build a future that is rooted in equality and liberation, you must imagine and pretend that it is possible. And the key part of imagination is joy. Joy is an act of resistance, it's revolutionary. The fact that our people have survived all that we have survived, and thrived, defying expectations and insurmountable odds . . . that deserves to be celebrated. So yes, I can still be a part of the fight for Black liberation while I travel, dance with my friends, laugh, and drink tea with my students."

I nod, sipping my tea.

"Some people choose different revolutionary roads to travel on," he continues. "No journey is wrong. But judgment of each other's roads has led to some divisiveness and fracture in our communities. That is why you, standing at this crossroads, feel so pivotal. Because the road you might want to take may be different than the road your friends or even your family have taken."

I think of Kevin. How the road he wanted to go down led him straight off a cliff. I stare out the window again and sigh.

"My roommate's older brother moved into our dorm. The chemtrails, the toxins, the Lynch papers . . . that was all him. He's been . . . using us."

Using seems like such a basic word to describe what we've been through but it's all I have in me.

Dr. Barnes takes a deep breath, his eyes never leaving me.

"Technically," he starts. "I'm not allowed to talk to you about this. It would mean the university had knowledge of what was going on and leave them open to a lawsuit."

"Well, why hasn't the university done anything about it?"

He picks up his mug. "It's a question of whether this is a roommate squabble or criminal activity. If it's a roommate issue, it would be under the Dorm Counsel and Housing to look into. It's a student's right to have visitors."

"And if there is criminal activity?"

He raises his hands with a dramatic shrug. "He's careful. Neither you nor any of your other roommates have filed an official complaint. Any violence reported wasn't done by him, it was done by other students. He hasn't disrupted school activities, classes. Hasn't damaged school property. He's never spoken to a single professor or administrator on campus."

"But people see him walking around! How can they think he's a student?"

"We have students of all ages. From as young as sixteen to

as old as seventy-two in various departments from Fine Arts to Dental School. This is the perfect place for him to hide in plain sight. He's toeing a fine line."

"So he's just gonna get away with this and Frazier is going to just let a cult be formed on its campus?"

"Ah! I wouldn't necessarily say that." He stands, moseying to the corner of his office to a small black kettle, clicking it on. "There is one way to kill a fire before it spreads."

A fire . . . before it spreads . . . and destroys more lives. Something I should have done from the start.

I straighten with resolve. "How?"

Dr. Barnes refreshes his cup before turning to me with a smile. "Deprive it of oxygen."

I walk out of Dr. Barnes's building with my head held high, ignoring the stares that my battered face and pixie cut draw. I think about those times I've fallen off the balance beam. The brutal thump your body makes as it hits the mat, the "Oooo" then judgmental silence from onlookers. But you can't focus on the fall. You have to spring back onto the beam and slip back into your routine like nothing ever happened.

I grab my phone out of my pocket and dial.

"Hey! Are you okay?" Vanessa asks, oozing with uncertainty. "I heard what happened. I swear I had nothing to do with—"

"Can I talk to Devonte. Please?"

"Um. Okay. One second."

There's a ruffling on the line, muffled words exchanged, before his voice comes through, silky smooth as ever.

"Jordyn. Are you alright?"

"Yes. I'm fine." I keep my own voice light and upbeat.

"Well. Good. You did the right thing, calling me. Is there something you wish to say?"

He's looking for an apology. The audacity.

"Yeah." I take a deep breath. "'Lions are not concerned with the opinions of sheep.'"

Devonte is silent for a moment. "What . . . what did you say?"

I wish I could see his face but the crack in his voice is just as sweet. "You heard me."

"Where did you hear that?" he snaps. "How did you—"

"I need to see you in person. Alone. It's important."

"Stay right there. I'm coming now!"

THIRTY-TWO

I PACE AROUND my room in fresh jeans and a T-shirt. Modest. Virtuous attire. I iced my face as much as possible, hoping the swelling would go down. My hair is a patchwork quilt of clumps that the only thing I could do is wash and wear it natural.

Devonte breezes through the door, stopping to take me in.

"Hello Jordyn."

"Um. Hey," I mumble, voice cracking. "Would you like some tea?"

He smiles appreciatively and I know because he likes my curly 'fro.

"I . . . asked Vanessa to give us a moment," he says, taking off his jacket, laying it over my chair. "So we can be alone. Like I promised."

I fold my hands, waiting. I've learned his habits, know his likes. Men are to speak first, women are only secondary in nature.

Principle number fifteen: Let the other person do a great deal of the talking.

He stalks forward. "'Lions are not concerned with the opinions of sheep.' Where did you hear that?"

"You've said it before. Once, when we were working on—"

"No I didn't," he snaps.

"Oh. Well, I guess I've heard it somewhere," I say, fluttering about the room, pushing the chair into my desk, keeping my back to him. "Maybe some white man stole it from you. But it sounds like something you'd say."

I grip his jacket, taking in the scent, and can feel him watching my every move.

He grabs my wrist, pulling me close. "Why are you lying, Jordyn?"

My neck is on fire and I think of the way Nick avoids questions. "Can you tell me what it means?"

Devonte gives me a dead-eyed stare and I'm almost positive he can read my mind. He sits on my bed, patting the space next to him. It takes me a moment to unfreeze my limbs to join him.

"It means," he starts. "Kings weren't meant to starve. They were meant for riches."

Principle number eleven: Show respect. Never say, "You're wrong."

I pick a piece of lint off the bed. "Are you . . . a king?"

"No, love. I'm a God."

The answer is so final and absolute, his inflated sense of self-importance is remarkable.

Devonte leans closer to me, heat radiating between us.

"I want you to be honest with me, Jordyn."

I meet his gaze, pushing myself.

"I want you to be honest with me too," I coo.

He smiles triumphantly. "I meant what I said . . . about you being different. You are different. I could sense that about you from the moment we met. It's why I fought for you. You don't need to be a lawyer. You can be anything you want with me. You don't need your family holding you back. You have me to lift you up."

I swallow hard, curling inward. He places a finger under my chin.

"I want to make you my queen. Put you above all the rest. Us together, with our family . . . the love between us could change the world. Don't you think?"

I bite my tongue, his touch revolting.

"I love you." He laughs. "Damn, I don't think I've said that in a long time."

My head is spinning. "You . . . love me, but you let Kerry punch me that night?"

He shrugs, gently touching my hair in awe. "Some lessons need to be felt, not taught."

"If you love me . . . then why did you send those girls to get me?"

He hesitates. "That . . . I didn't do that."

"I could've died. They cut my hair!"

"That wasn't a call I made. I swear to you." He frowns at the floor. "Anger always results in sloppiness."

I take a quick glance at the computer on my desk, the screen black. "Did you mean what you said . . . about my writing?"

He brightens. "Yes. Yes, absolutely."

Even as I sit here hating him with every fiber of my being, I ache to have this one morsel to be true.

"I need my credit cards. I need to buy a new wardrobe. They tore everything I had to shreds."

He waves me off. "You don't need those material things. You'll start fresh, new."

"I want to start new now. Can we go?" I ask, trying to persuade him out the door.

He smooths a hand down the back of my neck. "Love, you must practice patience. We just need to tie up a few things here. Then we'll go. Just you and me."

He doesn't sound like himself. His head is up in the clouds. Like . . . he's really in love.

"Um. Okay. Where will we go?"

He pulls me tighter against him. "To Virginia, like I said. We'll break ground on Emancipation. Become sovereign citizens."

I pull back to look at him. "You're . . . serious about that?"

His laugh is deep. "I'm serious about that like I'm serious about you. The land is in my name. Bought in cash."

I feel rocked off my balance beam. Because it almost feels like he's telling the truth. Maybe not everything out of his warped mind is a lie.

Just like Loren said.

Devonte loops an arm around my waist, pulling me tight against his hip.

"This has all been very difficult for you. I understand. It's easier to be led in the wrong direction than the right one. The path to true enlightenment isn't painless but worthwhile. You'll see. You just give me what I need, I'll give you what you need."

He bends down, kissing my cheek just as the front door creaks open. Devonte turns with a glowing smile that quickly drops at the sight of three plainclothes police officers strolling into the room.

There's no sense of urgency in the officers. He's already been caught.

I pull the wire taped to my bra out of my shirt.

Devonte tracks the wires in disbelief. The officers are talking, searching his jacket, finding the credit cards that he took out in my name. The ones that came in the mail that he never opened. The ones I slipped into his jacket.

Neither of us are listening to the detectives. Too busy glaring each other down. But then, suddenly, he smiles. It's not a sinister smile.

It's a smile that says he's won.

THIRTY-THREE

THAT WAS TOO EASY.

I pick at my nails, the thought running through my head over and over again.

That was too easy.

It's the prevailing feeling I have. His steps have been too calculated and meticulous. To trap him without breaking a sweat doesn't seem plausible. More impossible. Nothing in life is that easy. If it seems too good to be true, then it probably is; that's my dad's motto. Kevin hated the saying. I wonder if he was thinking it . . . in his final days.

That was too easy. What am I missing?

So caught up in my own pseudo-failure, I barely notice Nick ripping into the men facing me.

"How does a guy like that make bail and you LOSE him?" Nick snaps, standing behind me in a conference room at the police station.

"He has the means," Mr. Richard says, the lawyer my parents hired.

Devonte wasn't kidding when he said he had friends in high places and favors to cash in on. He was out on bail in less than twenty-four hours.

"And now he's gone! Free to come and attack Jordyn!"

Gone seems like such a simple word. *Gone* implies he's no longer around but Devonte feels omnipresent in every sense. I can still smell him, his scent baked into our clothes and all over our dorm rooms.

"Devonte's last been seen jumping on a flight to California, probably trying to make a run for Mexico," a detective explains. "He won't be back here anytime soon, I'm afraid."

The hope was that with him off campus, the fire that is his growing cult would simmer and die. The university is already trying to come up with excuses to avoid any pending lawsuits.

That was too easy.

But I keep thinking about that smile on his face. What does he know that I don't?

A chill rips through me.

"What if he comes looking for me?" I ask to no one in particular.

Nick sits beside me, holding my hand under the table, a thumb tracing over my knuckles.

"I'm not gonna let anything happen to you," he whispers softly.

"We have an all-points bulletin and a car set outside the dorm," the detective says. "The school has replaced the entire security team. Cameras are up to date. Jordyn, you're safe."

Nick's frat brothers used their connections with dorm security and found out one of the guards had edited footage out a week before Thanksgiving. In the missing clip is Kammy walking out of the dorm, her wig back on, nervously checking around her. Two minutes later, Devonte emerges, seemingly following her. There's no footage of Kammy returning. Just Devonte. He's now a prime suspect.

Between confirmation of my whereabouts and cell phone records, I've been cleared of any suspicion.

But it didn't matter. My parents insist on taking me out of school.

On one hand, I almost don't blame them for their overprotectiveness, especially after losing a son. On the other, I feel like I've failed, like I'm letting Devonte win. I was ready to take the stand, tell the whole story, share everything I knew. I wanted to see the look in his eyes when he realized he'd lost. But that smile on his face . . . is unnerving.

The only hope left for justice is through Vanessa.

THIRTY-FOUR

IT'S AMAZING THAT I never noticed how my dorm room resembles a prison cell. The grayish walls, the narrow window with little light, the bare minimal furnishings, the stifled air, the energy left over from Devonte's reign.

The lack of personality is my own doing.

I stuff my bedsheets, pillows, and towels into garbage bags, amazed that over the last few months, I hadn't amassed more belongings. I was so focused on making it work, on sticking to the plan, that it didn't leave much time for shopping.

I glance out the window down into the courtyard, watching other students head up to campus, toward the Malcolm Center for dinner, and I wish so badly to be one of them.

Instead, I'm wrapping up the short chapter in my life. A bittersweet ending.

I walk into the kitchen, taking my Frazier mug off the shelf with a small smile. I didn't expect to fall in love with this school. With the culture, the professors, my classes . . . I still had other people's opinions clouding my judgment. Who gives up Yale for a Black school?

Me, and I would do it all over again. Except do it right.

Whatever time I had here has been marred by controversy. I can't possibly make new friends now. Who would trust me? Devonte is gone, Kammy is still missing, and I'm still a person of interest in public opinion, despite proof clearing my name.

My phone buzzes on the desk. An unknown number.

Maybe it's Devonte, I think, and answer quick.

"Hello?"

"Hi, this is Detective Gates. Is this Jo?"

I freeze in the middle of the room. "Uh, yeah."

"You called me a few weeks back about Devonte Saunders. Sorry I'm just getting to your message now. His parole officer called. Sounds like he's in the wind. First, let me ask, are you okay?"

"Um, yes. Yes, I'm fine."

"Good. On your message, you mentioned something about him running a credit card scam?"

"Yeah. And that's what he went to prison for, right?"

"Yes but . . . it's not that simple. You're a college student, right?"

"Um yeah," I mutter, kicking myself for not coming up with a better fake name on the fly. He could easily find me now and if he tracks this number, he'll know more about me than anyone on this entire campus.

"Did you turn in any evidence to the DC police yet?" he asks, and for some reason I sense the urgency in his voice.

"No. Why?"

"You need to do that right now before they miss their chance to catch her too."

"Her? Who?"

"Devonte's not the one you have to be worried about," Gates says. "He's just a front man. His girlfriend is the one pulling all the strings. They've been considering building a federal case against her. Racketeering, extortion . . ."

I do a mental check, thinking of every girl I've seen walk into our suite. No one stands out among the rest.

"I don't think we're talking about the same guy," I snap, annoyed that after all this time, he'd call back about the wrong person. "I haven't met any girlfriend. I only know his sister, Vanessa."

There's a brief pause on the other end. "That's not his sister."

The world goes silent as the floor drops from beneath me. "What?"

"Her name is Shameeka Foster. She goes by Vanessa, or Nessa, sometimes. She's thirty-two years old but doesn't look it. They've been together pulling this shit since they were sixteen."

Keys jiggle in the lock. The suite door opens and in walks Vanessa. She smiles brightly, book bag slung on her shoulder, and waves, heading to her room.

I stare at the empty space she left in the hall, my arms numb.

I turn to the window, lungs shrinking down to the size of lima beans.

"She's dangerous," Gates says, and I realize he's been talking to me the entire time. "Back sixteen years ago she was the prime suspect in the murder investigation of a young college girl. Everyone suspected she was the one who did it. Devonte wasn't even near the crime scene but had been seen with the girl previously. He made a better headline. The last scam those two ran resulted in a young college boy—"

A knock on the door makes me jump. I spin around and quickly end the call, hands shaking.

"Hey," I croak out.

Vanessa stands at my bedroom door, leaning against it with a smirk. "Hey. You said you wanted to talk?"

THIRTY-FIVE

VANESSA GLANCES AROUND the room at my packed belongings and sighs.

"So this is it, huh? Heading back to your parents?"

His girlfriend . . .

It's hard to think after a brain implosion. The scattered pieces jiggle around in my skull.

"Uh, yeah," I say, forcing myself to seem as normal as possible. I have to stick to the plan. "I wanted to stay but after . . . everything that's happened, it just makes sense for me to withdraw."

Vanessa's lips wiggle as she gazes at my suitcases.

"Damn, I feel like this is all my fault." She takes a deep breath. "Look, I'm sorry for . . . everything. I don't know how I let it go so far. And Devonte, well, maybe prison just messed him up real bad."

I stare at her, speechless.

"So can we . . . well. You're my sister! With Kammy gone

and Loren sick . . . you're all I have left. Maybe we can just . . . start over?"

His girlfriend . . . His girlfriend . . . His girlfriend . . .

"O-kay," I sputter.

She smiles, rubbing her shoulder. "I'm gonna make us some tea. It's so cold. You like mint, right?"

I lick my lips. "Yeah. Mint."

I turn around, trying to control my breathing as the earth spins off its axis.

His girlfriend . . .

All this time . . . I thought they were brother and sister. How did I not know this. How did I miss it? I go over everything I saw, everything I know, and nothing makes sense.

His girlfriend . . .

In the kitchen, Vanessa hums as she pours boiling water into our school mugs, then steeps the tea bags.

"You gotta wait at least two to three minutes," she sings. "That's the proper way to make tea. Or so I've been told."

The shape of her body, her smile, the way she can seduce a spoon to bend to her will . . . you only learn those types of skills with time and age.

Vanessa holds the mug out. "Here you go."

I steady my shaky hand to take the cup from her.

"Thank you," I mutter.

"Oop! One more thing."

She runs into her room and returns with a small plastic bag

full of white powder. My stomach drops.

"What's that?"

She reads my reaction and laughs. "Girl, relax, it's just sugar! I had to stash it away. Devonte would KILL me if he caught me with this shit."

She pours a little in my cup and stirs it with a straw. "There! That should be perfect. Come on! Sit on the sofa with me. One last time!"

The white powder evaporates in the swirling water.

"Uh, one second, let me just grab my phone."

I rush into my room, trying to stay focused on my breathing. Outside, I see the unmarked police car but I have no way of reaching it.

His girlfriend . . .

The sick, demented things they've done. The hearts they stomped over. The lies . . . I grab my phone to shoot Nick a quick text. Maybe he could—

"Girl, hurry up!"

I jump in my skin, dropping the phone on the table.

Don't panic. Pull it together.

Except this feels like the perfect time to panic. With a deep breath, I grab the laptop out of my bag.

She laughs as I return, handing me a mug. "Always working, this girl."

I watch her back as she strolls into the living room, carrying such effortless grace. She's had years to perfect it.

She sits on the sofa, holding up her steaming cup. "Cheers, bitch!"

I join her and we clink mugs. I stare into the cup, mouth parted open, but can't bring myself to take a sip.

"OMG, are you serious?" She shakes her head, shooting her mug out at me. "Here, girl, drink mine if you're so worried. I ain't gonna poison you."

"I know," I say with a nervous chuckle. "It's just . . . you know ever since that night during homecoming . . . teas taste so different to me now."

She shakes her head, grinning. "Drink, girl."

Even with the switched cup, my nerves are too fried to trust anything this woman says or does. But I know it's the only way out of this.

Play along and act fast.

I take two big gulps. The hot water sizzles down my throat. Vanessa watches me intensely then smiles. For a moment, it feels like old times, us sitting on the sofa, drinking out of mugs. Even without Loren and Kammy around, Vanessa just puts me at ease. It's a superpower. One I fell for easily.

I glance at my phone, realizing I didn't press Send on the message to Nick. No one knows we're here.

Alone.

"But for real, I'm really sorry about everything that's happened. Like, I can't believe he set those girls up to jump you!"

"Anger always results in sloppiness."

He'd never do anything crazy on campus. He was too careful, tight roping around the loopholes. Vanessa isn't as careful. She leads with emotion.

"Have you heard from him?" she asks. "Text or anything?"

"No. Thought he didn't like cell phones?"

I take another drink. She watches my mouth and licks her lips. Satisfied with something unsaid, she sips more of her tea.

"He doesn't. Well, sometimes he uses mine. It's just . . . weird 'cause the last time I talked to him, he was meeting up with you."

I keep my face emotionless, though my heart is racing wildly. "Oh."

"He said you said something very specific. Something no one would know about him."

I glance at the front door. It's just us in here. For the first time ever. I'm not trapped. I can escape. But I still feel pinned by an invisible force.

"Well, we spent a lot of time together writing." I look at her. "Does that . . . bother you?"

"Psst! Nah!" she laughs. "He's my brother! A bit of a 'ho at times but who isn't. I . . . guess I just really believed he needed me, you know. The world's been so unfair to him that I feel I always have to protect him."

"He's my brother." She said that so many times. I gag, covering my mouth to stop the threatening vomit.

"Hey, you okay?" she asks, lightly touching my arm.

"Yeah," I say, trying to think of a way to create some space between us. "Can I have more sugar?"

She grins. "Yeah. Hang on."

Vanessa stands too quickly. She wobbles, falling back onto the sofa.

I place my mug on the coffee table. "You okay?"

"Yeah," she slurs with a frown. "I . . ." She touches her numb lips as the shock spreads across her face. She grips the sofa cushion, realization sparking in her eyes. "I . . . I . . . NO!"

Then suddenly she's on me, hands gripping around my neck with a tight squeeze, my head hitting the sofa arm. She lunged so fast I didn't have time to let out a scream. I beat my fist against her arms, desperate for air. We roll off the sofa, tea mugs crashing onto the floor with us, water scalding our shoulders. I grab the mug and swing but she dodges it, returning with two punches to my right eye, sending shooting stars around my vision. She pushes against my bruised ribs and I howl in agony.

Her hands return to my neck. My legs run in place, sneakers squeaking against the tiles, but I can't move. She screams, pressing down harder, a rage in her eye I've never seen. She's stronger than she looks.

And she's about to kill me.

Slowly, as life leaves my body, her arms become tough noodles. I arch my leg up and knee her in the stomach. She cries out, her hands loosening, and with the last of my energy, I shove her off and she thumps onto the floor, all dead weight.

I cough out a gasp and roll over to my back, my ribs throbbing.

The drug finally slipped into her system, weighing down her veins, leaving her motionless.

Holding my side, I manage to make it onto my feet, wincing through the motions, and drop on the sofa, straightening what little hair I have left. Vanessa stares at me from the floor, trying to catch her breath, reminding me of a dying trout on shore.

"You know," I begin, the words scratchy, and nod at the computer. "This isn't mine. It belonged to my brother. Kevin. You remember him, right?"

Her eyes grow huge as she wheezes, trying again to move, to stand, to do anything. I watch her squirm and open the laptop to the photo album, turning it in her direction.

"This you?"

I tap the selfie he took while lying in bed with her, smiling, cheesing, laughing into one another. He looked so damn happy that it breaks my heart, thinking of his heart shattering as he slowly learned the truth about the one person in the world he was willing to give up his family—his sister—for.

"You didn't even bother to learn who his parents were or what they looked like. Hearing my last name didn't ring any bells? Or maybe you just fucked over SO many Kevins that you forgot? Just another drop in the bucket."

Vanessa's eyes toggle from me to the computer, shaking her head with a whimper.

"I know. We don't look alike. He was much cuter than me. Everyone said so."

"Please," she slurs, gurgling a throat full of saliva. Maybe she'll choke on it, maybe she'll die.

"'Lions are not concerned with the opinions of sheep.' That's the line your stupid brother swore he made up when he just stole it from a TV show. *Game of Thrones.* Ever heard of it? It was a show my brother knew by heart. That's how he figured out you two were full of bullshit. Oh, I'm sorry. Not your brother. Your BOYFRIEND!"

Her mouth gapes wider, lips trembling as she struggles to stay awake.

I lean closer to her, shaking in rage. "You took EVERYTHING from me. He was the one person in the world who understood me, the one person I had to lean on, and you took him."

The terror in her face isn't as satisfying as I thought it would be. She manages to moan a small "help" before slumping to the floor, passing out cold. I study her for a few moments. The woman my brother was so in love with, the woman who crushed him. I put two fingers to her neck. There's still a pulse.

Good.

I close Kevin's computer and walk into Vanessa's bedroom, noticing how it smells just like Devonte.

THIRTY-SIX

THERE ARE FIVE stages of grief with a few of my own additions: denial, anger, bargaining, depression, acceptance, boomerang, and then finally . . . revenge. Most people would think I was just stuck in the anger stage. Anger is just the weeds that grow out of that lump of dirt that used to be a heart when it's grieving. But revenge . . . revenge is the sweet frosting on a yellow cake.

I arrived at the revenge stage four months after they found Kevin's body in his dorm room closet. I came home from another stint at therapy, utterly numb and decided to open up Kevin's computer, still tucked away in the corner of our garage with the rest of his belongings. There was no way I could accept that he killed himself without reason. Despite what everyone told me . . . that maybe he hid his depression, that people change when they go to college . . . I knew him better than I knew myself. Something had to have happened. Something drove him toward his death. And if I didn't search for a reason, I would be in a perpetual loop of grief. I didn't want to boomerang. I wanted someone to pay for what they'd done.

I dug through his computer, every file, every folder, until I found one titled "Emancipation." In it were various notes from Devonte's rhetoric, the lion quote with a question mark beside it, credit card statements, and then pictures . . . of Vanessa. He was in love with her. Or the version of her he thought he knew. A girl we never heard of or from, even after he died.

I found text message threads and email conversations with people from other schools that suffered at the hands of Vanessa and Devonte. I could almost imagine Kevin putting two and two together, slowly learning the truth. The heartbreak he must have felt, the shattering, after finding the community he was so desperate for, all for it to be a con and he found himself lost once again. Devonte brainwashed my brother, Vanessa sucked him dry of the will to live.

I couldn't show my parents what I had found. They were already disappointed that Kevin had stolen so much money from them. They would be even more knowing he had fallen into the trap of scam artists. *Stupid* would be the first word they'd use. And even if I did show them and we went to the cops, it wouldn't be enough to act on.

I called two of the people Kevin had reached out to, delivering the news about his death. Neither seemed surprised, and neither wanted to come forward to share their story. Either too scared or too ashamed that they had been fooled. One admitted he traded sexual favors for an "outstanding bill" he owed

Devonte, the other estimated she gave upward of fifty thousand, all borrowed from her parents.

Devonte would fall under two-strikes-you're-out parameters. But Vanessa seemed untouchable, her hands never truly dirty. She may have done a few pathetic years of probation. That wasn't good enough. Not for her taking my brother, my best friend. For any real justice to be had, I had to find a new victim that would be willing to testify.

That's when the plan started to build in my head.

Wherever Vanessa would go, Devonte would follow. All I had to do was track her down. Kevin's friends mentioned her talking nonstop about hoping to go to Frazier. When I found the mug in Kevin's belongings, I knew that's where she'd end up.

Once I learned Devonte was doing two years for credit card fraud (a mere stroke of luck with his slip-up), I suspected Vanessa would lie low and had an alert set for his release, the timing working serendipitously with my upcoming graduation.

The last part was the most difficult. Contacting the head of Student Housing, Ms. Rogers, to make sure I was room-matched with Vanessa. Buying her cooperation and silence cost ten thousand dollars. But it was worth it.

Everything else fell into place naturally after that—Vanessa practically gave me full access to her computer, with all the evidence I needed neatly planted.

Principle number nine: Make the other person feel important—and do so sincerely.

I left my door open from time to time, allowing them opportunities to use my credit cards and open new ones. It also gave them access to plant their subtle threats and bogus evidence in my closet.

After the police searched our suite looking for Kammy, I noticed the misplaced tile in the bathroom ceiling. I found a burner phone, Kammy's wallet, a bag of cash, and roofie pills. The same drug Devonte slipped in my drink that night at the party, probably so he'd have another hold over me. Like he did to Kammy. Like he did to Loren. I switched the pills with aspirin. Slipping the real pills into my own mug that day was easier than I thought. Amazing how they both underestimated me.

"That's how you are taken advantage of. Appearing like easy prey instead of a worthy adversary."

The cash they siphoned, almost seventy-five thousand dollars, was comically stuffed under her mattress. I took the money and planted whatever additional evidence, including the full list of people she swindled, on her computer to rack up the charges. As she was being detained, she screamed how I stole from her, that this was all a set-up. But there was no way to prove it. I don't know if I would have had the guts to go through with this plan if I knew they were capable of murder.

My parents, stunned by this "coincidence," stepped into lawyer mode, threatening to sue the school for not ensuring our safety and letting a predator roam around campus freely. People were fired, articles were written, life moved on.

What I didn't expect was how good Devonte ended up being. I almost swallowed up the bullshit he was feeding us that it's believable anyone else would too.

If I had known how quickly the spell he cast would work on us, of course I would have prioritized the girls' safety. But Devonte called me out right, I'm not a good friend. Because what kind of friend am I not to warn them of the hell he would unleash on our lives? They seemed so strong, so street smart, never falling for boys' bullshit. I thought they would snap to their senses. I misjudged the power of his magic, and they ended up being casualties in a war they didn't know they were a part of. The guilt sickened me to the point that food only tasted like garbage juice.

He's good. A little too good.

Jack: Hey.

Me: Hey.

Jack: So I heard you found her.

Me: Yeah. I did.

Jack: But you're still going to stay?

Jack didn't know exactly what I was up to, not the real plan. He knew I wanted to find my brother's girlfriend, he just couldn't understand why, and to his credit, despite the bitterness, he didn't tell anyone. And he never will. Revenge is a universal language.

Yes, I found Vanessa, but I found so much more here at Frazier, and I'm not ready to let it go.

Me: Yeah. I am.

THIRTY-SEVEN

SPRING AT FRAZIER brings a different kind of energy. A change in the air mixed with the pollen and heat, the thrill of something new. The cherry blossoms are blooming puffs of white and pink, the sky powder blue. The euphoric rush tackles everyone on campus with a blissful high. Or it could be the end of finals that's giving us all the giggles. I finished my last final a few hours ago, redeeming my academic standing.

Nick and I stroll hand in hand through the Quad, heading for the Rec, as workers set up chairs and wooden bleachers, facing a massive graduation stage.

"This is gonna be us in a few years," Nick says, nodding at the stage decked in our school colors. "Then, law school for me and an MFA in creative writing for you."

I sigh. "It's gonna be so weird."

"What do you mean?" he asks, curious.

"I don't know. We'll be real adults in the real world. We won't have this to look forward to every day."

He nods, his face growing serious. "I know. We'll have to interact with white people again on a daily basis."

I laugh, giving him a playful shove. He stops in the middle of the Quad to kiss my forehead, trailing down to my nose, then my lips, fingers gripping my new microbraids.

But it's true. Some people don't ever want to give this up. Some people try to stay in college forever. It makes me think of Emancipation. Devonte really had a plan to build a utopia for himself on the backs of college students. How many colleges would he have hit if they weren't stopped? What would he have become?

"Hey, have I told you how proud I am of you?"

I gaze up at Nick and chuckle. "What? Where'd that come from?"

"I don't know, just thinking back on everything that's happened this year. You came to college, the one your brother wanted you to. You made friends, even if they were insane. After all that, you kept going. You handled your grief better than I ever could. Even with the trial coming up, you're ready to face your fears. And I just can't get enough of you."

He nuzzles my neck and I swallow down the guilt burning my throat. As the new trustee, Nick is lobbying for more mental health programming and stricter rules on dorm visitation. I tell myself that one day, I'll tell Nick the truth. I just hate the idea of him knowing what I gave up for revenge. Or who I gave up. It doesn't taste as sweet, mostly sour.

Vanessa's trial will start in the fall. Alongside the trial of the two officers who murdered an unarmed man. Both predators on the Black community, just in different ways. Loren agreed to be a witness. She dropped out of school to move back home to New York. I wasn't surprised by this. People were more surprised that I wanted to stay at Frazier. And why wouldn't I want to be around such Black excellence? I'm even in Dr. Barnes's class next year.

Despite my parents' offer to buy me my own condo, I decided to move into another dorm. I want a chance at starting over, making new friends. No way to do that holed up alone in an apartment. Besides, Nick plans on getting his own place so I'll be staying there often. We still don't sleep well without each other.

Mom came down to help decorate my new room, a single with its own bathroom. We made up for lost time shopping. She even sat in for a group therapy session. The possibility of losing another child made her drop all expectations.

On the Quad, sororities and fraternities are stepping, and a few students turn up their music on a bench, dancing. A professor passing by stops to chat, laughing along with them. I remember while touring Yale, a group of boys dressed in khakis and blazers tossed around a Frisbee on the old campus grounds, a spitting image of my high school. Looking out today, I can only laugh at the striking difference.

Dad still doesn't understand how I can choose Frazier over Yale. He's just never experienced the glorious energy of truly belonging. He'd rather continue fighting for a seat at a table that won't serve him.

Everyone knows that monsters are real, that they don't just live on the outskirts of our imaginations with the tooth fairy. What we were never told, never fully explained, is how the monsters can roam among us, hidden in plain sight, with nice teeth, gorgeous skin, and breathtaking smiles. How they have the power to manipulate, the power to persuade, the power to siphon the life out of you.

I want to believe that Kammy is still alive, somewhere. That Legacy is just back home with his family and lost his phone. But Vanessa refuses to talk and Devonte is out there, floundering without her helping to plan their next score. I don't know what the future holds for Nick and me once he learns the truth. But there's one thing I know for sure:

Kevin would have loved it here.

ACKNOWLEDGMENTS

THIS IS MY first YA project out of the postpartum mud, and I have to say it was a tough one. So to my editor, Jennifer Ung, who was tender with me despite me being *insanely* late delivering this book, I appreciate our team work.

To my agent, Jenny Bent, thank you for supporting me and being willing to stop down to talk out career stuff.

Huge shout-out to the School & Library, publicity, social, design, events, sales, and marketing teams at HarperCollins. Thank you to Quill Tree Books for being my new cozy home.

Thank you to my super last-minute beta reader, Nic Stone, who gave me notes when I felt like I didn't nail the landing.

Thank you to all the readers, reviewers, bookstagrammers, and TikTokers for the endless support. I literally would not be able to be the mom of my dreams, living my dream, without you.

Thank you to all my friends, both authors and not, who held me down while I found myself again. You popped in on me at events while I was weeping at being away from my baby, and you sent encouraging messages, food, toys, and random memes. I will never forget how you covered me. To my family, especially my mom and dad, thank you for flying down and helping to take care of baby girl. I love seeing you becoming grandparents. To my bae and my baby girl, I never imagined life would be this sweet.

And if you stopped by my dorm room in the West Towers at Howard University and had some of my food, this book is for you.